High praise for

MORTA

"*Deliverance* by Dakota Banks delivers everything I love in suspense fiction: great characters who jump from the page; a smart, layered plot; and pacing that screams. This is the kind of book that makes you look forward to a rainy day."
JOHN GILSTRAP, author of *Damage Control* and *Nathan's Run*

"Passionate, fascinating . . . packed with action and history. Three hundred years ago, Maliha Crayne was burned at the stake. Now she's in a race against time to save the world and her soul, and you'll be with her step by step."
DAVID MORRELL, *New York Times* bestselling author of *The Brotherhood of the Rose*

"Seductive, sophisticated, and imaginative . . . a labyrinth of fast-paced suspense."
STEVE BERRY, *New York Times* bestselling author of *The Jefferson Key*

"*Mortal Path* is to be savored for both its edge of suspense and the pure joy of its storytelling. . . . Not to be missed!"
JAMES ROLLINS, *New York Times* bestselling author of *The Devil Colony*

"Chilling, thrilling, and a page turner!"
HEATHER GRAHAM, *New York Times* bestselling author of *The Killing Edge*

"Edge of your seat, breathtaking action . . . a must-read."
DAVID DUN, author of *The Black Silent*

By Dakota Banks

Mortal Path

Book 1
DARK TIME
Book 2
SACRIFICE
Book 3
DELIVERANCE

DELIVERANCE

MORTAL PATH

BOOK THREE

DAKOTA BANKS

HARPER Voyager

An Imprint of HarperCollins *Publishers*

HARPER Voyager
An Imprint of HarperCollins*Publishers*
10 East 53rd Street
New York, New York 10022-5299

Copyright © 2012 by Dakota Banks
Cover art by Don Sipley
ISBN 978-0-06-204998-8
www.harpervoyagerbooks.com

First Harper Voyager mass market printing: April 2012

Harper Voyager and) is a trademark of HCP LLC.

Printed in the U.S.A.

10 9 8 7 6 5 4 3 2 1

*To someone who's always there
for me, through joy and heartache:
my husband Dennis.
Love you, sweetie.*

About morals, I know only that what is moral is what you feel good after and what is immoral is what you feel bad after.

—ERNEST HEMINGWAY,
Death in the Afternoon

Author's Note

Deliverance, the third adventure of Maliha Crayne and her friends, is an intensely personal book, digging into Maliha's mind and her relationships with her friends and lovers (past and present). She realizes she's not an independent force anymore, and has to open the door further to allow for her friends' participation in her life. You'll find that this book offers the same rich experience of action, paranormal elements, and drama as the previous two books, in addition to Maliha's growth in relationships and personal understanding. Maliha's caught in moral dilemmas at nearly every turn as she is forced to challenge long-standing ways in which she thinks and operates. She must adapt or die. Writing the book was an emotionally draining experience for both Maliha and for me.

Visit me at www.dakota-banks.com for more information about the Mortal Path series, including its mythological background. Send me an email via the website, and you'll get a prompt, personal reply. I'd love to hear from you!

D. B.

DELIVERANCE

Chapter One

Maliha Crayne placed her feet carefully on the old clay-tiled roof. Freezing rain made the passage treacherous. Xietai, the man she was chasing, seemed as sure-footed as a gazelle. She had already sent a tile sliding to the street six stories below.

It was three in the morning, and although New York never sleeps, the residents of this neighborhood did. Most of them, anyway. As another tile clattered to the sidewalk, a window was flung open and a woman's head appeared, her neck twisted to look up at the roof.

"What's goin' on up there? Think yer goddamn Santa Claus or somethin'? Get the fuck off my roof!"

With flat roofs all around, he has to choose one with tiles. Should have gone around and picked up his trail on the other side. Maliha—0, Xietai—1.

Xietai had been in her sights twice before, and he'd eluded her. He ran a human trafficking ring, bringing Asian girls to America, and then sending American girls to Asia. Round-trip profits. Complicating matters was that Xietai was the son of one of Maliha's dearest friends, Xia Yanmeng. Maliha planned to bring Xietai to justice, but with his record of confrontation, it was possible she'd have to kill him.

Kill Yanmeng's son. Not sure how he'd feel about that, even though the two of them are estranged. If my daughter,

*Constanta, had survived her birth and grown up evil, would
I be hunting her?*

Maliha came to the end of the tiled roof and paused
briefly. Xietai's footprints led her on into the moonless
night. Using her ability to view auras, she could see the
outline of his footsteps and the tendrils of red and black
twining together, rising from them. Normally she used her
aural vision for a few seconds at a time, a quick check to see
if someone was lying or to make sure she faced a truly evil
person before plunging her sword into him. Constant viewing, as she was doing now to track Xietai, was draining.
His aural footprints were clear, but her surroundings were a
little out of focus. As long as Xietai kept out of her normal
sight, he had an advantage.

Maliha felt a touch on her shoulder, as soft as if she'd
been brushed by a bird's wing. Yanmeng was a remote
viewer, and he was signaling her that he was viewing her
now. He'd been trying to increase his remote presence to the
point where he could move objects. He'd made some progress but it was erratic. She could extend her arm and make
an *L*-shape with her fingers, the sign they'd agreed upon for
him to withdraw, and he would immediately stop remote
viewing her. At least, she trusted that he would.

She didn't make the withdrawal sign.

*It's his son. Yanmeng's not going to like this, but it's not
right to hide it from him.*

She swung over the edge of the roof, hung briefly by one
hand, and dropped down to an adjacent flat roof. Landing
with a forward roll to break the momentum of the fall,
she put out a hand to avoid sliding on the patchy ice. She
scraped the side of her hand raw on the rough roofing material. She wasn't an accomplished *traceuse*—tracer—so
her hands weren't calloused. The man ahead of her was a
highly skilled practitioner of *parkour*, a method of crossing
obstacles in the most efficient way and shortest time.

She ran barefoot, with loose black shorts, a black T-
shirt, a belly bag with a few throwing stars secured inside
so they couldn't shift and hurt her, knives strapped to her

thighs, and her thick black hair flowing behind her. It was late November, and an icy rain pelted her face and other exposed skin. Maliha wasn't prepared for this pursuit, but when Xietai crossed her path, she had to try it.

Maliha jumped to a building a dozen feet away. She rolled, then ran and dropped to the fire escape.

Could he be Ageless?

Her bare feet landed lightly on the fire escape's icy stairs, and at each landing, she vaulted the railing to the next run of stairs. She dropped the last ten feet to the ground. Thin red wisps spiraled eerily up from slushy puddle he'd passed through. She cleared the puddle in a small hop. Ahead a wall loomed. He'd taken her down a dead-end alley. Using the momentum of her run, she stepped up the brick wall to a balcony, used a spring from the rail to power another handful of steps, and reached the next balcony. Eight balconies later, she muscled up to the roof.

No good. Blind corner . . .

Anticipating a trap, Maliha threw one of her knives, then ducked and rolled as a sword swung powerfully where her neck should have been. She lashed out with her second knife, scored a deep gash in Xietai's calf, and felt the splash of hot blood on her hand.

That should slow him down a little.

Xietai took off into the night, running away before she'd come fully out of her roll. She retrieved her thrown knife from where it had landed. Her opponent took them down to street level. She was gratified to see a blood trail in the pale cone of light from a streetlamp.

He bleeds too much to be Ageless.

Then she spotted Xietai on the roof of a run-down theater, standing next to the marquee with its hundreds of broken bulbs. His aura was blacker than the night sky washed by city lights, and the spidery electric red web of his anger had intensified since she'd wounded him.

This is it.

One of them was going to die.

She sped toward an alley a few buildings away on the

theater's left, using a burst of superhuman speed, a remnant of the time she spent as an Ageless assassin beholden to the Sumerian demon Rabishu. When she was a demon's slave, she could maintain that pace effortlessly. Now she would grow weaker as she used it and have to rest before speeding again.

Melting into the alley's entrance, Maliha hoped that Xietai hadn't seen her. At roof level, she paused to make sure her target hadn't joined her there, and then found a secure observation point on the roof. Xietai was still there, with impatience starting to work on him. The pursuit had changed from a fast traverse to stealthy tracking, and she didn't have to use her aura vision.

Finally, advantage: Maliha.

Maliha checked the rooftops for possible launching points. The only thing that caught her eye was a dilapidated billboard sign on the roof where he waited. She did the gap jump followed by a drop, her bare feet moving as silently as a sigh, taking her right to the base of the billboard. She climbed a few feet up the cross timbers of rotten wood.

Xietai had moved out onto the metal frame of the marquee, facedown on one of the supports, peering around at the ground. He must have thought she was down there on the street. There was a sword fastened tightly across one shoulder blade, slanting toward the small of his bare, muscular back. From where she was, the scabbard looked bent, as though it conformed to his skin, something that would allow him flexibility for *parkour.*

Maliha had two throwing knives and three stars. She could plant five bladed weapons in his back before he had a chance to rise. She had her throwing knives in one hand and stars in the other when Xietai suddenly rotated onto his back.

Their eyes met. He pulled the sword from its scabbard and it came out in loose sections. A flick of his wrist brought the sections into alignment as a formidable weapon, longer than its scabbard.

I want one of those.

He strode onto the roof. Maliha threw her three stars to

distract him as she got down to roof level. She saw with dismay that he swatted away the stars with his sword, and had to remind herself that he wasn't Ageless, just superbly trained. The cloth dripping with blood wrapped around his calf was proof he was mortal. If he was Ageless, blood would have stopped flowing from his wound and it would have healed by now, leaving no trace. She ran toward him faster than his human eyes could follow. Veering away just out of reach of his sword, she swung around him and slashed behind his knees, going for crippling blows. Neither knife connected.

He'd spun around and blocked them.

He heard the rush of the wind when I used Ageless speed. Can't sneak up on him. I'm in deep shit.

He began fighting with both the sword and a knife he'd pulled from somewhere. Soon Maliha's bare legs and arms ran with blood.

Retreat? Master Liu says that humility is the best way to handle being overmatched. But not yet . . .

On her knees, Maliha saw a way for one of her knives to weave in close to the core of his body. Feinting with the other knife, she closed in. If he didn't go for the feint, her head would be too close to his knife to think about.

She felt her knife strike in his gut, twisted it, and shoved it upward as far as she could.

She caught a glimpse of metal as his knife descended, aimed to slip between two vertebrae in her neck and sever her spinal cord. With the power of his evil and anger behind it, she knew she would suffer a mortal wound.

Instead of striking her neck, the blade's angle changed a little.

Yanmeng!

He must have exerted all of the new force he'd been working on to give the knife a shove and save her from a fatal blow. She managed to slip away from the continuing path of the blade, but not before it ripped across her back, dragging its cutting edge, and peeling back her shirt, skin, and flesh.

Xietai slumped to his knees, and she saw him wide-eyed

and slack-jawed, surprised at being stabbed. She yanked her knife from just below his sternum and gave him a shove. He fell heavily to the rooftop. Immediately she straddled him and severed his spinal cord for a quick death.

Maliha took a deep breath and savored her victory. She picked up Xietai's sword, which was unresponsive in her hands. She couldn't get it to collapse to the way she'd seen it hugging his back. Satisfied that the weapon died with its owner, she left the hilt cradled in his hand. She did take his knife, though, the one that had inflicted the painful tear on her back. Handling it reminded her that Yanmeng had faced a terrible decision—loyalty to her or to his own flesh and blood.

Maliha used her ragged T-shirt and torn bra to bind her back wound. It left her in only a band of cloth across her breasts, black shorts and an empty belly bag, but that would have to do. The chase had taken her far away from her hotel, into an area where cabs weren't swarming the streets, especially in the middle of the night. She would have to make it back on foot, keeping out of sight.

She took a few steps experimentally. With her wound bound, she wasn't losing much blood. Her back hurt like hell, but her feet were steady enough. She could do it, especially knowing that her wound would cease to bleed along the way.

She thought about calling her editor, Jefferson Leewood, who knew her only as the fabulously successful novelist named Marsha Winters. She'd stopped in New York for a meeting with him yesterday, a meeting that now seemed far away in time and place.

Jeff's nice, but he'd insist on picking me up himself, and then he'd freak out when he got a look at me. He's better off with his last view of me leaving his office, looking like a bankable author.

On the sidewalk in front of the theater, Maliha gasped and staggered back against the brick wall. She slid down the wall, scraping her already torn back against the bricks, but barely noticed the pain.

Chapter Two

Maliha's scale was in motion.

She carried on her body a depiction of a balance patterned after the scales of justice, carved into her flesh by the fiery claw of her demon Rabishu. One pan of the scale held tiny images representing people she'd killed while serving as his assassin. The other pan held images of people whose lives she'd saved since she defied the demon and went rogue. The pans were seriously out of balance. Maliha was a long way from saving as many people as she'd killed, which was the only way she could reclaim her soul from Rabishu.

As she sat transfixed by pain on the sidewalk, small figures left the "lives taken" pan and walked across her belly, leaving a trail of small footprints burned across her belly, like a splash of acid. The miniatures climbed into the "lives saved" pan, and the scale swung through a small arc on her skin to reach a new balance point. The reward for stopping Xietai's slavery operation had been generous.

Then came the aging. Whenever her scale rebalanced, she aged a little. The amount wasn't always in proportion to lives saved, so she never knew what to expect. It was Anu, the main Sumerian god, pulling the string that tugged her through time. She judged by the strength of the pull that she'd aged only a month, if that.

She gathered her legs under her and stood, now aware of the pain of her back, wounded by Xietai and freshly scraped by bricks. If any challenge presented itself on her way home, she wouldn't be able to give a full-force response. There was no hurry to leave the area. It wasn't likely that Xietai's body on the defunct theater roof would be discovered until it began decomposing. Maliha moved into an alley and found that she had company, a homeless man snoring in a makeshift tent. Maliha didn't cringe from the homeless, as some did, because she'd been in similar situations herself during her more than three centuries of life. She was no stranger to living alone or living off the land when it served her purpose.

Easing her body down to the ground at the entrance to his tent, she decided that she'd stay a few hours to recuperate. Scooting backward, she ended up just inside the filthy, torn fabric that served as the tent's flaps. The odor assaulted her, the unwashed man, the alcohol, the tent that could have been a corpse winding, and the smell of urine. She tugged one of his blankets over to cover her cold legs and feet.

Not too bad. Smells better than a demon, anyway. A lot better.

She synchronized her breathing to the old man's snoring first, then gradually slowed it and entered a healing meditation she learned from Master Liu. Giving her body the task of healing her back, she let her mind walk the loops of the glowing, golden infinity symbol she used as a meditation aid. As her mind filled with the radiant glow, what healing ability she had left from the time she'd been Ageless went to work, stopping the bleeding on her back and starting to knit together the edges of jagged tears in her skin.

Coming out of the trance later, she stood and stretched. Her back made it clear to her that healing was nowhere near complete, but she could start back to her hotel with confidence without needing a cab. There was a bottle of water in the makeshift tent, and after she assured herself that the contents weren't anything else questionable, she cleaned the blood from her limbs and face as best she could. The tent didn't have a closet full of clothes, but she managed to find a ripe, rumpled T-shirt that she pulled on.

She felt like a reverse Robin Hood, taking from the poor and giving to the rich, but made plans to return the next night. She hoped that he'd still be here, so that she could bring blankets, clothing, and some money. He'd slept through her entire intrusion.

It was an overcast morning with a slight drizzle that washed away most of the thin ice coating. She pushed away the chill in her bare feet and took off at a moderate walk that worked up to a jog. She couldn't wait to get back to her hotel for a hot shower and a change of clothes. She didn't have a room key or identification with her, and she smelled like a wet dog.

No problem.

But before cleaning and refreshing herself, she would see that her knives were spotless. Master Liu taught that comfort never came before showing respect to the weapons that kept her alive.

Maliha Crayne had originally gone to New York City for a happy event. Her new car, a black Zonda F, had been at a customizing shop. The previous car, a McLaren F1, had given its all in a crash. The shop had finished installing her custom-designed safety package of cockpit nets and expandable foam, plus other items that she'd found useful in the past.

The Zonda F coupe was made by the Italian manufacturer Pagani. It was light and fast, and looked like a black panther ready to spring. Maliha fell in love with it. Amaro, another friend of hers, had negotiated the purchase, a thrill for him, but this was the first time Maliha had seen the car.

It was all hers to drive home to Chicago. The drive wasn't as fun as it was supposed to be, especially with her back wound. She had to concentrate on her driving and keep the pain suppressed as well as she could.

She pulled up in front of the Harbor Point Towers in Chicago, her lakefront home. The past few weeks of bodily injuries, guilt, and deaths on her recent case plus her pursuit of Xietai had taken their toll. She needed time to work on those things, physically and emotionally. She hadn't alerted her friends to the exact time of her arrival, even her more-than-friend Jake Stackman, an agent of the Drug Enforcement Administration.

Not that she wasn't thinking of him, fantasizing about another night in his arms.

Jake, her Ageless lover, had already told her the plans he had to cheer her up. While the plans sounded enticing, they didn't include any rest for her, unless she counted short naps between periods of lovemaking. Maliha's girlfriend Randy Baxter had a habit of assigning nicknames to her lovers based on anatomical features or talents in bed. Getting into the spirit of it, Maliha had dubbed Jake "Repeater."

I'll be ready for him in two or three days. She had a delicious thought. *In the meantime, he can bring me takeout dinners. I'll meet him at the door in next to nothing and just take the food.*

She smiled for the first time that day, thinking about how her idea might play out. While she and Jake had some problems in their relationship, they were great in bed. But Jake had a few years mysteriously missing in his past. That left Maliha with the impression that he'd done something bad—so bad he couldn't tell her about it because it would make it impossible for her to love him.

What if it was so terrible that we couldn't stay together?

The thought of having a life with him was almost too much to hope for, but in the deep recesses of her heart, she knew that was what she wanted most.

She felt a phantom child growing and kicking inside her, as her daughter Constanta had until she was stillborn in a dark, dirty jail cell, a small and helpless casualty of colonial injustice. Maliha put a protective hand over her flat abdomen to cradle the life within, but the illusion of pregnancy faded. Decades, then centuries, of living since then came rushing at her. She saw the split-second decision she'd made to become Rabishu's assassin and felt the new Ageless power rushing through her blood after her first kill. Her training with Master Liu turned her into the perfect stealth killer, with a heart armored against feeling the human suffering she inflicted. Years rolled by and the killings became a blur, until she felt she was turning into an evil creature like Rabishu, sprouting claws and carrying the stench of death. Finally there was the one assignment that repelled her so much that she couldn't carry it out. Defying her demon had been at once the most terrifying and the most liberating thing she had ever done.

The attentive doorman called for a porter and a valet. The porter unloaded Maliha's three small bags on the curb, heading first for the rear of the car until she waved him to the front. One carry-on bag, a garment bag, and a grungy, beaten-up hard-sided case that weighed about a hundred pounds. It was her weapons bag. She'd gone to New York by commercial airliner, so the weapons she took had to be in checked luggage. She used to carry plastic knives with her on the plane, but with full body scans in some airports, there was no reason to take the risk since she didn't really need them.

The doorman was unfamiliar, even though it was Arnie Henshaw's shift. Maliha had a long-term relationship with Arnie. He didn't know all the details of her life, but he understood that she fought crime. He helped her in the subtle way that a doorman could, such as warning her when someone was waiting for her. Arnie also knew about the two homes she had in this building. One, on the thirty-ninth floor, was her public home where she received guests. The other, on the forty-eighth floor, was her private haven.

The new man took care of the luggage efficiently and it was all going to the thirty-ninth floor, so there was no problem.

She turned to the valet, who couldn't keep a big grin off his face at the prospect of parking her car.

"It's the private garage on Level One."

"I know, Ms. Winters. Didn't you used to have a McLaren? I'll take good care . . ."

"Yes. No drooling on the leather." She tossed him the key and turned her attention back to the doorman. "Is Arnie taking a day off today?"

The doorman's face got serious. "You haven't heard, then?"
She shook her head.

"Arnie disappeared a couple of weeks ago. No one's
heard from him since."

Surely he didn't quit. He wasn't old enough to retire.

"I'm sorry to hear that. We were friends."

"I think he got tired of the job and took off for some place
warmer. There's a shitload of people, excuse me, who'd love
to live the fantasy."

"You don't have to excuse yourself. My ears aren't tender."

He leaned in close and whispered, "Seems as though the
police are looking into foul play, though."

"Really? You'll have to let me know if they turn anything up."

"Will do, ma'am." He put out his hand to shake hers.
"Sounds like we'll get along just fine. I'm Chester Rafferty,
the new day-shift manager. Call me Chick. Anything else I
can do for you right now?"

"No, thank you, Chick. Please call me—"

"Marsha. You're Marsha Winters, right? The author?"

Maliha nodded. "I'll just go upstairs."

"You need anything, you let me know," he called after
her. "Including anything . . . medicinal."

Maliha realized she'd been walking a little hunched over,
favoring her back.

I look like I could use a stiff painkiller.

She straightened and turned around before she got to
the elevators. "No thanks, and I should mention that my
boyfriend's—"

"A DEA agent."

"How did you know that?"

"Just building gossip. I seem to be kind of a magnet
for it." He gave her a lustrous smile, and then rounded his
thumb and forefinger into an "OK" sign.

She punched the elevator's UP button.

"Oh, wait up, Marsha."

Maliha turned back and headed for the doorman's station.

"There's a package for you. Came today. Just a minute."

Chick rummaged through the desk and came up with box about a foot square and four inches high.

On the way up in the elevator, carrying the box, she wondered if Arnie had taken off for somewhere with a tropical breeze. Maliha had tipped Arnie generously over the years for his cooperation and silence about her activities, and given him investment advice.

He'd be a millionaire by now. No reason he couldn't live his dreams. I'm surprised he didn't say good-bye, though. Maybe he sent me a postcard from Bora Bora.

She remembered the considerate way Arnie had kept her from meeting Jake with blood on her face, early in their relationship when Jake didn't know much about her.

"There's a DEA agent in the lobby waiting for you, Ms. Winters. I told him you weren't home and I couldn't buzz him in, but this guy doesn't take no for an answer. I think he's prepared to sit in the lobby for days. He had a sandwich delivered from Dave's Deli and read the Tribune."

"You'd think he'd have better things to do with the government's time. Thanks for your efforts, Mr. Henshaw."

Arnie stretched his neck to look around her at the lone figure sitting in the lobby and shook his head. "You want to go up the back way?"

He meant the loading dock and a service elevator.

"No, I'll take care of it. I wouldn't want him to grow roots in there." She turned to walk inside.

"Wait. Ms. Winters, you've got a little spot of . . . er, red paint under your right ear."

She held still while he dampened a blindingly white handkerchief from a bottle of water and dabbed at her face. The handkerchief came away streaked with red.

"Don't worry. I'll take care of the, er, paint rag." He folded the handkerchief and tucked it in a compartment of his desk.

She realized that Arnie had cared for her, maybe even loved her in a fatherly way.

I hope I was never unkind or indifferent to him. Didn't know I'd miss him so much until I was stuck with Chick.

By the time she reached the door of her condo, images of people she cared about who'd died during her last case were occupying her mind, their faces in life and in death vividly remembered.

That was an advantage of being the demon's killing machine—never looking back.

Her bags were outside the door, at her request. The door opened before she could do it herself, and Hound drew her inside. She put the box on a table and slipped into his welcoming embrace. She rested her head against his lopsided shoulder and pressed against the slightly hollowed right side of his body, remnants of injuries he'd gotten in Vietnam. He pushed her back to arm's length. The pink scar that traversed one side of his black face looked like the Grand Canyon had been carved there, not in millennia by erosion but in the split-second impact of a piece of jagged shrapnel. She could see concern in his wrinkled brow and expressive eyes.

"Hold on while I get everything inside."

She watched as he checked the hallway, then pulled her luggage inside and closed the door. The two of them carried everything into her bedroom. He took her hand and led her to a sofa. Her home was large, since she'd purchased the condo next door and combined the two to make one residence. She had a master-bedroom suite, three guest bedrooms, an expansive living room where she could entertain, and an eat-in kitchen that could handle all of their needs when she had a full house. Since it was her public home, where she might have to meet anyone, from the press to her publisher, the furnishings were expensive but neutral, so the space wasn't personalized. There was also a hidden armory and a supply room that held everything from ink cartridges to disposable phones.

"Sit down," Hound said. "I can tell by the way you cringed with my hand on your back that you've been wounded. Want me to look? Yanmeng thinks he's better than I am at this doctoring stuff, but I just humor the old guy."

She turned her back to him, and he gently raised her shirt. For travel, she'd wrapped layers of bandages around her torso. She flexed her shoulder blades. The wounded area felt stiff.

"I should change that bandage," he said.

"Knock yourself out."

Hound went to retrieve her well-stocked medical kit. While he was gone, she unwrapped the old bandages and stretched out on the sofa, belly down.

His gasp when he came back into the room told her that her back wasn't a pretty sight.

"Christ, you look like you've been through a fucking wood chipper."

"Felt more like a buzz saw, but I'm feeling better. How's my tattoo?"

Maliha had a tattoo of a hawk across her shoulders, put there as a sign of respect by Master Liu.

"Let's see . . . it's intact. The wound starts below it."

Hound cleaned her back with warm, wet towels, applied an antibiotic treatment, and put on new bandages.

"Mmm, thanks," Maliha said. "You can rub my back anytime."

"Be more fun if your spine wasn't almost showing. Dampens the mood. Is it my imagination, or are you healing slower these days?"

When Maliha was Ageless, her healing was instantaneous. Since she'd broken her contract with her demon, she healed slower, and as she aged, she healed slower still.

"You're right. Ten years ago, a wound like this would heal in a day. Now a deep wound takes a day to close up on the outside and a couple more to finish healing the inside. Something with a lot of skin loss like this one—" She shrugged.

"Doesn't that prolong the pain you feel when you get injured?" He put a hand on her shoulder in sympathy.

She shook his hand roughly off and lowered her eyes so she couldn't meet his. "I don't need sympathy. Pain is part of my job description. Master Liu says . . ."

"Fuck Master Liu! He's some ascetic hermit who counts snowflakes on a mountain in China and dips his balls in ice water for the hell of it. You're not Liu. You live in the real world."

Maliha couldn't help smiling at the mental image of Master Liu running around naked, counting snowflakes, with a container of ice water clasped to his groin.

"Okay," she said. "You have a point. As long as I remain worldly, I can't approach Master Liu's way of living. He would say I have barely started on my spiritual journey."

"So you heard about Arnie leaving?"

Maliha nodded. "I don't know what to think about the new guy, Chick, yet. It's strange the way he finishes my sentences. Does he do that to you, too?"

"Yeah. Weird."

"I want to track down Arnie. The police are treating this disappearance with suspicion and we should too. You and Amaro could get together and start tracing his credit card usage and phone calls."

Hound looked indignant. "I don't need the little squirt's help for that. I'm a licensed private investigator. A dick and proud of it."

Maliha laughed. It felt good. "Okay, I won't tell Amaro you called him a little squirt if you can make sure Arnie's absence is intentional. On top of everything else."

"I know. You're thinking about Lucius."

Maliha hesitated. She hadn't revealed to anyone her last words to Lucius as he died in her arms. *I'll do it. I'll do it for us. I'll kill the demons and then we'll be together.*

Lucius was in the private hell created by his demon Sidana, suffering constant torture. "I told him I'd bring him back, Hound. I don't have the slightest idea of how to do that. Even if I kill the demons, does that mean he's free? Or that he finally dies? Even thinking about what he's going through . . ."

"Listen, you still have me and Yanmeng and Amaro. And Jake. You still have your goals. Maybe in time you'll figure out how to free Lucius."

Hound was a close friend of Maliha's, one of three who worked with her and understood her situation of trying to wiggle out from under Rabishu's thumb. Hound had been a medic in Vietnam. He didn't know that Maliha had been responsible for saving him after shrapnel had left him looking like Swiss cheese on the battlefield. Years later, she hired him as a private investigator. They had a history as lovers, too, but that had cooled as Hound's relationship with his girlfriend—and now fiancée—Glass, heated up.

Get a grip, woman. This isn't a soap opera.

Maliha straightened up. "Arnie's disappearance isn't the only piece of news. Xietai's dead."

"Finally caught up with him, huh? So was he Ageless like we thought?"

"No. I'd sure like to know who trained him, though."

"Get some rest. I'll tell Yanmeng and Eliu."

Maliha stood up. "Yanmeng already knows and I'm sure he's told his wife by now. I brought his son's knife back for him."

It would be up to Yanmeng and Eliu to decide if they wanted a memento of their son's life or not. If it were Maliha's choice, she'd say no, but she wanted to be able to give Xietai's parents a choice.

"I have something else I want to work on. Lucius gave me a key right before he, uh . . ."

"Was pulled into his demon's hell," Hound finished for her.

"Yes. He said the key would lead me to a lens shard he took from me."

Maliha sought not only to balance the scales on her body but also to eliminate the Sumerian demons left on Earth. To do so, she had to collect shards of a lens made by the chief Sumerian god, Anu, then broken by him into seven pieces and scattered across the world. When she had all seven shards, they would seal together into a round diamond lens that would allow Maliha to read the words on the Tablet of the Overlord. By speaking them aloud, she could kill the demons one by one.

Maliha possessed two shards already, plus the Tablet of the Overlord. She'd retrieved a third shard, but Lucius had taken it from her, following the orders of his demon Sidana.

She pulled a key from her pocket. "It has a number on it, but I don't know how to find the place it comes from. Once we do, it should be an easy retrieval."

"Nothing seems to be easy where those shards are concerned. What if Sidana knows where the shard is and has guards set up around it?"

"A trap, you mean? I'll have to deal with that if it comes up. The first obstacle is just finding the location. To start, send Amaro an image of the key and see if he can come up with anything."

"What was Lucius's full name? He might need to know if it's the name on the key's record."

"Lucius Antonius Cinna. He used 'L. A. Cinna' as a public name. He said the Roman first name was for intimate use." She handed the key over to Hound.

"So the rest of us are supposed to call him L. A.?"

"You can call him the Great Pumpkin if you want. Where he is, names aren't needed."

Amaro Reese, another of Maliha's assistants, was a computer specialist. She'd saved his life and his sister Rosie's life when they were in danger from a gang in Rio de Janeiro. Amaro discovered that he had a knack for working with computers, and now had a business breaking into the supposedly secure computer systems of large corporations and governments. They paid him to find the weaknesses in their systems, and Amaro never disappointed them. Or maybe he did disappoint them by the ease with which he penetrated their computer security. Amaro was a world-class hacker.

"You get some rest, and I'll start checking out Arnie. Maybe Amaro can come up with something on the key," Hound said.

"Is he staying here?"

"He'll be here in two or three days. Oh, and Jake's called several times. He left a message that he'll be traveling for a few days."

"Working?"

"Yes."

Maliha sighed. It seemed like there was nothing to do for

a while. She and Jake had a pact that there was no return contact when one person was working because of the dangerous situations that might be interrupted. Since Jake was Ageless, she didn't worry about him when he was out of touch—he should be able to handle anything that came up in his work.

Lately, time for reflection hadn't been bringing her peace. She'd been missing workouts, too. She'd been hoping Jake would be available to talk and bring her dinner.

Hound hugged her, avoiding touching her sore back. He didn't release her right away, and she felt a hardening in his groin pressed against her. She pushed him back.

"How's Glass doing?"

"Off on a food drop in Africa someplace. She won't be back for another three weeks."

"I see. You think we can fool around because she's on a mission."

"Crossed my mind."

Maliha pulled away. "Good night, Hound."

"Jesus, woman . . ."

Maliha closed the door to her suite, cutting off Hound's lament. In her private, soundproofed area, she opened her weapons case and spread everything out on the bed. Each blade was inside a locked case. She inspected everything carefully, and all were freshly oiled and gleaming. She was satisfied.

Skipping a shower to keep Hound's treatment of her back dry, she got in bed and pulled fresh, cool sheets up to her neck.

I'd rather be out there with Hound. No, scratch that. I wouldn't want to hurt Glass. This "good girl" business doesn't come easily.

She sighed into the darkness. *Good girls sleep alone. Where's Jake when I need him?*

Just before falling asleep, she remembered the box that Chick had given her. She retrieved the box, got a knife, and cut its well-taped edges. Inside was Arnie Henshaw's service cap, with the shiny black brim. There was blood, lots of it. Her eyes fastened on the note pinned to it: *The first one rests in peace. Or is that pieces?*

She slipped on a robe and called Hound into her bedroom.

"Change your mind?" he said. "You're not wearing anything under that. . . ."

"Oh, shut up. Arnie's dead."

She held out the box with the cap. He took it from her and examined everything, including the note.

"Nothing like a murder to spoil the mood," he said.

"It's terrible. Why send this to me when it's too late for me to do anything to help Arnie?"

"Fuck. I guess Arnie was considered expendable to send you a message."

"That's what I think too. But what's the message?"

Chapter Three

It was hours later that Maliha made it back to bed, after she and Hound put together a plan to investigate Arnie's death. She tried to set aside the sad event and instead started thinking of Jake. She pulled his pillow over and hugged it, thinking she could at least imagine his presence. A vague scent of her Ageless lover remained on the pillow, and she drew in a deep breath to hold it inside her. It was comforting and drew her thoughts further from Arnie's seemingly senseless death.

Jake Stackman was an immortal assassin beholden to the demon Idiptu, but he claimed that Idiptu had long ago lost interest in giving Jake assignments. That contrasted sharply with Maliha's demon, Rabishu. In Jake's case, he had no reason to rebel, since he had all the advantages of being Ageless without a demon interfering in his life. She talked to Jake about it, and he made it clear that he wasn't going to walk the mortal path with her for the sake of some point of ethics. He enjoyed his immortality, great speed, and nearly instantaneous healing, and he argued that he might be of more use to her in her quest with his abilities intact. She had to admit there was logic to that.

Since when has logic been an element of love? Or am I so out of practice I don't even recognize love anymore?

Maliha had been married once, over three hundred years ago in the American colonies. Then she'd been accused of witchery and treason, and given the special punishment of being burned at the stake. In the Salem witch hysteria, witches were hung, but in her case, she was also accused of planning to kill her husband to use his blood in her heinous practices. Lies, all of it. But the townspeople, her good friends, and even her husband turned against her in a trial during which she was gagged to prevent her from uttering curses.

Tied to the stake with the fire snapping at her toes, a demon's offer of immortality was too good to resist. After that, she'd taken up the Ageless way of life, killing on demand, gathering wealth, and enjoying sex on her whim and her terms with men, from kings and sheiks to the blacksmith who shod her horse. If her partner grew too attached, she moved on. Lasting love wasn't in her behavioral repertoire.

After rejecting the demon's control, Maliha became a mortal with benefits. It took her fifty years to learn how to reach out in friendship. Falling in love with a man was a lot harder.

Not so much the falling part, just the trusting part. I love Jake, at least I think I do. But . . . there's always some worry in the way. He still kills, according to his moral code, which he won't clearly explain. He won't give up immortality—isn't that selfish? There are things he won't talk about, and all he'll say is that they have something to do with his moral code. Can I live with that? I've already trusted him with my whole story but there might always be things hidden from me. He can keep his job secrets at the DEA. They're not what are bothering me.

And then there's Lucius.

Bits of their brief time together flitted through her mind. The crossbow bolt Lucius shot through her shoulder . . . the shimmering of his armor in the moonlight . . . their first kiss in a dark alley after he'd saved her life . . . the bloody heart outline he'd carved on a tree for her in the wilds of Ethiopia. She'd thought he was her true soul mate. Lucius was in his demon Sidana's private Underground. Even if she collected all the shards and destroyed the demons, she had no idea how to retrieve a person from a demon's fortress in hell. Wasn't it likely that when she snuffed out a demon, everything the demon possessed would disappear with him in a puff of smoke?

Sidana owns Lucius for eternity. I love Lucius as my one true love, my soul mate. But he's a shadow now, a dream I can't touch. No soul mate for me here in the Great Above, but there's Jake. As long as I keep Lucius locked inside my heart . . . Why not? I could be normal with Jake. He talks about a house in the mountains and kids. . . .

She hugged the pillow to her chest and let the tears flow, and was finally able to sleep.

She woke just a few hours later with the rest of the condo quiet. Hound was either gone or resting, so she took some time to work on her latest book in the Dick Stallion series, *Hot and Bothered.* The books were something she'd taken up to have a visible means of support. Maliha had accumulated wealth over quite a few normal lifetimes: precious metals and gems, art, collectible items, and investments. Still, she liked to have a job that explained away at least the tip of the iceberg of her vast wealth. The Dick Stallion books were designed like pulp detective fiction from the 1930s, down to the garish covers and the cheap, yellow paper. To her surprise, they became wildly popular, and she couldn't write them fast enough to keep up with the demands of her agent and publisher.

In this passage, Dick had gratuitous sex with an airline attendant somewhere over the Atlantic Ocean, unaware that the attendant was a recruiter for an international sex ring of bored housewives. She reported him to the Guiltless Orgasm Society as a candidate. After deplaning in Paris, he proceeded with his improbable adventure of saving the kidnapped daughter of a fabulously wealthy philanthropist while evading the Paris chapter of GOS.

Later, she removed Hound's bandage and took a shower. She adjusted the spray as hot and hard as it would go, sending liquid needles into her injured back. It was painful but in a good, cleansing way. Then she turned her face up to the water and accepted the pummeling for unspecified sins past and future.

Wrapped in a thick cotton robe, Maliha went into the kitchen. She hadn't eaten in a long time. There was a bag on the counter full of fresh croissants from Watson's Bakery in the lobby area of her building.

"Thank you, Hound!"

"Hound didn't bring them."

"Yanmeng?"

"Guilty."

She made some tea for the two of them and brought several croissants and a couple of plates over to the table.

Xietai's blood is on my hands.

She picked up a croissant and began to eat it in her favorite fashion: by pulling off one tip and then gently unraveling it. No butter or jam. Watson's Bakery made their croissants from scratch rather than using frozen ones, and the only thing wrong with these was that they were already an hour or two out of the oven.

"I'm sorry about the loss of your friend," Yanmeng said.

Maliha nodded. She didn't want to talk about it now.

"Yanmeng," she said between mouthfuls, "do you believe in unconditional love?" It was her indirect way of asking how he felt about his son's death at Maliha's hands.

Yanmeng's method of eating croissants was to bite them straight through, one end to the other, no mercy. He had a few flakes of pastry caught in his white moustache. The corners of Maliha's lips turned up, until she remembered that this was a solemn conversation.

"No."

There was an awkward silence. She'd hoped for more from him.

"You told me once that you loved me," Maliha said. She'd been riding a camel at the time and had nearly fallen off, until Yanmeng made it clear he wasn't talking about romantic love. "What did you mean by that?"

"I meant that you have earned my love, my respect, and my loyalty. I have given myself over to your cause. I would die for you."

Maliha lowered her head. She couldn't take the intensity

of the look that Yanmeng was giving her, a look like an X-ray reading her inner truth. "Wouldn't you consider that unconditional love, then?"

"No, because if you return to the service of the demon Rabishu and assassinate at his will, I would be betrayed."

"You have my word I will never do that," Maliha said.

"You are a worthy person, regardless of your past," he said.

A few minutes passed during which Maliha unraveled another croissant. All of sudden it struck her that this was Yanmeng she was sitting with, Yanmeng who could already walk different planes of existence, Yanmeng who was on his way to joining the god Anu in the highest plane. She viewed his aura and was stunned at the beautiful white and gold light radiating from him. He'd progressed far since the last time she'd looked.

With a gasp, she bowed her head. "You honor me."

He waved his hand. "We're just two friends talking. And cut out that aura viewing. My wife Eliu says I already have a big head."

"I killed your son." *Duh. He already knows that.*

"You removed a scourge of evil from the world. Xietai betrayed Eliu and me a long time ago. What kind of son turns his parents in for death sentences to gain favor for himself with the government? Our love was broken!"

"Thank you for saving my life. I brought home something of his, a knife. Do you want it as a memento?"

Mixed emotions played across Yanmeng's face. In spite of his words, pain showed in his eyes. "No. We're finished talking about Xietai. Hound mentioned that you had some scraped skin on your back. I've got just the thing for it, some salve my grandmother used to make. Let's take a look. I hope he didn't mess anything up."

The stars sang of adventure and Maliha's ears were tuned to them. It had been three days since her arrival home, three days during which Hound and Yanmeng had alternated treating her back. The wound was healed enough by her standards, yet Yanmeng kept putting on gray gooey stuff that smelled like fish, and Hound kept washing it off in favor of antiseptic cream. Finally she mutinied and declared that no one would attempt to heal any part of her, ever.

Hound had nothing definitive to report about Arnie Henshaw.

"Arnie made few phone calls, most of them for food delivery. He'd purchased a one-way ticket to Antigua, one of the Leeward Islands in the Caribbean. The building management said he'd given written notice two weeks before his disappearance, saying that he was retiring to some peace and quiet, no forwarding address given. Then he'd taken accumulated vacation days for the two weeks of his notice, so the day his resignation letter came in was the last day anyone saw him," Hound said.

"I wonder what the rush was. If he'd been planning this retirement for a while, he could have worked the last two weeks," Maliha said.

"He was within the letter of the regulations to pull that trick, but it was the act of someone not concerned about getting a good reference for his next place of employment. Someone retiring and leaving the country and his former life behind. Human Resources was concerned that they had no place to send his last paycheck."

"They do know he's dead, right?"

Hound sighed. "The police aren't certain of that. Now they say it looks like Arnie needed to get out of the country fast and wanted people to think he was dead."

"Meaning somebody was after him and he sent the hat and note to me himself. I can't believe he wouldn't have asked me for help if that was the case."

"You might have it wrong. Maybe the bad guys made it look like *you* were the one after him. Arnie was too scared to approach you. He didn't know who to trust."

Maliha shook her head. "We've got to find him, if he's still alive. Whatever his problem is, we can . . ."

"Make it go away?"

Maliha nodded. "Or find out who killed him and why."

"One more thing. Arnie's financial holdings were liquidated and sent to a private Swiss bank account."

"Interesting. Maybe he really is out there, living off the grid," Maliha said. "I'd sure like to think so. That note creeped me out, though. 'The first one rests in peace.' The only way I can interpret it is that there would be more deaths. Why would Arnie write that if he was behind this?"

Hound shrugged. "Who knows? To make a convincing disappearance. Say he was trying to make it look like a sociopath had written the note." Hound latched onto a thought, his brows furrowing. "Maybe he *is* a sociopath."

"Oh, I can't believe that."

"I'd be happy to hop down to Antigua to look around for him." His face took on a hopeful look.

"I'm sure you would." Hound's smile disappeared. "Did Arnie actually board that plane or just buy a ticket as a ruse? Amaro's coming in later. Let's see what his electronic approach turns up."

When Amaro arrived later that day, he brought news on the key Lucius had given her—the one that supposedly led to the hiding place of the third shard. The three friends pounced on the search for Arnie and the latest about the key, and that left Maliha with time on her hands until there was something actionable.

She decided to make herself useful.

She dressed wanting to be prepared for anything and opted for her leathers. She tied her hair in a thick braid, with a black silk scarf wound around her head. Flexing the skintight black gloves on her hands, she moved toward her weapons collection.

The cache was in a small room that served as an armory for the team. In her private haven, nine floors up, there was an entire wall devoted to displaying weapons openly. With the possibility of visitors down here, the goodies were locked out of sight.

She ran her hands over knives, swords, guns, and axes. The gleam of the two *sai* caught her eye. They were three-pronged edged weapons with the middle prong longer than

the other two. She'd made leather sheaths for when she
didn't want to wear them tucked through her belt. Strapping
them on her back, she was pleased that the handles didn't
show over her shoulders. From the front, she looked like an
unarmed, though oddly dressed, woman.

Maliha was all curves and sharp edges, like a sexy porcupine. She went out through the main lobby faster than any
human could run. Chick, if he was still on duty, would have
to be broken in slowly to the idea of her leaving at night in
this type of garb. Maliha slowed her pace as she ran along
the lakefront. It was Friday night, a good time to visit night-
clubs near Division Street. Her scene wasn't the clubs, but
the dark alleyways where muggers could lurk.

The temperature was mild for a December night, probably in the upper forties. It was 1:30 A.M., and the district
was pulsing with life. Cabs turned the street into a traffic
jam, accompanied by the shouts and gestures of cabbies
with their windows open. The target of their animosity
was generally the suburbanites who'd driven their cars
downtown, but sometimes they railed at each other as
one cab slipped in front of another with an inch to spare.
Music poured from the crowded bars and bouncers managed velvet-roped lines. Maliha wouldn't mind dancing,
and she'd gone to a few of the clubs with her friend Randy
Baxter. Randy was Maliha's window into normality, a
twenty-something friend who knew nothing about Maliha's
background. But Maliha only drank on rare occasions
and almost never to the point of intoxication. The stakes
were too high. She didn't want a stupid accident or a slow
response to land her in Rabishu's hell forever, her quest
overcome by a few giant margaritas.

Maliha's heart beat faster at the prospect of some action.
She prowled the alleys. For the next hour, she saw nothing
except some couples who'd slipped into the entranceways
to make boozy love. Heavy clouds moved in, followed by
a brief downpour. People on the streets ran for cover and
did their best to crowd into the clubs, leaving the sidewalks
less crowded. Maliha waited out the storm in the shelter of

a recessed doorway. Rivulets of water ran down the alley, sending the filth down another block. Two condoms and a banana peel floated by near her feet. The storm ended as suddenly as it started, but colder weather had come in behind it. Maliha considered going home. With the sidewalks less crowded, the likelihood of finding someone in trouble decreased.

I'll give it a little while, but it's not exactly a starlit stroll anymore.

As she rounded the corner of a new alley, suddenly a motion-activated spotlight came on about halfway down. Two men stumbled into the light. One pinned the other up against the wall, and she saw the glint of a knife in the light.

"Stop!" She ran toward the men, racing the movement of the knife. She yanked the man's knife hand back sharply and twisted it, hearing bones in his arm break. She banged his head into the brick wall and stepped out of his way as he fell to the ground unconscious. Damage had already been done by the attacker. The victim slid down the wall, bleeding heavily from a wound to the abdomen.

Maliha searched the victim's pockets, found a cell phone, and called 911. After the call, she put pressure on the injured man's wound. She'd have to stay until an ambulance arrived, not an ideal situation, but the knifed man's only chance.

She heard a whimpering noise from outside the lighted area and turned her head to check. Just as she did, a man came hurtling out of the dark at her.

"What did you do to my brother, bitch!"

He collided with her. She was on her knees in the wet alley, bent over the man who was bleeding, and his impact sent her sprawling. Then he was on top of her and punched her in the side with his fist.

"I'm going to kill you!" he screamed in her face.

She brought her elbows up and hit him sharply on both sides of his head. She pushed him off her and scrambled to her feet.

"I don't have time for this," she said, dragging him over to the wall. "Sit still and shut up." A quick punch to the face ensured that he did just that. Maliha went back to compressing the blood flow from the man she was trying to save.

The whimpering got louder.

"Is there someone else out there? An ambulance will be here soon. If you can come over here into the light, do it."

The wounded man opened his eyes, half slits filled with pain. "My wife . . ." Blood dripped from the corners of his mouth.

Maliha heard a dragging noise and then saw a woman, mouth gagged, wrists tied, bone projecting from an open break at her ankle, trying to wriggle across the ground.

"Your wife's fine," Maliha said. "She's here with me. Hang in there. Help's coming."

Maliha pulled the woman over close to her, removed the gag, and cut through the plastic ties.

"Oh my God! Is Steve dead? Is my husband dead? Oh my God!"

"Calm down. He's not dead. What's your name?"

"Belle."

"Belle, do you think you can press here," Maliha said, indicating the bleeding wound, "if I move you closer?"

"I think so . . ." Belle slipped into unconsciousness.

Maliha heard two sirens approaching.

Time to get out of here. She ripped off a strip of the shirt of the man she'd told to shut up, folded it into a square, and pressed it on Steve's wound. It was saturated with blood by the time she unwound the scarf from her head. She ran the scarf under his body and tied it over the cloth square as the sirens grew louder. The delicate silk and soaked cloth didn't provide enough compression. She squatted next to Steve. If she didn't keep manual pressure on, he would bleed out. Maliha glanced at Belle, wishing she hadn't lost consciousness.

I'll bet they're tourists. She comes to Chicago happily married and goes home a widow. Not if I can stop it.

Headlights turned in at the end of the alley, reflecting in the puddles and giving the impression of four headlights staring her down. The police car was first, followed by the ambulance. The muscles in Maliha's legs ached to do what she'd always done—run away, keep her secret.

The car pulled up close, adding its lights to the alley spotlight. Two officers got out, weapons drawn, and remained behind their open car doors. Maliha kept her face down.

"Move away and get down on your knees!"

Looking at it from their point of view, she knew it looked bad. Here she was armed, bloody-handed, with four bodies on the ground.

"I'll move as soon as the paramedics take over. Four people are alive, this man is critical," she said.

"Medics will move in as soon as you're down on your knees. Do it now!"

Reluctantly Maliha moved away several feet. She knew the next step was to be handcuffed and taken in for questioning, and she couldn't allow that. Every second of delay meant more of Steve's blood where it didn't belong, on the outside of his body.

Nothing else to do.

She turned and ran at Ageless speed toward the empty end of the alley. The human eyes watching saw her vanish.

Shit! The camera in that patrol car doesn't have human eyes.

Several blocks away, after her scale rebalanced for two lives saved, she considered going back and destroying the camera in the patrol car.

Too late now. It's up to Amaro to save my skin.

Chapter Four

"Are you out of your mind?" Amaro said. It was 3 A.M. He was tapping away at his computer, trying to hack into the Chicago Police Department's files, looking for the digital images of Maliha's retreat. "How do you know there was a camera in the squad car? Do they upload wirelessly?"

The edge in his voice triggered a low, dangerous tone in hers.

"I stopped to help people in trouble. I do that. The man was injured and his wife was going to be raped. They would probably have been killed. Sound familiar? I didn't hear any complaints when I saved Rosie."

Amaro grunted. "Do all of the squad cars have dash cams?"

"I don't know. I think so. The PODs are wireless, so maybe the dash cams are too. That's your area, not mine."

PODs, or police observation devices, were surveillance cameras in public areas throughout Chicago, ranging from obvious ones the size of mailboxes with flashing lights to micro-PODs, unobtrusive cameras mounted on rooftops or light poles.

"I have to get the POD stuff too?"

"No. I'm sure I've shown up there dozens of times, but I know where they are and I never show my face uncovered while wearing this." She had not changed out of her leathers and Steve's blood was starting to dry on her. "So I'm just another freak running around this city."

"You know what," Hound said, "I think you just got restless and went out looking for trouble. Now we're going to see your lovely ass frame-by-frame on YouTube. You know, we've all broken the law for you. You get caught, so do we."

"Why, do you think I'll break under questioning and turn you all in for a few lollipops? You're missing the point here. What do you think would happen if the military got hold of me? I'm a readymade super soldier, and they're not going to listen to any crap about demons. I'd be drugged and experimented on to find out how I work. Wait till they find out I live a long time, too. They could pass me down from one generation of scientists to the next."

She pictured herself strapped to a table, a group of scientists clustered around, and sharp instruments gleaming within reach.

My own death by a thousand cuts.

"You think I don't fear the same thing?" Yanmeng said. "China, Russia, and America have studied remote viewers as intelligence tools. My only advantage if I'm caught is that I'm already halfway into the grave."

"Hey, don't talk like that," Amaro said. "You're gonna be around when I have great-grandkids." The conversation veered into Amaro's lack of a wife to get the whole great-grandkids thing going.

"I'm going to go get cleaned up," Maliha said. Her friends were back to being themselves.

As she headed for her room, Maliha wondered why no one had asked about what seemed to be her most glaring failure of the night.

Why didn't I get rid of the camera as soon as I saw the headlights of the patrol car? Speed to the car, blast the camera, and speed away. The second mugger shouldn't have caught me by surprise, either. Losing my edge?

Maliha cringed at the thought of having been sent sprawling by such an unworthy opponent. It was so unsettling she hadn't mentioned it.

Mishandled that man's wound, too. He was just bleeding, damn it. A loss of focus? Maybe I should go back to Master

Liu's for more training. Too ashamed to tell him the reason, though. Her cheeks burned at the thought of facing him.

By the time she came back to join the conversation, Maliha had made a decision.

"Hey, got some results," Amaro said as soon as she entered the room.

"Tell me the bad news."

"I found the digital upload on the department's servers and squashed it. I wrote over it with some military-grade static. The segment was still on the hard drive in the squad car, so I deleted it and gave it the static treatment. No one's going to recover anything from it."

"Great. Amaro to the rescue!"

He frowned. "Not exactly. The video segment was viewed before I erased it. We could still be okay, unless the viewer made a copy on something like a flash drive I can't reach."

"Oh."

There was silence that stretched out uncomfortably.

"I think we should all get the hell out of here," Hound said. "Scatter."

"I second that motion," Amaro said.

"Third," Yanmeng said.

"Let's do it," Maliha said. It was the decision she'd come to earlier, but she was pleased that they'd come up with it by themselves.

Chapter Five

Elizabeth put her face close to the window of the Nine Lives Pub in Washington, D.C., looking in. It was a rainy Wednesday evening and only 8 P.M., a time more suited for dinner at one of the many restaurants in the Adams Morgan neighborhood rather than staking out territory in a bar. Pub crawls didn't build up until later at night. There were a few customers at scattered cocktail tables, their heads close together, their eyes displaying the shine of alcohol and desire.

Couples stopping for a drink or two before heading home to make love. They're already paired and don't need to join the flesh parade later on.

She breathed on the window and drew a heart on the fogged area with a blood red fingernail filed to a point. Pulling open the heavy wooden door, she stepped inside. The air smelled of cheese dip and salsa. There were bowls on each small table, along with a basket of chips. The walls hadn't been painted for years, and since the place was formerly a smoking establishment, they were coated with a smoke film that looked substantial enough to support the ceiling all on its own.

She flipped back the hood of her raincoat, revealing blonde hair that fell in loose curls to her shoulders. Her skin, which she prized above all, was as white as if the sun had never kissed it, and free of imperfections. Elizabeth slowly unbuttoned her coat, shook it out, and hung it on a peg on a rack near the door. By the time her stunning figure, in a sheath dress the same color as her fingernails and lips, had been displayed fore and aft, she could have her pick of men in the room. But that wasn't why she was here tonight. When she did prowl, it wouldn't be in a bar with congealed cheese dip on the tables.

Elizabeth sat at the bar. The bartender, trying to be non-chalant, finished wiping a section of the bar before he came over to take her order.

"What can I get you to drink, honey?"

She waved away the prospect of a drink order with a small gesture of her hand. "I'm here for a meeting in the back room."

The bartender went to a curtained doorway and spoke to someone behind the curtain. He waved Elizabeth over with a nod of his head.

Behind the curtain were three security guards. One grabbed Elizabeth's arms and raised them over her head. Another searched her with a metal detector wand followed by a lingering, manual search. She pursed her lips and put up with it.

If my demon Tirid hadn't ordered me to do this, I'd . . .

She allowed herself images of her pale skin streaked with the guards' blood and their brains splattered against the walls, but it wasn't as satisfying as the real thing.

"Passport," the oldest of the guards said.

"Sorry, didn't bring it. Doesn't go with my outfit," she said.

The guard tensed and drew back his hand as if to strike her. His face reddened.

Let the fun begin.

Her nostrils widened and she noticed a fresh scratch on the man's arm. She could smell his blood. Her eyes dilated with pleasure. *Come to me, Red.*

One of the other guards pushed Red away. "No damage to the package."

Red's shoulders drooped in disappointment. He had no idea what had just been averted. The three huddled around a computer monitor, looking at her and then back at the screen. They had to be satisfied with the visual match to whatever grainy photo they had of her on the screen. Red motioned her forward, and she walked with him down a short hallway. At the end was a steel door with a retinal security scanner and an intercom. Red pressed the intercom switch.

"She's here, sir. She's uncooperative and wouldn't show any ID. I recommend you not see her."

There was a slight pause, and a smile began to spread across Red's face.

"Send her in."

Red grumbled under his breath, but moved his eye up to the retinal scanner. Elizabeth was thinking along the lines of poking out his eye and holding it up to the scanner herself if he wasted any more of her time.

It'd work as long as the eye is fresh. After a while, the vitreous clouds up so the scanner can't read the retina through the murky gel. I wonder if the dead eye could be refilled with fresh fluid. After all, they do it on live people. I'll have to experiment with that sometime.

The steel door slid back. Red grabbed Elizabeth's arm and tugged her inside. She reached out with her other hand and drew her fingernail across the back of his hand. Blood welled and he let her go, startled. He pushed her ahead of him instead.

The room was sparsely furnished with a conference table, soft lights that circled the ceiling, gleaming steel walls, and a small but well-equipped bar in a far corner. One man sat at the table. There was none of the dinginess of the Nine Lives Pub that fronted this place.

"That'll be all," the man at the table said.

"But . . ." Red started. The man's raised eyebrows convinced him to close his mouth and leave.

Elizabeth sighed.

"Sorry to put you through that, Elizabeth. Do you have a last name?"

"Yes."

When the name wasn't forthcoming, the man said. "You can call me Fred. Fred Smith."

She knew *exactly* who he was, and his name was *not* Fred Smith. She'd worked hard to find the channels that led to this meeting, and she would have walked out on anyone else.

No harm in playing along with this little identity game for now.

Elizabeth walked over to the bar, poured herself a double Chivas Regal, neat, and sat opposite Fred at the table. A chill rode up her spine, a very enjoyable one.

This is a place where deals are made, where power oozes out of the walls, where lives are built up or torn down.

"A Scotch drinker, eh? You should have asked. I would have gotten out the good stuff."

Elizabeth shrugged. She wasn't picky about her drink and had just taken something to appear companionable. She was going to be spending a lot of time in this man's company.

He poured himself the same drink, came over to her side of the table, and perched on the edge of it. They toasted to friendship. He looked down her dress while she checked out his flat stomach and broad shoulders.

Not bad. At least the sex should be tolerable.

Elizabeth put her hand on his knee, answering the unspoken question. She wanted Fred relaxed and confident that he'd already charmed his visitor.

"I have something to offer you," she said. "A secret weapon to use against your opponents."

"What makes you think I need a secret weapon? My relationships with my enemies are all civil. We manage."

"Then why did you use the term *enemies*?"

"It's a common . . . what are you selling, some new type of armament?"

"In a way."

"Get to the point, or I'll get the guard back in here to soften you up. Come to think of it, it might be fun to do it myself." Fred shifted positions enough to show that he was wearing a shoulder holster underneath his jacket. She'd already spotted it, but having it in view made her next move easier. She rose from the table, snatched the gun, and pointed it at him. It all happened so fast that he didn't even feel the touch of her hand slipping into his jacket. When he got the picture, he put his drink on the table and raised his hands.

"That wouldn't be wise," she said, "for you or the guard. I can take care of myself."

Her voice was calm but devoid of warmth, and carried the utter certainty that she would follow through.

She put the gun on the table. Fred went back to his chair and sat down. She was pleased to see that he was cautious but not overly intimidated. He wasn't so much yielding to her as wanting her out of his space. When he sat down, he reached for the gun. Her hand shot out and claimed it, but then she let him take it back, knowing he was doing so with her permission. She glared at him across the table for a moment and then continued as if nothing had happened. He picked up his drink and sipped it, reevaluating her over the rim of the glass.

"The secret weapon is an assassin. An unstoppable one."

"Why unstoppable?"

Elizabeth went to a laptop computer at the other end of the table and plugged in a USB flash drive. Fred leaned over her shoulder—too close—as she started up a video.

"See the woman kneeling on the ground? Watch her."

In a moment, the woman vanished.

"Are you seriously trying to sell me some goddamned magic act?"

"No. Watch again, slower this time."

"My God! Does anyone else have this video?"

Elizabeth shook her head. "It's been destroyed. Thoroughly. Do we have a deal?"

"You haven't said what you want in return."

"I want to be your advisor. As you rise, so do I."

Fred tipped his glass to her. "Deal."

"Deal."

Chapter Six

With her team scattered because of the police video, Maliha decided to leave her Chicago home in her private jet. For once the jet happened to be located in the United States, if not in the state of Illinois. She had a habit of leaving it in foreign locations. Indianapolis was less than two hundred miles away, so by the time she'd packed a few essentials and taken a thirty-mile limo ride to the Gary Jet Center in Gary, Indiana, the jet had arrived. The jet center was an FBO, a fixed base operator, that served as a truck stop for private planes and jets. Her pilot preferred to avoid major hubs like O'Hare and Midway.

The second refueling stop, this one in Lisbon, almost sidetracked Maliha from her destination. Although it was December, it was sunny and mild, 62 degrees the day she was there. Very nice for a lingering meal outdoors at a café or a quick visit to the beach. The water might be too cold to enjoy swimming, but the sand would be warm. Maliha closed her eyes and imagined lying on the beach without a care in the world.

With Jake. I haven't seen him since I got back from New York. She sighed. *Some other time.*

They took off into blue skies with another 2,500 miles to go, a nonstop flight for her midsize executive jet. The drive from the Ben Gurion International Airport in Tel Aviv to her friend's home was 9 miles of steady rain in a cab where the windshield wipers had only one speed: super slow. She wondered how the driver could see in the long intervals between swipes, but she wasn't about to get out in the rain to switch cabs.

Fingering Lucius's key to the shard in her pocket, she hoped she might get information about it and come home from this trip with the third shard. It had special significance to her because it marked both her first and last time with Lucius—when he'd stolen the shard from her and when he'd freely given her the key to its hiding place.

The cab let her out at a white apartment building that stood up on piers, as if flooding were a concern. It was a cooling device, not necessary at 40 degrees but welcome during the brutal summer heat. Winds sweeping under the buildings eased the temperature and the residents liked to think they made the humidity more bearable.

Maliha glanced up. Her friend, Abiyram Heber, was sitting on his covered balcony. He appeared to be looking elsewhere, but she had no doubt that he'd seen her, even in the gloom of the rain and approaching darkness. He was a retired commander in the Mossad, the Israeli intelligence agency. At the age of sixty, the only thing retired about Abiyram was that he no longer went on field missions. Maliha had turned to him for tracking down some information on her last case. It was a touchy situation.

Abiyram had known her thirty years ago, when they'd worked together on a number of missions and had been close friends. Then she turned up three decades later looking the same. She had to give him some vague hints about her story and told him that perhaps he could join her band of do-gooders.

She had also asked him, in payment of a life-debt for a time she'd saved his life, if he would try to find out about Jake's past. She hadn't heard anything from him about that, so she assumed there was no success.

He opened the door to her with a warm smile on his face. They hugged. He was still a lean and hard desert man of action, and his eyes, though now set in a wrinkled face, showed that thirty years hadn't diminished the spirited man inside the physical shell. His breath smelled of olives and his clothing of the sun.

"I hate to just show up like this," Maliha said. She glanced down at the luggage at her feet. "The heat's on a bit in the States. Mind if I stay with you for a few days?"

"My friend, you are always welcome in my house. Come, wash off the dust of the journey."

Do I look that dirty?

Chapter Seven

Maliha remained out of contact with her team, but she did check Internet news. The only thing that showed up said that a female suspect might have fled the scene, although one of the victims claimed the person wasn't a suspect but was helping the injured. No description of the fleeing woman was given, and Belle was disputing that there was even a woman present. She said the person was a black man.

Atta girl, Belle. Although she might have fainted before figuring out what sex I was, and only saw the color of my clothing.

There was no mention of the camera in the police car. One of the brothers confessed to the attack. The police had played them off against each other. She was glad to see that Steve had survived. Steve and Belle Hanson were tourists, as she'd guessed, and they would be going home to Kansas City as soon as Steve was discharged from the hospital and paid his parking tickets.

So far, so good. Amaro's got them running after their tails.

Abiyram didn't press her for any reason for her visit. After dinner, she decided she was ready to give him all of her background and recruit him for her team—if he was still interested. In the past he'd told her that, as dedicated as he was to his country, it was time for him to do something of his personal choice.

They relaxed after dinner, sipping Nescafé, the popular

at-home coffee. Maliha didn't care much for instant coffee, but she knew better than to complain to her host.

"I have something I'd like to talk about," she said.

"Me too."

"You go first, then." Maliha was glad to have the extra time to phrase her thoughts as best she could.

He sat with her and said nothing for a time. The streets they could see from the sliding door to the balcony were filled with cars with their headlights on. If she relaxed her eyes just right, she could get a streaming effect that was very pleasant to watch.

Like liquid cars flowing along in a highway river.

"It's about Stackman."

Maliha's eyes closed and her heart sank. His tone wasn't happy.

"I can stop at this point and forget that you ever asked me."

She gave it serious consideration. Without Abiyram's help, it was unlikely that she would come up with anything independently. Even Amaro had spun his wheels.

An unbidden whisper in her mind: *Do I need to know or want to know?*

And another: *Why can't I trust Jake to tell me when the time is right?*

"Continue."

Abiyram sighed and sat back in his chair. He reached to the side and in a moment, she saw that he was tamping and then lighting his favorite pipe.

"I was very lucky to find anything on him. His partner during that period is dead, killed on the first leg of the missions. Stackman continued on alone."

"But what are the missions? For whom?"

"Ah, that has cost me dearly. I hope the information is of great value to you. First, let us go back to 2001, the first year of Stackman's vanishing act. By the way, at no time were his actions unknown to a few in the U.S. government. A few at the top. What occurred that year? Besides 9/11, since he's clear on that one."

I have no time for guessing games. In a desultory tone, she said, "SARS."

"First thing I looked at. Was the introduction in China deliberate and did it come from outside? To the best of my knowledge, no. Look to a different continent. In the Democratic Republic of the Congo, President Laurent Kabila was gunned down inside his office, supposedly by a bodyguard, but the details are slippery. He was succeeded by his son Randall, who some say was not his son at all, and in fact not even born in D.R. Congo. Details? Again slippery. Randall managed to put an end to the Great War of Africa that had six different countries' armies and a couple dozen militias traipsing around his country. Peace at last, or at least a better situation."

"I know my history." *The Great War of Africa was chaos wreaked by the demons, with humans paying the price— like so many events in our history.* "What . . ."

"What does your man have to do with it? The assassination of the elder Kabila was blamed on a bodyguard in the room with him, but the shot came from outside the room, fired by a sniper. By Stackman."

Maliha's mind was racing. "Is that so bad? It was a targeted assassination to put into power a man who eventually was able to bring a semblance of peace to the region."

Abiyram puffed on his pipe for a while before continuing. The aromatic smoke drifted her way and she inhaled. Even though she was a nonsmoker, she loved the scent of a pipe.

"In 2002, President Hugo Chávez of Venezuela was thrown out of office by a coup. Two days later, he was back in office, restored to power by the loyal Presidential Guard. Much fuss was made about possible U.S. involvement in deposing him, at the very least prior knowledge, at the most collusion. Stackman worked his way into the Presidential Palace. The Guard retook the palace with little resistance because Stackman had prepared the way for them. He was instrumental in getting Chávez back into office, and quickly."

Maliha opened her mouth to ask questions, but Abiyram held up his hand to forestall them.

"2003. Military men took over a hotel in Manila in the Philippines and raised a mutiny against President Gloria

Arroyo at a sensitive moment in her young presidency. The hotel was rigged with high explosives. Some hostages were let out, but the press and others remained. One mutineer decided to blow the place, actually pressed the button, but there was no detonation. Stackman, posing as a journalist on the inside, had defused the bombs. After killing the firebrand, he then talked the rest of the mutineers into surrendering."

He puffed on his pipe while Maliha bit her tongue.

This is a good thing too, isn't it?

"2004. The Sudanese government and the militia group Janjaweed—"

"Stop! Skip this one."

Abiyram's eyebrows rose but he did as she wished.

"2005. The year following the tsunami. The central government of Indonesia had a long-standing issue with a northern territory named Aceh, where rebellion brewed for independence. Aceh happened to be the closest point to the earthquake's epicenter and was particularly weakened by the tsunami. Many of its rebels and military died, and quite a few of those who weren't killed by natural causes or the Indonesian army were killed by Stackman in a systematic wipeout. The citizens of Aceh, hit by the double whammy of nature's devastation and no defensive capability, decided that peace was in their interest and an agreement was signed ending twenty-nine years of war. That was it. In 2006, Stackman resurfaced at the DEA."

"The things you're telling me don't sound completely negative. I'm confused. Why didn't you want me to hear this? You know I'm not naïve about black ops missions. We have done these same things together and separately."

"You're looking at these as individual events. You need to put them together to see the big picture, the pattern. D.R. Congo, Venezuela, the Philippines, Sudan, Indonesia. What links them? Put your brain into it."

She thought for a while. "Gold."

"Excellent. You've heard of blood diamonds?"

Maliha didn't want to know where this was going, but she nodded.

"Beginning in roughly the year 2000, the dirty little practice of using siphoned-off diamonds to fund arms sales and rebel activities began to get the spotlight on it, in the UN, the diamond industry, and elsewhere. There are still conflict diamonds on the market now, but they are greatly diminished. The world spotlight sent the cockroaches scurrying, only to emerge elsewhere. Gold from these five countries and others is flowing into maintaining some of the most heinous dictatorships and presidents-for-life in the world. That's not all. I know there's a link to America. Gold is flowing there but I haven't been able to find the end of the rainbow yet. In some cases the gold-producing countries know about it, in other cases all that was needed was a stable environment to support the shadowy operation. Stackman was crucial to the setup. To turning on the faucet."

"Blood *gold*?"

"If you wish."

Not Jake.

"Any chance you're mistaken?"

"None whatsoever. I would stake my life on this."

Maliha remembered something he'd said at the beginning of the conversation: *At no time were his actions unknown to a few in the U.S. government. A few at the top.*

She leaned back in her chair to think while Abiyram puffed on his pipe. Suddenly the pipe smoke revealed the pencil-sized red light of a laser gun sight. Her hand flashed out to tip his chair, to move him out of the way, but it was too late. As her push propelled him and the chair over, there was already a bullet in his brain.

Maliha turned the table on its side to block the sniper's view through the window, and then she crouched next to Abiyram and felt for a pulse.

"Old friend," she said. His eyes lost the light of life as she watched, helpless to stop the shutdown of a brilliant mind.

When a violent death happened, there was a psychic scar left at the location. As Maliha understood it, the victim's spirit left a remnant of itself behind in the sudden transition to its next destination. Most people would walk through the location and not notice anything, but Maliha could detect the imprint if she was paying attention. It was similar to her ability to see auras, but this viewing was intensely personal. It required her to go through the death experience of the victim.

She pushed Abiyram slightly out of the way so that she could lie down in the spot he died. She shifted slightly, and she found the correct spot. Her eyes remained open, but the input to her sight and other senses lessened dramatically. She relaxed and let another scene come into focus. Slipping into his death experience, she looked through Abiyram's eyes as he sat across the table from her in the last moments before his death.

From his perspective, she saw that he was scanning around him, an old habit for a Mossad operative. Through his eyes, she saw the origin of the laser sight through the sliding door. It was a window on the top floor of a building a block away. She dropped the pipe. Then she felt pressure and pain on her forehead as the bullet arrived and penetrated her skull. Right after, so close in time they seemed to happen as one, she saw a hand as a blur in front of her eyes. Her head snapped back and she swayed and then tumbled out of the chair to the floor. She heard the comforting words "old friend" before her vision went black and she felt her heart beat for the last time.

Maliha remained in position and in a moment, Abiyram's traumatized, scattered spirit coalesced around her like a loving embrace, grew whole, and moved on.

She called a friend in the Mossad, explained what had just happened, and said she would stay until he arrived to make sure no one looked through Abiyram's office. Although Abiyram kept most of his information in his head, she couldn't guarantee that there weren't secret documents in his home. She found out that Abiyram had a younger brother, something she'd never known, and that he would be brought in to be the guardian of the body so that it was never alone, a Jewish custom. As a friend, she stayed with Abiyram until the brother arrived.

A man like Abiyram must have enemies, but he said that this information had cost him a lot. What did he mean by that? We were talking about Jake's past. Was Jake the sniper? He has the skill to do it. He could have found out that Abiyram was poking around in his past. Do I find him and try to force the answer out of him? If I did that, it might break us both.

Maliha shuddered at the form such a confrontation would take. The Ageless felt pain, as she well knew, but their rapid healing made them ready for another torture session in a short time.

If he's not guilty, he'll hate me for suspecting him and going behind his back to learn about blood gold. Can there be another explanation? If he is guilty . . . what then?

When the Israeli agent arrived with the younger brother in tow to take over from her, she packed her few things. Then she left without a word, her eyes bright with unshed tears.

Chapter Eight

The next day Maliha attended Abiyram's funeral. The Mossad had photographed his body and removed the bullet for their investigation, then released his body for burial. In accordance with Jewish custom, he wasn't embalmed. There was no viewing, and his body was wrapped in a shroud inside a plain wooden coffin. His body was in the ground fifteen hours after his death.

Later Maliha investigated the top floor of the building where the sniper's shot originated. She found several scratches on the windowsill. An experienced sniper left no trace—the scratches indicated that the rifle had been moved around, as if the shooter was hesitant.

An experienced sniper like Jake wouldn't hesitate, she couldn't help thinking. *Is this proof enough that he wasn't here?*

In the aftermath, she found that Abiyram had changed his will to include her, since she came back into his life. Anything in his apartment related to the intelligence business was hauled away by the government, as expected. Abiyram's money went to his brother. What was left, the personal accumulations of a brilliant, worldly, and well-traveled man, belonged to Maliha. Unable to stay in his apartment to sort and appreciate her newly acquired treasures, she had everything packed and sent home to Chicago on her jet.

Reeling with the notion that she was a destructive force ripping through the lives of others, she wondered if this might be a good time to break up her team. They all had had lives of their own before they aligned their goals with hers. Maybe it was just too dangerous. In a short period, she'd had to deal with the loss of two old friends, Arnie and the Israeli. Although Arnie's death wasn't a certainty, she didn't hold out much hope for finding him alive.

Why not turn them loose? None of them need me to survive. We're friends, but time and distance could take care of that. Maybe it's time for my cover identity to meet an unfortunate death or just vanish. Bye-bye, Marsha Winters.

Maliha had gone through numerous reinventions in her long life. She couldn't remain in the same identity and stay young while others around her aged. So periodically, she would have to move on and establish a new life, usually by moving to a different country. Setting her new life up well took a year or two of planning, but in the meantime, she could live in isolation on the island she'd inherited from Lucius. Unfortunately, the first time she'd visited there was after he'd kidnapped her in an attempt to gain her trust, but they'd smoothed that over after she'd broken his neck.

And Rabishu's offer for her to return to being an Ageless assassin was still open.

No emotional attachments. No tragedies. No concern about friends, because I wouldn't have any. No more pain, because of instant healing. Immortality. Sounds like a damn good package.

She'd told Yanmeng she'd never do it, though, and he'd called her worthy. Balanced against all the temptation, Yanmeng's respect was enough to hold her back.

I will stay rogue. There's more to this than balancing my scales and regaining my soul. Only a rogue has the motivation and skills to retrieve the shards and kill the demons. Without my commitment, how long will the Earth have to wait before there's another rogue stupid enough to try?

She decided to call Amaro for an update. He didn't answer his phone, so she tried Hound, using an encrypted line.

"Hey, Hound," she said. "Do you know why Amaro isn't answering his phone?"

"Yeah. He's on a cruise. Took along some dancer he met name of Trixy, with a y. I told him he'd have to have a pole installed in his cabin, and last I heard he was considering it."

"Oh. So he probably hasn't left his cabin, yet."

"If you really need to talk to him, I can get him on the ship's radio, but I wouldn't recommend it. Don't send him an email either, unless it's encrypted. Shipboard Internet security sucks, or so he tells me."

"He just told you that to keep you from bothering him."

"I'd go for that. Listen, it looks like the whole incident is blowing over."

"I've been searching for news. Seems like the police have egg on their face and they're not going to pursue it anymore. They've got two thugs to put in jail, so they'll make do with that. But I've got something to tell you."

She filled him in on her stay in Tel Aviv, leaving out everything she'd learned about Jake. She hadn't processed the information enough to feel like sharing it with anyone, even Hound. He was shocked to hear that Abiyram was dead.

"I'm really sorry to hear that. Are you sure the bullet wasn't meant for you?"

"We were sitting four feet apart. A sniper wouldn't miss by four feet."

"Wasn't he the guy you were going to bring onto the team?"

"Yes, but I never had a chance to confirm it. Hound, do you . . . do you think maybe we should all go our separate ways? Make this scattering permanent?"

"What the fuck for? 'Cause I tried to get into your pants again?"

"Oh, please. There are bigger issues here."

"I don't know. You didn't see what you turned down."

"Smart ass. I'm serious."

"I've yet to hear a reason."

"You know the reason. Danger. It's my job to deal with

whatever I stir up, but I've involved you guys too long. You and Glass are getting married, starting a life together."

"Yeah? Where'd you hear that?"

Maliha bit her lip before responding. "It might have something to do with the engagement ring she's wearing. The ring you gave her."

"Technically you gave me the diamond, so I wasn't acting of my own free will."

"Would you please just shut up, you exasperating man! You're getting married, Yanmeng is getting older, and Amaro will get married . . . eventually."

Jake and I . . .

"Amaro is already married—to the Holy Motherboard. And if Yanmeng heard you call him old, he'd wipe the floor with you."

"Not a chance!" Maliha paused. She was falling into Hound's verbal trap, allowing him to lead her away from the main point.

"Okay, seriously. I have no intention of cutting off my work with you. I believe in what you're doing. You'll have to do a better vanishing act than you did in the alley to leave me behind, and then I'd spend the rest of my life looking for you. Besides, I couldn't live like this if I wasn't in your condo."

"You're where?"

"I hid out in a dump of a motel out in the suburbs. They had a sign that said 'No Bedbugs, No Crabs,' and they were halfway right. I slept in my rental car. Have you ever considered with the prevalence of nasty critters in even respectable hotels lately that rental cars . . ."

"You're in my condo."

"I figured if there were going to be any repercussions it would happen fast, at the speed of YouTube. I stayed at the bedbug paradise a whole four days before crawling back. Don't take that too literally."

"Since you're there, you should know that a shipment of around fifteen boxes will be arriving. Please accept them and put them in the living room."

"Are you mad at me?"

How can I be mad at someone who just pledged loyalty like that? She examined her feelings and found that she felt more light spirited than she had in a while.

"No . . ."

"Sorry about your friend," he said.

"Uh-huh."

"Hey, Amaro sent me something on the key before he took off. He said it's from a resort in Greece."

"That makes sense. It would be near the island Lucius owned. How did Amaro know that?"

"Microengraving on the inner surface of the hole where you'd attach a key ring. It's the resort's logo. It's their way of making sure no one duplicates the key."

"This must be some ritzy place."

"Caters to the ultra-wealthy. They must have an expensive spa or something."

"You wouldn't believe the cost of some massages. Wait a minute—Amaro got all of this from a picture of the key?"

"Um, we have a 3D digital camera and some software that lets him view the image from different angles."

"Oh. Why doesn't anybody tell me things? What's the name of the club?"

"The Royal Dawn Hotel on Crete."

"Hound . . . thank you."

"Aw, shucks. Maybe you won't say that next month when the credit-card bill comes in." He hung up before she could respond.

Maliha had an American Express Platinum account with cards for her team members. She'd recently switched to the black card for herself, partly because she liked the official name of it: Centurion, the rank Lucius had held in the Roman army.

Well, I guess Hound is having a good time in Chicago.

Chapter Nine

Elizabeth almost snorted at the pathetic conversation, but caught herself in time. She was talking to Fred, and he was giving her suggestions on how to, as he put it, "secure the assassin."

Stay out of what you don't know, asshole.

She was relaxing in her bathtub, talking on a speakerphone. Fred had wanted a video connection, but she'd refused. She wasn't about to let him invade the privacy of her home, at least not yet. Both of them wanted to be making the decisions, so Elizabeth had to carve out her territory. She'd held off his sexual advances so far, but she knew that eventually she'd have to give in.

When I say so.

"I appreciate your suggestions, Fred, but I have a plan that's already in the works."

"You're not a very good communicator. I need updates on this project daily."

Project—he calls planning assassinations a project? I wonder if he's ever gotten his hands dirty.

She dipped her hand in the bathwater, rose-scented and pale red, and dripped some between her breasts. She was in a slipper tub, a claw-foot tub with one end raised and sloped for support for her back. The tub was located in a room adjoining her master bedroom, on the second floor of a redbrick home in Wildwood, in northwest Chicago. It was a family neighborhood, filled with trees, meandering streets, and parks, and it was adjacent to the Bunker Hill Forest Preserve. The bicycle trail, prairie, and woods of the preserve would have been convenient hunting grounds, but Elizabeth had learned her lesson about soiling her nest.

"What if nothing happens on a particular day? You expect me to call you and say nothing happened?"

"Sarcasm doesn't wear well on your pretty face. Tell me your plan."

She slid down into the tub until the water was neck-high.

"I should have an update on that for you soon." She ended the call smiling. She liked keeping him on edge and pissed off at her.

The bathwater was getting a bit cool. She waved over her bath servant, a seventeen-year-old runaway.

"Run some hot water."

"Yes, Lady." The girl ran enough to warm the tub and went back to her position kneeling near the door. As she walked away, Elizabeth could see blood striping the back of her thin dress. The girl—*what was her name? Debbie? Deidre?*—had been whipped earlier in the day. She hadn't done anything wrong. It was just her turn. Elizabeth needed to keep her servants in line so they knew that their situation was hopeless.

Hanging above the bathtub, upside down, was a naked girl whose pitiful body showed whip marks, bruises, and broken bones. Her throat and wrists had been slit, and her blood drained into the tub. Elizabeth lifted her right foot out of the water and let the blood drip between her toes.

Ashley didn't do anything wrong. It was just her turn.

Chapter Ten

Maliha flew into Heraklion International Airport, the largest one on the island of Crete. The Royal Dawn Hotel, built into a rugged hillside on the eastern coast, was pleased to welcome internationally best-selling author Marsha Winters, including the expansive gesture of sending a car to pick her up at the airport. Maliha had been there several times before, and once had rented a villa for six months to soak up the Mediterranean sun and Cretan hospitality.

In December, there were fewer tourists, and the eastern coast of Crete was not as well developed for travelers. That might have had something to do with the hotel's expansive welcome of her. Maliha used the hotel's priciest accommodations and its restaurants, shops, spa, personal trainer, and concierge service often, and tipped well.

"Welcome, Ms. Winters! We are delighted to see you again," the manager said. He'd met her at the front desk. Mr. Eliades was about fifty, angular, had a moustache that looked as though it had been dipped in olive oil, and darkly tanned skin. He always wore a black suit, a white shirt with an open collar, and monogrammed cufflinks. His eyes came up to Maliha's chin, and he had either an affectation or a nervous tremor that made him look like a bobblehead.

Never did like this suck-up. He strikes me as the kind of guy who'd rifle through the guests' underwear drawers while they were at the pool.

"You haven't mentioned how long you'll be staying with us," he said.

"Let's start with a week and see how things go from there."

"Certainly, certainly. If you don't mind my saying, it doesn't seem like you've brought enough luggage for a week. Are you expecting more to arrive?"

Maliha had only a garment bag and her metal case full of sharps. "I plan on picking up some new items at the hotel's boutiques."

"Excellent. Will you be coming down for dinner or do you want room service?"

"I'll call later. Right now, I'd like to wash off the dust of the journey."

If only sorrow could be swept away so easily.

He tilted his head sideways, like a robin eying a worm, but she kept her face unreadable. He drove her in a golf cart around the paths that cut through the hotel's dramatic landscaping to spare her the walk to her villa, which was perched on the edge of a cliff overlooking the pebbled beach. He left the cart for her convenience, and walked back to the hotel lobby. If he'd known that she planned a cross-country marathon run that night, he would have taken the cart for himself.

Fresh flowers greeted her on a table just inside her door and a bottle of wine with a cheese and fruit basket stood on the counter. It was impressive that the staff had gotten them there before Maliha's arrival, and it didn't seem that Mr. Eliades had tried to delay her. Maliha took a shower, wrapped in a luxurious robe, and relaxed with the wine, fruit, and cheese. She had a beautiful view of the sea as the sky darkened and the round moon gradually became visible. The hotel was known for its spectacular sunrises, but Maliha always found the descent into night intriguing.

Lucius was here at this hotel, maybe in this very room.

She was hungry and could have devoured the entire contents of the basket, but she needed to eat dinner later, so she set aside the food. Dressing casually, she drove the cart to the hotel's shopping area. Two hours later, she'd made several clothing, shoe, and jewelry salespeople very happy, and followed that with getting her hair, nails, and makeup done. She hadn't felt so decadent since she was on the arm of royalty at a state dinner.

I could live like this. It's fun getting pampered here, and there are places I'd love to revisit. Dissolve the team, no matter what Hound says, take a new identity, and travel the world. They might find me, but I just wouldn't let them back into my life. After all, I was saving lives before I had a team, and I could do it again.

Maliha changed in the dressing room of a shop where she'd made a large purchase, while the attendants fussed over her as though she was Cinderella going to meet her Prince Charming. The dress was red and low cut, front and back, to show off her assets. Resting just above her breasts was a diamond pendant that would give a cat burglar a heart attack, and an inch-and-a-half wide diamond cuff circled her wrist. She had the rest of her purchases boxed and sent to her villa. When she went to pay for her purchases, she found that her jewelry was already paid for—a gift from Jake.

Very thoughtful. He's keeping tabs on me. She couldn't help thinking about the red laser sight appearing on Abiyram's forehead.

Her final preparation was to put on a dead woman's fingerprints.

Maliha had a large supply of prints from a time before they were widely used for identification. She'd foreseen the use and had been collecting fingerprints from unclaimed corpses starting about eighty years ago. Amaro used them to set up her fake identities, and she had them made into "skins," thin sheaths that covered her fingertips. They were very responsive to body heat, and in a minute were smooth, undetectable, and sealed to her skin.

Maliha went to the dining room. It was a large space with tables around a dance floor, and a glass dome over all. She scanned the room quickly.

He's not here.

The maître d' approached. She requested a table for two. Heads turned as she made her way to the table. Fifteen minutes later, a waiter led Amaro to her table.

"About time," she said, after the waiter left.

"Do you have any idea how much a fucking tuxedo costs in this place? You better have a damn good reason for pulling me off that cruise."

"You're the only one who could do this with me."

"Is that like I'm the only ship in the quadrant or something?" His voice was starting to get loud.

"Shush. Yanmeng's off somewhere meditating, and Hound can't dance. Not on this dance floor, anyway, because he only dances naked."

Amaro rolled his eyes. "Too much information. So Yanmeng's daydreams are more important than my cruise?"

"Some cruise. It was a sex romp."

"We had ports of call with archaeological interest. It was educational."

"I'll bet it was. Did you have the pole installed in your cabin?"

He crossed his arms and looked petulant. "No. And Hound shouldn't have said that. That was guy talk."

"We shouldn't be looking like we're having an argument. We're supposed to be a romantic couple."

Amaro forced a smile on his face, leaned forward, and took her hand in his.

"Is this better? What's the mission?"

"We're retrieving a shard. It's in the hotel's safe."

Amaro's eyes lit up. "Robbery?"

Maliha shook her head, and then blew him a kiss.

"Mayhem at least?"

"I hope not. I'm planning to use good old deception. But if things go wrong, you may get your mayhem."

"I've never been on a field op before. I'm always at home base working on a computer."

"That's another reason you're here. In case of mayhem, I'll need you to destroy some computer records."

She explained her plan and the two made a show of

flirting while eating a fine dinner. They danced a few slow dances under the dome that showed a velvety black sky with stars scattered by an otherworldly hand. They left, his arm around her waist, and headed for the hotel's front desk. Everything she had planned led up to this moment.

Mr. Eliades was behind the counter talking to the night clerk.

Doesn't he ever sleep?

"How may I be of service, Ms. Winters?"

"I'd like to put my jewelry in the hotel safe. Sweetie, do you mind waiting a few minutes?" she said to Amaro.

"Each guest area is equipped with a locking safe."

"Into which I will put my pocket change. The hotel safe, please."

"Yes, of course. I'll have to get a key made for you."

She had been counting on his cooperation, and he came through. He took Maliha into a small room where she had her fingerprint scanned and her photo taken. A few minutes later, a guard handed her a key, then gave her a slip of paper with her safe box number on it. She memorized it and he threw the paper into a shredder.

"No one else can use this except you. Let's go try it out." They went to the vault room, where there was an armed guard posted.

"I'm impressed with the security here," Maliha said. Mr. Eliades beamed.

I hope I don't have to kill him. He may be a creep, but he's been a useful creep.

She inserted the new key into a slot near the door and pressed her finger on the pad. Up popped her photo and a positive identification. The guard swung open the thick vault door.

I'm in.

She considered the situation for the worst-case scenario. She'd have to take out the armed guard first. Mr. Eliades was next. Last, she'd have to go back to the room where her key was made and kill the guard while Amaro removed her information from the hotel's computer.

Three possible deaths for this one shard. Deaths of people who aren't killers. Wonder what Anu would think of that, if it all goes wrong.

Amaro remained by the door, talking to the guard and Mr. Eliades. He was creative with small talk, and kept their attention focused.

Maliha removed Lucius's key from her handbag. The box number was encrypted in the microengraving, but Amaro had deciphered it. She went to that box and opened it with Lucius's key. Inside were a letter and a diamond shard. She tucked the letter into her bag, but stared in dismay at the shard. It was roughly rectangular, about two inches by twelve inches. There was no way it was going to fit into her small evening bag. It was also a shock because it meant that the lens was bigger than she thought. From the pieces she'd already retrieved, she thought it was about seven inches in diameter.

There must be some whopper pieces out there. Makes sense, since the Tablet of the Overlord is a foot high. I had this shard in my hands once before, but didn't remember the size. Too busy trying to get out of the sucking sand pool.

Like the other shards, this one was a quarter of an inch thick. It had a glossy surface and underneath there were thousands of facets reflecting light, as though it had been carved from the inside.

"Sweetie, would you come over here? I could use your help."

Amaro excused himself and came into the vault, blocking the view from the doorway with his body. She pointed at the shard and he saw the problem right away. He picked it up, tucked it under his vest, and slid it into an area covered by the jacket. Maliha quietly pushed the box closed and removed the key.

Then they moved a few steps away and inserted Maliha's key in her numbered safe box. Amaro unfastened the diamond pendant and bracelet Maliha was wearing and put them in the box. The two men near the vault door were now watching.

"Your selection of jewelry shows a perceptive eye, Ms. Winters. The shopkeeper asked me to convey his appreciation of your taste," Mr. Eliades said.

"Thank you. These pieces are already among my favorites."

She and Amaro walked out together, Amaro with a little less grace than usual, one arm pinned to his side.

Amazing. Body count 0.

Chapter Eleven

Maliha stayed at the Royal Dawn Hotel for three more days, making certain that there wasn't the slightest suspicion that she'd raided a safe box that didn't belong to her.

Technically, it did, because Lucius gave me the key willingly. Proving it would be tough, though.

Amaro stayed with her in her villa, arrangements any romantically inclined couple would make. Most of the day he spent working from her living room, but was on call for making appearances around the hotel with her. They had one very public kiss for authenticity, and there was a lot of touching of arms, shoulders, waists.

When she'd rescued him he was sixteen years old, and he spent a lot of time around her. Predictably, he developed a crush. After all, despite her true age, she appeared only a few years older than he was. When his sister Rosie married young and moved out of Maliha's care, she pushed Amaro out on his own, too. No way was she going to become the ultimate cougar, three hundred years older than her inexperienced prey. Amaro discovered girls his own age, and the crush faded. Maliha thought he still had feelings for her, though, at his age of thirty-four.

Staying with him under these conditions, she was afraid his interest would be renewed. He was no longer a naïve boy, but a handsome, worldly, and well-built man.

Charming and sexy. Looking more irresistible by the

hour. Damn, I haven't been laid in a long time. But he's the baby of the team. Hands off. I've got enough trouble in my love life. One man in hell and another one who maybe belongs there. What am I going to say to Jake when we finally get together?

So they staged a pretend breakup. Amaro moved out and took his own accommodations. She told him to stay two or three weeks and enjoy himself. She'd seen the way the women eyed him and figured he'd have his hands full as soon as the word of the breakup got around. She really did owe him something for breaking up his cruise with Trixy.

Maliha called Hound. He said Yanmeng had checked in from Sri Lanka, where he was staying with Buddhist monks. His wife, Eliu, was in Hawaii working on a free-lance story. Maliha told him about Amaro's situation.

"One thing that's still up in the air is Arnie Henshaw," Hound said. "No living relatives, no girlfriends that I've been able to find. He's dropped off the grid; so far he didn't even leave a shadow behind. Sure you don't want me to go to Antigua?"

"Keep looking locally. I have a very bad feeling about this. I don't think Arnie's sipping drinks on the beach."

"Okay, but it's going to have to be a backburner job. I have a high-priority case."

Hound's work as a private investigator included secret work that he did for the government. She'd found out about that not long ago. Hound liked to joke that he got the job through Affirmative Action. For all she knew, it was true. After all, he was an African-American veteran.

"I hope they're paying you well," she said.

"More than I earn from you." He hung up before she could respond. She didn't pay the members of her team. They survived on perks like the credit cards, some cash bonuses, access to her condo, and her support anywhere they needed to travel. Amaro and Hound had their own outside incomes. Yanmeng didn't, but his wife still worked.

By choice or necessity? I'd better make sure it's by choice. Why aren't I paying these people for their time? Just because they're my friends doesn't mean they should lose money by helping me out.

Maliha made a dignified exit from the scene, before Amaro could start playing around with the other female guests. She retrieved her jewelry from the vault, and had to suffer through Mr. Eliades's exuberant sympathy for her romantic spat.

He's mourning the fact that I cut my visit—and my spending—short.

She joined a charter tour to Beijing and paid the guide to let her go off on her own and explain to the others that she'd taken ill and was in a medical facility. She took buses on roads that grew less maintained, and finally walked the last fifty miles to her destination, the XiChan Monastery. She hadn't been to the area since she was twenty-six years old, yet the surroundings looked familiar. Maliha wasn't interested in the landmark monastery.

After pausing to set aside her warm clothing, she started up a nearby mountainside wearing thin white pants and a matching shirt, barefoot. She followed a trail that few could perceive. It was snowing by the time she neared the top.

Maliha saw a figure standing up ahead, obscured by the snowfall. The mark on her left arm, the Chinese character *shou,* meaning long life, began to heat up and glow, just as it had on the day it was branded into her skin. It was the mark of her martial arts school, and it had never healed like other wounds to her Ageless body. She stopped a few feet from Master Liu. She could see him clearly now, a young bare-chested man wearing white pants as she did, in prime condition. He had a bucket in one hand. He'd been picking berries from bushes where only a few remained this late into winter.

Maliha dropped to her knees and bowed her head.

"Grandfather," she said.

"My child."

When she looked up, Master Liu was clothed in heavy robes. His face was wrinkled and wisps of white hair stood up from his head. His white, rheumy eyes fixed her with a blind stare. One of Master Liu's abilities as an Ageless was to change his appearance. She believed she was looking at the true version now.

"Master, I seek your wisdom," she said.

"Come in out of the wind," he said. "It's good to see you." He held out his arm to her and she took him by the elbow as if she were supporting a frail old man.

She flashed back to Hound's description of Master Liu: *He's some ascetic hermit who counts snowflakes on a mountain in China and dips his balls in ice water for the hell of it.* She almost giggled. Almost.

He took her inside the school, where a student maintained a small fire. It didn't do much to warm the large room. Master Liu taught tolerance to the elements and humility in the face of nature, which is why Maliha had worn only thin clothing.

"Student, bring a warm robe for my guest. She is a disciple of this school."

Maliha raised her eyebrows in surprise.

Master Liu shrugged. "I'm mellowing in my old age," he said.

The student, a boy of about sixteen, returned with a heavy robe and slippers for Maliha. She wondered who his demon was, since Master Liu only taught the Ageless.

He was the oldest Ageless Maliha knew, at least five thousand years old. He had been a priest of Anu's in Sumerian times. He didn't want to turn against his demon, even though he hated the evil works he participated in by training assassins, because he wanted to remain immortal. He was convinced that Anu would return to Earth someday, and wanted to be alive at that glorious moment so he would once again be Anu's priest. Although he wouldn't turn rogue, he supported Maliha by taking no action against her. They both knew that if his demon ever ordered him to kill her, he would do it.

"I've come here because I . . ."

"You've come because you are soft," he interrupted. "I

felt it in the way you moved when you walked next to me. Did you think I needed your arm to steady me? Your first task will be to join the advanced students."

I have missed a few workouts, and when I was fighting Xietai, he had a few moves I hadn't anticipated and should have.

"When you are no longer soft, we'll talk."

Maliha returned to her white-uniformed student days of training, discipline, and humble work at the school. He was right—she was soft. After three weeks of hard training, she knew the refresher had been good for her.

She talked to Master Liu about the recent events in her life, everything from the tide of deaths in her last case to killing Yanmeng's son to Abiyram's death and her suspicions about Jake. His answers left more questions in her mind—he told her she was walking the mortal path, something she will eventually see clearly in her mind, as clearly as the lines created by the Nazca people in the plateaus of southern Peru.

Images floated into Maliha's mind of huge forms in the sand that made sense only when viewed from above. The lines were made by removing the pebbles that covered the plateaus to reveal white or pink sand underneath. Intricate hummingbird, spider, and lizard patterns, among others, might have been sacred paths for people to walk as they prayed for fertility or rain in the near-desert climate. At least, that was one theory. Others involved alien landings at Nazca, with some lines serving as landing strips and the multitude of glyphs as welcoming sights for aliens to see from above.

"I recommend the Condor for you," he said. "You must walk it without rest and without water. It's a complex glyph and a challenge, but there are times you will see with wonderful clarity. Your feet may tread upon sand but your mind will not remain on this plane of consciousness."

"You talk as if from experience."

"The Nazca people were contemporaries of mine. The rest you must discover on your own."

He's not much for practical guidance. Looks like I'll have to walk the Condor in the future.

"Tell me about Jake," she said. "He came here for training, yet you didn't accept him into your school. He doesn't carry the shou." She touched the symbol on her arm, which remained warm—sometimes hot—whenever she was with Master Liu.

"You took a pledge the night you got that symbol."

"Come here, student."

She hesitated, not sure Master Liu was talking to her. No one else moved, so she walked forward and knelt.

"You have proven yourself worthy. Today you become a disciple of this school. My other disciples,"—he indicated the line of people standing behind her with a nod in their direction—"have gathered from around the world to witness this ceremony. Let me hear your pledge."

Pledge? I don't know any . . .

Her mouth opened anyway and words tumbled out. "I swear to honor you as my grandfather, to do nothing to bring shame to you or the school, and to never stray from the teachings of this school."

The senior disciple, standing next to Master Liu, approached her, and suddenly she saw that he had a glowing branding iron in his hand.

"This is the character shou, meaning long life," the senior disciple said. "It is the symbol of this ancient and proud school." He pulled up her left sleeve and pressed the iron high on the outside of her shoulder. Pain shrieked through her, but she didn't cry out or move. Her Ageless skin didn't heal the branding mark, nor was her pain diminished after the brand was removed. There was a price to becoming a disciple of Master Liu. She knelt, dry-eyed, as wisps of smoke rose from her flesh.

"I accept you as my daughter," Grandfather said.

"I remember," Maliha said.

"Jake Stackman did not take the pledge."

Maliha felt as though she'd been stabbed through the heart by an icicle.

There is nothing in that pledge that he should object to. . . .

"Why not?"

"I cannot say."

"Can't or won't?"

"The subject is closed."

"Did he kill Abiyram Heber? Should I stay away from Jake?"

Master Liu closed his blind eyes. It was a signal of dismissal.

"May I ask a different question?"

His eyes opened. She was free to continue.

Thinking ahead to a time when she might have all of the shards assembled into the Great Lens, she asked Master Liu what would happen if all seven of the demons were destroyed. She was thinking primarily of Lucius, trapped in his demon's hell, but the question was bigger than that: What is the future of humanity without the chaotic and deadly hindrance of the *Utukki*, the demon offspring of Anu?

"Will all the inhabitants of a demon's hell die with him?"

"They are all already dead. You are asking if they will all be brought back from death. My question to you is what would happen if the population of the Great Above suddenly surged by billions of people, most of whom knew nothing of the modern world and were barbaric in nature? How could we cope? The Underground is not a physical location in a cave somewhere. It has an unlimited capacity for damned souls. To absorb them back into the Great Above would be the end of things."

He's right. It would be a bloodbath.

"Anu could put them somewhere."

"Now you are presuming to tell a god what to do. Learn humility, my daughter. It is enough that Anu has given you the Great Lens and the tablet, the means to free the world from the demons' evil work. Look to the future, not the past."

Maliha hung her head. It was the clearest answer to the fate of Lucius that she'd heard so far, and even worse, it made sense.

Master Liu reached out and touched her hand. "I have news to give you. My disciple Daniel Harper possesses a shard. You will have to pry it from his hands if you are to retrieve it. He will be difficult to overcome, but if you approach him as a woman rather than a rogue you may have better luck."

"Thank you for your advice and help, Grandfather." A tear slipped down Maliha's cheek

"Come, daughter," he said, gently wiping away the tear, "let's spar. Movement and discipline will keep your mind focused."

She walked to the training room, to find him already there, in his guise of the young bare-chested man. His earthy appeal made warmth blossom in her center.

When I get my hands on Jake! I don't care what kind of bad stuff he's been doing—at least not until I've worn him out. I'm ready for that challenge.

"You must have been a real lady-killer in your time, Master," she said.

"A stain on my spirit." He closed his eyes for a moment, and when he opened them, he was swinging a sword at her.

He thought I meant that literally.

After a dogged three hours of sparring as a final test, Master Liu was satisfied that Maliha was no longer "soft." He pushed her back into the world by telling her that his school was not to be used as a tourist hotel. She took the good-natured hint, bundled the few items she'd brought with her in a backpack, and headed out on foot across China in the middle of the night.

Chapter Twelve

Back in Chicago, Maliha went to her haven, the second condo she owned in the building, on the forty-eighth floor.

The lock to the room used retinal identification. Maliha put her eye to the reader and the door slid open. Bright spotlights came on inside, bright enough to blind Maliha if she hadn't prepared by closing her eyes and covering them with her free hand. Letting a minimal amount of light in through her fingers and opening her eyes in slits, she sprang across a steel-lined foyer and tapped a code into a panel on the opposite wall at lightning speed. That disabled a shower of darts propelled from the ceiling.

The door slid shut behind her. She went down a short hallway, rounded the corner, and came out into the open space of her haven. On one wall was a weapons cache. The wall that faced Lake Michigan arced in a half circle. There were windows there, but they were covered with blackout cellular shades.

"Soft lights." The voice-activated lights came on to her defined level.

Display cases scattered around the space held items she'd collected. The black ceiling had low-voltage lights all over, so that it looked like a night sky. She kicked off her shoes and wriggled her toes in the deep carpet. The haven began to work its magic on her. She glanced over at her sleeping area, the one living area that had a wood floor instead of carpet. It held a straw tatami mat. After her shower, she'd unroll a futon and sleep in a rejuvenating space.

First, she had some important business. She got the newest shard out of her backpack. She opened the floor safe she'd installed and put the shard in with the other two and the Tablet of the Overlord.

Four to go and I know where one of them is. I'll have to learn about this Daniel Harper Master Liu mentioned.

The next morning, she went to her public condo. She found an envelope on the floor inside the door. It was white with no markings on the outside, no sign of having been mailed or delivered by courier.

A flash of foreboding chilled her.

Her fingers operating on automatic, she slit the top of the envelope. Fumbling it a bit, she saw something shiny slip out and fall to the floor.

It was a man's gold ring, familiar because she'd given it as a gift. She read the inscription on the inside of it: *Wisdom grows with years.*

It was Yanmeng's ring.

Oh no. No!

She checked the ring's aura and found its elemental resonance overlaid with the seething black aura of the hand that had last held it. Maliha put everything down and called Eliu.

"Have you seen Yanmeng lately?"

"We're both back in Seattle. He went to the Seattle Asian Art Museum yesterday, then I got a text that he'd met a friend there and was going to stay at his house last night."

"Is that unusual?"

"Not at all. Our friend Shing's wife passed away two months ago. Yanmeng has been keeping him company at times."

"Did you try calling him?"

"No. Why? Do you need to talk with him?"

"Yes. It's . . . urgent."

"Just a minute."

Eliu put her on hold. When she came back, she said, "I

just tried reaching him on his cell. It's turned off, but he always does that when he goes into the museum. Sometimes he forgets to turn it back on. So I called Shing's home phone. He hasn't seen Yanmeng in days! What's going on?"

Yanmeng can defend himself. He wouldn't give up his ring or anything else to a typical mugger. Something's wrong here.

"Eliu, was he wearing the ring I gave him?"

"Always. I'm sure he had it on when he left yesterday morning. Why? You're starting to scare me."

"Has he been in touch by remote viewing?"

"Not since lunch yesterday! Tell me what's wrong! Should I call the police?"

"I received a box a few days ago with Arnie Henshaw's cap in it."

"The doorman? I thought he retired. What's that got to do . . ."

"Arnie's hat had blood on it and a note inside said he was dead. Then just now I received an envelope with Yanmeng's ring in it."

She hated to be so blunt, but there was no way to protect Eliu from the implications of Yanmeng's ring being delivered. There was silence on the other end of the phone. It occurred to Maliha that Eliu might not share her husband's view about the death of their son Xietai. Maybe to his mother, Xietai was not a scourge of the Earth. Maybe she did believe in unconditional love and had never stopped loving her son, despite his betrayal of them and his subsequent evil activities. And now here Maliha was, the son-killer, getting Eliu alarmed about her missing husband.

"Still there?" Maliha said.

"Yes. Should I call the police?" Her voice was very frightened.

"I think that might not be the best thing to do. If it were an ordinary kidnapping, the ring would have been sent to you, followed by a ransom demand. I think this has to do with me and the way Yanmeng helps me."

"Then what can I do?" Eliu sobbed, "No, no, no . . ."

"I think you need to get away from your home. Come here. You could be in danger, too. Get here as fast as you can."

"I have to stay here. He might come home. He could be injured."

"If that's what you have to do, I'll get security guards for you. Just say the word and they'll be outside and inside with you."

"He's not coming home right away, is he?"

Maliha didn't want to let her own fear into her voice. "Maybe not right away. We have to work on this. I promise I'll do everything in my power to bring him back safely. Everything."

"Wouldn't it put me in more danger if I came to your home? I'd be more exposed to the kidnappers there."

"You'd also be with us. We can protect you, I swear."

There was a brief pause while Eliu thought about her options. As the pause stretched out, Maliha was sure Eliu was going to turn down the offer.

If she doesn't come, I'll be sick with worry. I need to have her in my sight. I might have to force her to come here, even if she'd hate me for it.

"I trust you," Eliu said. "I'm coming to Chicago. I know Yanmeng would want it that way."

Maliha let out the breath she was holding. *What a relief!*

"Then pack a few things," Maliha said. "In twenty minutes I'll have security personnel at your door, a man and a woman. Ask them for their passwords before opening the door. The woman should say 'pumpkin' and the man 'lightning.' I'm going to set this up right now. They'll get you on the first plane out of town, so you may hit a few other cities before you get to Chicago. Take care and see you soon."

Maliha immediately dialed another phone number. A man picked up.

"Marcus," he said.

"I need an escort to Chicago, the subject may be in great danger. Marcus, I want you and your wife to take this one personally. The subject lives a few minutes from your office." She gave him Eliu's name, address, and the passwords, then heard a woman's voice in the background, giggling.

"Not in my office. How much time have I got?"

"Less than twenty minutes."

"Damn, it's gonna be tight. Hon, get the travel bags."

"Marcus." Maliha was on the verge of tears. "She's a dear friend. I'll triple your fee. Just get her here safely."

"You got it."

Maliha hung up the phone and collapsed into a chair. She shrieked and pounded her fists on the wooden arms of the chair, splitting the arms to splinters. She cried for a few minutes, and then her resolve hardened.

After I bring Yanmeng back, I will tear his captor to pieces. I swear it.

She called Hound and told him that Yanmeng was in trouble. He said he'd drop the high-priority case he was working on and be there as soon as he could. Amaro said he'd arrive in a couple of hours.

When Amaro arrived at Maliha's public condo, she was wearing a white uniform, soaked with sweat, and using two swords. She was doing lunges to skewer an invisible opponent and fierce swings that sent an invisible head flying across the room. Items from the kitchen cabinets had been lined up on a counter and systematically destroyed as though someone had taken a chainsaw to them. She'd been practicing with her whip sword, a deadly weapon she wore coiled in a sheath around her waist. The whip sword had two long, flexible blades that an expert user could snap and swing at terrific speeds, severing limbs or whatever else was in the way. It was a vicious weapon and she used it with great skill.

"Okay, I can see you're seriously pissed," Amaro said. "Tell me about it."

His voice broke into her trance. She stopped and lowered the swords to the floor, making sure she caused him no injury. Amaro moved closer.

"Seeing you like that was kind of scary," he said.

"So is what's in that envelope." She nodded her head in the direction of the packet on the counter.

He examined it, then sat down and put his head in his hands. "Is this a kidnapping for ransom?"

"I might suspect that, if it hadn't been for the note. Arnie was the first one resting in peace. Yanmeng has to be the second, then. They're not asking for money."

Maliha sat on the floor, crossed her legs, and pulled a sword into her lap. She had her cleaning kit next to her, and began removing the old oil and sweat from the swords and then re-oiling them. She didn't want to discuss anything more right now. Amaro went into his guest room to see if there was any chatter among his hacker friends.

Hound arrived with pizza, and the three sat around talking. Emotions were running high—one of their own was missing. Maliha took a slice of pizza on a paper plate, but she had no appetite for it. With the strenuous exercise she'd been through plus the stress of the situation, she avoided making eye contact with the slice.

"You going to eat that?" Amaro said.

Without a word, she passed him the paper plate.

"Do you think Chick had something to do with this? He had opportunity both when the box and envelope were delivered," Hound said.

"I don't know. I was surprised to see him when I first met him, and I didn't think to view him," Maliha said.

"Uh, view him? This is different from seeing him?" Hound said.

Maliha hesitated. She looked at two inquisitive faces and sighed. "Okay, I can view auras. They're like energy fields surrounding everything. I can tell from the color and activity in the aura whether a person is good or evil, lying or telling the truth, angry or calm, and other things. Jake's the only one I've talked to about it."

"Have you viewed me?" Hound said.

"No . . . yes."

"And?"

"You wouldn't be here if I didn't trust you completely. You too, Amaro."

Hound snorted. "That's a vague answer. We've got privacy rights, you know."

"I know," Maliha said. "And I needed to feel comfortable before I shared my story with you. I can't undo what I've already done—once—but there's the door if you feel violated."

"Hound, shut up," Amaro said. "Your so-called privacy is violated worse than that every time you get on the Internet. Like when you bought that black lingerie for Glass."

"What the fuck! How did you know about that?" Hound said.

"If you'd think for one second, you'd know. You used one of Maliha's credit cards. Who do you think pays the team's bills? Me, that's who." He poked Hound in the chest. "And you call yourself a private investigator," Amaro said.

"Could we get back to the subject?" Maliha said.

"Only if he doesn't spy on me anymore," Hound said. "Kid, anytime you want to finish what you started with that finger in the chest, just let me know."

If I didn't love them both, I'd kick them out.

"Do you two need a time-out in your rooms?" Maliha said.

There was no answer, but no more arguments, either.

"One of our friends is in mortal danger. Don't you think we should stay on topic?" Maliha said. "This is really going to impress Eliu when she gets here."

"Truce," Amaro said.

"Truce," Hound said. "You started it with that viewing business."

Maliha was about to speak, but Hound held up his hand to fend her off. He went over to the envelope. "I'm going to check for fingerprints, not that I think I'll find any." He retrieved a fingerprint kit from a case he'd brought with him and got to work.

"What about asking Jake for help?" Amaro said. "Maybe he can look for government involvement."

Maliha bit her lip. "I'll have to think about it. Why do you think the government's involved?"

"Just a hunch. It might have something to do with that video of you."

"That was a month ago. You might have a point, though.

Sounds like it's time for you two and Eliu to go to a safe house."

I could use their help but it's too much to ask. Too dangerous. One member of the team has been targeted—the others could be next.

"You're kicking us out when we want to help find Yanmeng?" said Hound.

"No way," said Amaro, shaking his head. "Uh-uh. Not this time."

Maliha frowned. "I don't have time to worry about everybody."

"Excuse me, Miss High-and-Mighty, don't you think we're worried too? We want to help and you're not shunting us out of the way. If you think I'm going to go sit in some tin can and chew my fingernails . . ."

"Can't you work from there? There are secure computers," she said.

"Hell, no! I was planning to catch a flight to Seattle, where I can act like a goddamned private investigator and investigate!"

"Amaro, you . . ."

Amaro's cheeks were flushed and his eyes narrowed. He shook his head.

"Who the hell's in charge here?" Maliha said.

Maybe breaking up this team can't come soon enough.

The room grew quiet. Another word tossed out and the tension would have ignited. Finally Maliha plopped down on the floor, unsheathed her whip sword, and began the delicate process of cleaning it—again.

Amaro went off to his room, slamming the door. Hound sat cross-legged on the floor, knee-to-knee with Maliha. It wasn't an easy position for him to get into, with his old injuries, but he managed with a little grunting.

"That wasn't intended as some kind of threat, was it?" he said.

"What?"

"Getting out that whip right at that moment. Asserting dominance."

"Of course not," she said.

"It's hard for me to know. We've been friends for a long time. We were lovers. But there are still things I don't know about you and know that I never will."

She lowered her head. "I can give you one simple explanation why I'm on edge about this. It's about guilt. Yanmeng's gone. Other people I loved have died, and I haven't been able to stop it."

Just as she ducked back into the shelter of the lab bench, she saw the tall man pick up a piece of broken glass from the floor.

Maliha knew his intent as though their minds were one.

She rolled out from behind the bench and planted a star in the wrist of the nearest gunman. He screamed and dropped the gun. As she passed by him, she finished him with a blow to the throat, and then turned her attention back to the real danger in the room. She launched a throwing knife at the tall man. He was in motion as she threw, and instead of skewering his heart, the knife landed in his arm. It didn't stop him from carrying through the action he'd started. He yanked Claire's head back and slit her throat with the piece of glass.

No!

Blood spilled and she knew Claire was gone.

Hound didn't answer for a while. She knew he had the same kind of memories from his days in Vietnam, and had been helpless to save some of the men he worked with every day.

"Things have piled up on you lately. It kinda comes with the territory, doing what you do," he said softly. "When you were Ageless, you killed without guilt. Now that you're partly human—or whatever you are—you experience both love and loss." He paused. "Would you do without love?"

"There's one form of love I almost wish I'd never opened up to. Lucius is gone, Jake is . . . maybe not the one for me."

Hound looked at her quizzically, but she didn't elaborate.

"I think I'm responsible for Yanmeng's disappearance,

and Arnie was just an opening act," she said. "If Yanmeng dies too . . ."

"Let's not put him in the grave, yet. Maliha, you've got to bend on this. Let us help in the way we need to."

Trying to calm her fears, she said, "All right. Just remember I can't be everywhere at once."

"We've never expected you to be."

"What about Eliu—the safe room for her?" Maliha said.

"What do you say we leave it up to her choice? The new democracy."

Maliha felt something slipping through her fingers that she knew she'd never get back. She was letting go of some degree of power she'd held because of her abilities.

Master Liu told me to learn humility. Maybe this is part of walking the mortal path.

"Okay."

There was a knock at the door. Eliu didn't have a key. Maliha assumed it was she, even though the doorman was supposed to announce guests. She ran to the door as Hound told her to slow down and check it out first.

It wasn't Eliu. A small box sat right outside the door. Hound shoved her aside, looked each way down the hallway, and then headed for the emergency stairs at a run.

With her heart dragging the floor, Maliha brought the box in and opened it.

Inside, wrapped in paper towels, was Yanmeng's index finger. She recognized the scar he'd gotten a long time ago in a tactical knife fight. There was a note demanding her presence at a meeting spot, alone.

Chapter Thirteen

Maliha wrapped the severed finger in a clean cloth and put it on ice in a cooler in the vague hope of reattachment, making sure that the flesh didn't rest on the ice. It would be ready for transport immediately, but she didn't think Yanmeng would be recovered in time for that. There had been a clean removal with a sharp instrument, perhaps a skillfully wielded knife or even a sword.

She grimaced. *I've seen it all too often, a finger or hand cut off and sent to someone to intimidate. I should know—I've done it.*

Her phone rang. It was Chick.

"Got a lady name of Eliu to see you, with luggage. Okay?"

"Yes, send both up."

"Christ," Hound said. "Should we hide all this?"

"I suggest we put the box and envelope away and tell her everything. She can decide what she wants to see," Amaro said.

"Sounds good. Use my bedroom."

The box, envelope, and cooler were spirited away before Eliu arrived. She waited until her two small bags were brought in before giving Maliha a tearful hug, then giving one in turn to Hound and Amaro. Maliha made some tea while the two men led her to a sofa and sat on either side of her trembling body like bookends.

"Has Yanmeng viewed you?" Maliha said, when all four

of them cradled hot cups of fragrant tea. She wanted to know if he'd attempted to contact her via remote viewing.

Eliu shook her head. "It's not a good sign. Usually we're in touch several times during a day, sometimes for hours at a time."

"Hours? I didn't know he could sustain that."

"That's only been for the last few months. For him not to contact me in so long a time, he must be . . ."

"Don't jump to conclusions," Hound said. "He could be knocked out."

"My husband's mind is very powerful. He would have to be deeply sedated, I think. Like for surgery."

"That's an idea. He could be in a clinic somewhere," Maliha said.

"The clean cut that took off his finger could be from a surgical instrument," Amaro said.

Eliu looked startled. "What does this mean?"

"Way to go, big mouth," Hound said. "You must've lost your tact pills."

"I'm sorry, Eliu," Maliha said. "Since we last talked on the phone, a box arrived. It was your husband's finger."

Eliu bowed her head. "Oh no," she said in a small voice. "How do you know it was his?"

"I recognized the knife scar on his index finger."

"I want to see."

"Are you sure? It isn't necessary."

"It's necessary to me." Eliu straightened up and her voice was steadier. She'd made it clear that she wasn't going to be sheltered.

Plenty of time for grieving later, if it comes to that. No, don't think about that. I have to believe he's alive so that I can bring him back home.

Maliha nodded at Hound. He picked a few items out of his fingerprint kit and then took Eliu into the bedroom.

When the two of them left the room, Maliha glared at Amaro. "Well, that could have been handled better."

"You're right. I messed up."

There was no use in belaboring it. "This building has

security cameras in the hallways. Why don't you see if you can find out who delivered our surprise package?"

Amaro headed for his room, where he kept most of his computer equipment.

Hound came out by himself. He wore latex gloves and carried the note in a clear evidence bag. "Eliu needs a minute. She confirmed your identification. I didn't get any latents off the box or envelope, so I doubt that this note will have any. It's worth a try, though."

"Let me see that note before you get started," Maliha said.

8:15 A.M. TOMORROW, CORNER OF DIVERSEY AND NEWCASTLE, HALF A BLOCK NORTH. COME ALONE OR HE DIES.

"Diversey and Newcastle . . . where's that?" Hound said.

"I know it. It's on the northwest side."

"Geez, woman, is there any part of this city you don't know?"

"I believe in knowing my surroundings so I can get from point A to point B using the shortest route."

"Get a GPS."

"I'm old-fashioned in some ways. Sometimes you forget I'm older than I look."

There was a knock at the door.

Maliha and Hound approached and pressed against the walls on opposite sides of the door.

"Who is it?" Hound said.

"Flowers for Marsha Winters." The voice was cheery and young.

"Leave them outside and go."

"Um, I need a signature."

"Leave them. Go."

A few minutes later Hound opened the door. There was a vase of two dozen red roses in the hall and there was no one around.

"What do you think?" he said to Maliha. "Bomb? A bug?"

"Who are they from?"

Hound squinted at the card tucked among the flowers. "Jake."

"I think we can chance it." She came over, picked up the vase, and brought it into the kitchen. The card said, MISS YOU MORE THAN I CAN SAY. CAN'T WAIT TO SEE YOU, LOVE, JAKE.

"I'm getting my kit," Hound said. "Check it out for bugs."

It's sweet. Am I wrong about him? Jewelry, roses, must be candy coming next.

It was 20 degrees and blustery the next morning. The gray clouds seemed to hang so low that Maliha could reach up, grab one, and squeeze the snow out of it. She dressed in loose jeans, a T-shirt covered by a worn sweatshirt, and a jacket with deep pockets. One jacket pocket harbored a Walther P22 short-barrel pistol and the other an automatic knife and a few extras. At Hound's insistence, she had a handheld GPS unit in the pocket of her jeans.

Woven into the neckband of her T-shirt was a wireless transmitter made of a new material, polyester fibers with a metallic coating twisted into strands or mesh. When an informant was wearing a wire, he was always in fear of being discovered by the bad guys. No one would suspect Maliha of transmitting information because her T-shirt looked like any other. Amaro would be listening to her conversations and recording them for later analysis.

She took a cab and got out a few blocks from her destination. Half a block north of Diversey and Newcastle there was an elementary school. Students were arriving, and Maliha tried to look like she was not lingering outside a school for nefarious purposes. A girl about nine years old headed toward her.

I don't like this at all. My contact is a little girl?

It was disappointing, because Maliha had been planning to extract information from her contact, as roughly as necessary.

"You Malehat?"

My name lost something in translation. Warily, Maliha nodded.

"Here." The girl handed her an envelope and turned to walk away.

Maliha wanted to grab her by the shoulders and spin her around, but she wouldn't do that to a child. *No wonder they sent me here. Very clever.*

"Wait a minute. Who gave you this?" Maliha said.

"I'm gonna miss the bell."

"Do you know his name?"

"No. He was here just a few minutes ago. He gave me five dollars."

Maliha flinched at the thought of the girl talking to someone associated with Yanmeng's captor. "What did he look like?"

"Not as tall as my dad but about the same age . . . old. I really gotta go now."

"Okay. Don't talk to strangers and especially don't take money."

The girl didn't hear her. She was already hurrying away toward the school entrance, and the wind carried Maliha's warning away. She opened the envelope.

CORNER OF FULLERTON AND LOGAN.

She stuck the note back into the envelope, inserted it into a plastic bag, and tucked it into her back jeans pocket. She didn't need a cab.

Here we go. One wild goose chase coming up.

Snow began to fall, insistent flakes that pelted into her face, driven by the wind. That was one thing about Chicago—it knew how to do a snowstorm right. She pulled up the hood of her sweatshirt.

As Maliha feared, the second location was another elementary school. This time a boy of about twelve separated from a group of friends and came over to her. The boys left behind shouted encouragement at him, as if he were about to charm the pants off her.

"You the Mailman?"

"Yes."

"I got somethin' for ya." His friends hooted as he pulled an envelope out of his pants. He purposely held it close to his body so that she had to step forward to take it.

"Who gave this to you?" she said.

"Some dude."

"What did he look like?"

"Talk wit some kinda crazy accent. Got one o' them ponytails." He swaggered back to his friends.

Maliha opened the envelope.

LAMON AND DICKENS. HUSTLE.

There were two more stops before she ended up at Lavergne and Maypole, at a boarded-up house across the street from a school. Her target was marked with a red *X* on the plywood covering the front entrance. Maliha was frustrated from the runaround and hoping to get her hands on the man with the ponytail. She was disgusted that she'd been given children to deal with, and didn't like the idea that some creep was using the children as intermediaries.

What was all this for? To make sure I'm not followed? It's criminal to mess with these kids like that, or ought to be.

There were no footprints in the snow leading up to the front door. She went around the back of the house. No footprints there, either. That meant her contact had been in the house before it started snowing.

Hope he's freezing his ass off in there. The temperature's dropped 10 degrees since I left.

She loosened one of the boards on a basement window quietly. Wary of a gunshot from the interior, she pulled a telescoping mirror from her pocket so she could get a look into the basement.

The mirror showed no threat. Maliha moved to the middle of the backyard, ran toward the window, and dove through it, snapping boards and the remnant of a broken pane of glass. She rolled when she hit the concrete floor, jarring her shoulder a little, and stopped behind a large desk that had been turned up on end. She drew her .22 and checked out her surroundings. Dust motes, disturbed by her flying entrance, floated in the pale light coming in from the window. All the drawers of the desk that sheltered her were gone and the wooden frame was split in several places as though someone had started to chop it with an axe and gave up. As a vantage point to survey the room, it didn't offer much cover.

The ceiling was low and the place was cluttered. In one corner, there was an old urine-stained mattress and an Army blanket with moth holes. There wasn't any sign of recent occupation. Not far away was a rusty barrel on the concrete containing ashes and some wood fragments. The occupant had been keeping warm by burning pieces of wood from the dilapidated furniture. The splintered pieces of a chair were stacked nearby, but the burnt smell was stale and barely noticeable. It had been a while.

"Up here, sweetheart!"

The male voice came from almost directly over Maliha's head, on the first floor of the house. The stairs were in a dimly lit area away from the only window. Several of the stairs creaked as she stepped on them, so there was no way to surprise the man waiting.

The door at the top was held in place only by its upper hinge, but had been fitted into the frame, another barrier to surprising her contact.

As soon as I pull on that door, I have a target on my forehead. This guy better be here to deliver a message, not to kill me.

She pulled the door open and came out ready for action. There was a battery-powered camping lantern hanging from a hook that had formerly held a hanging basket. She was in the kitchen, but there was little sign of cabinets. The squatter in the basement had gotten to them. The man she faced pointed a gun at her and for the moment she respected that. He was shorter than she was, dressed in dark pants and a black sweatshirt, and had a ponytail.

"Hello, Malehat," he said. "That is your name, right?"

She studied him before answering. He had a thick, powerful frame and shiny black hair that was oiled. He spoke English well enough, but she recognized the accent of his birth language, Quechua, spoken by indigenous people who lived in the Andes Mountains. Maliha had lived among the Quechua people for more than thirty years when she was

Ageless, exploring the Andes on foot. Millions of people spoke Quechua, but it was little known on the world stage because of the prevalence of Spanish in the Andean countries of South America. There were three variations of the language, and speakers from one region might have a hard time understanding speakers from a different region. She thought his native language was that of the central region, probably Peru.

"I want to know. I need to verify before I hand over the documents."

"I'm Malehat. And you are?" She edged closer.

"My name is Wayra, though we are not here to have a civilized conversation. On the other hand"—he let his eyes travel up and down her body—"there is no reason why I can't have a little fun before I deliver the documents. Put that gun down."

She followed his directions, waiting for her best opportunity.

"Take off your jacket and put it down on the floor."

Maliha smiled mentally and did as she was told. *This man has something to do with Yanmeng's disappearance, but he couldn't be the captor. He's just a thug with a gun.*

"Now the sweatshirt and pants."

Maliha stood in her T-shirt and panties. She trembled a bit, intentionally, to make her breasts shake. The coldness in the room did the rest—her nipples hardened, a spontaneous invitation that served her purpose.

It was all too much for Wayra. He gestured with the gun. "Take off the T-shirt."

"Why don't you come over here and do it yourself?"

He started toward her, his gun wavering in one hand, the other hand undoing the button of his pants and sliding down his zipper to free his erection. Maliha was ready to unleash the anger that had been building in her all morning, now that she had a target she could rough up instead of children. When he was close enough, she lashed out with her foot and knocked the gun out of his hand. Then she delivered a powerful kick, angled upwards, to his genitals, shoving his testicles into his torso. A second upward kick caught his erection. There was a popping sound that didn't bode well for Wayra's penis. A rapid third strike hit him in center of his torso, tossing him backward.

Wayra curled up on the floor in agony. She pushed him down with a foot in the middle of his back, but he was no danger to her anymore, so she removed her foot.

"Let's have that civilized conversation now," she said. There was nothing but moaning from the man. She found a battered metal folding chair, opened it, and dragged Wayra up into a seated position. There was blood on the front of his pants.

"First, where are the documents you were supposed to give me?"

"Damn you, bitch," he said in a weak voice. His breath was coming in painful gasps. "Call 911. You broke my fucking dick!" He clutched at his bloodied pants. "My balls are gone!"

"You'll get a doctor if you cooperate. The documents?"

Wayra nodded his head toward a corner of the kitchen, where there was a briefcase on the floor. Maliha retrieved it. There was no lock, but she was worried about a trap. She brought the briefcase to Wayra. His head was leaning to the side and he was starting to fade into unconsciousness. She slapped him with perfectly calculated force and he opened his eyes.

She pulled up his hands and put them on the briefcase, and he groaned. "Open this." She walked across the room. There wasn't enough space to get out of the way of a major blast, but it was better than nothing.

With effort, he flipped the latches and opened the lid. There was no trap. She took the briefcase away and examined it. Inside, Maliha found a dossier with photos and information about a man named Nathan Presser. There were clear instructions to assassinate Presser or Yanmeng would die. A flash drive in the bottom of the case had WATCH ME written on it. She slammed the briefcase shut.

So that's it. Someone's blackmailing me to do what I was

forced to do for Rabishu for three hundred years. Could it be Rabishu? He made me an offer to return to the fold, and maybe he's angry I didn't accept.

She turned her attention back to the man in the chair. "Who hired you?"

He shook his head. "Got a call. Threw the phone out." His chin drooped down to meet his chest.

"Why all the business with the kids?"

"Uhhh . . . told to."

She was sensitive enough to psychic activity to feel the pain flowing from him like blasts of hot desert wind. It was something she usually shut out completely, since she had enough pain in her life from sharing death experiences. She relaxed her eyes and looked through him, focusing on a point beyond him. His aura came into view, a luminous radiance in layers around his body extending about six inches on either side, with tendrils and spikes that could be a foot in length. The dominant color was brown, for deception and selfishness. There were tendrils of black for evil, but the man wasn't given over to it. She was more concerned about the increasing spikes and swirls of dark, ominous green that showed his injuries. They were fatal. In a few seconds, his aura began to fade and thin out, showing patches of ice blue with specks of soft light suspended in them like fireflies. Soon it would become gray and dissipate further. He was dying. No doctor could help him now.

Five or ten minutes left. That last kick must have ruptured something inside. Shit. I didn't intend that.

"All right. I'll get that medical help now," she said, hoping he could still hear her. She slipped behind him and snapped his neck to spare him a few minutes' pain. Pulling his body from the chair, she sat in it and went through his death experience, collecting the confused remnants of his spirit and sending them through the portal. Wayra was whole.

Maliha's anger dissipated. She felt guilty for killing the man, who was, after all, a hired messenger. She didn't know enough about his background to say whether he was an evil man or not. There was that indication of evil in his aura, but it hadn't been clearly defined, not like some of the auras she'd viewed. Not like her own.

He was going to rape me, but I've faced that before and stopped it without killing. Master Liu said that the one who strikes out in anger is the loser, even if by chance he lives.

She put her clothes back on, picked up the briefcase, and wiped down the folding chair. Searching the man's pockets, she found his wallet and tossed it into the briefcase to take with her. Waiting for Anu's displeasure with her, she went into the basement and sat on the floor. There was a penalty for a life taken without purpose. A figure on her scale would walk from the lives saved side to lives taken—a setback for her quest to regain her soul.

Although she judged herself harshly, Anu didn't feel the same way. Nothing happened.

Chapter Fourteen

Amaro had his feet up on the coffee table when Maliha came out of the shower. She was surprised that she had the urge to tell him to put his feet down.

What is this, kill a man, come home and act motherly? Twisted.

She sat next to him on the couch and put her slippered feet up next to his. He took no notice, but Hound, sitting across from them, raised his eyebrows repeatedly, like in a cartoon. The lower part of her robe had fallen open and was revealing a good deal of thigh. She rolled her eyes at him and tucked up the robe.

All I can say is Glass had better get back soon. Her man's about to explode like a volcano of molten sperm.

Eliu was asleep. Her normal sleeping patterns were disrupted by stress, and when she was able to fall asleep, she did so, day or night. Hound had offered to get some pills for her from Chick, but she declined.

Hound had started poking through Wayra's wallet without her. "Eighty bucks, three credit cards, a photo of his daughter maybe." He handed Maliha a picture of a girl about seventeen years old cuddling a newborn baby.

Ouch.

"Driver's license and Social Security card," Hound continued. "He's not supposed to carry that card. I'm going to have an easy time checking him out. Two theater ticket stubs. Might be a wife or girlfriend in his life."

"What play did they see?" Amaro said.

"Romeo and Juliet."

"Girlfriend," Amaro and Maliha said simultaneously.

Even rotten men can have girlfriends. I wonder if she knows about his tendency to strip strange women. His ex-tendency.

"See if you can find the girlfriend, but don't waste a lot of time on it. We have more urgent business," Maliha said.

"You didn't tell us much about your meeting with Wayra," Amaro said.

"Nothing much to tell." She turned her head away. "He intended to rape me, and I didn't take it well."

"So he's no longer among the living," Hound said. "Hell, Maliha, we could have gotten useful shit out of him. You said he wasn't the actual kidnapper, just some guy on the payroll, but still. If you're going to off every guy who looks at you with lust in his heart, well, there goes half the population of Chicago. I could've interrogated him and I doubt he would have worked up any lascivious thoughts about me."

"It happened fast, okay?" Her tone was harsher than she'd meant it to be. Hound clamped his lips shut and put an *I was only trying to help* look on his face.

"What Hound means is that he's sorry you had to go through that, as am I," Amaro said.

"What's up with the security cameras?" Maliha said. She was anxious to move on.

"I looked at the recording made by the building's cameras in this hallway and found nothing. The relevant portions of the recording were nothing but static. It's a military-grade disk wipe, just like I did on the dash cam video of Maliha running away," Amaro said. "I just finished installing my own high-speed camera system to watch the hallway and especially right in front of your door. There are four match-stick cameras out there now."

She looked at him in surprise. "I thought you installed those weeks ago."

Amaro shrugged. "Uh, it's done now."

"Hey! We depend on you. You could be more responsible."

"I could," he said, crossing his arms defensively. "Sorry."

From his tone of voice, she wasn't sure he was feeling apologetic. Her lips tightened into a sour expression, but she dropped it.

"What could do that kind of damage to digital recordings besides software?" Maliha asked.

Amaro shrugged. "Ultraviolet light. Magnets. Microwaves. Maybe heat. Static discharge, like when you rub your shoes on the carpet and then touch a doorknob."

"Aren't you supposed to be watching the entrances to the building?" she asked Hound. *Geez, a little democracy and the place falls apart.*

"Hey, I'm too valuable to sit around on surveillance. I got reliable assistant investigators who do that."

"What he means is that his legs get stiff when he sits too long," said Amaro.

Hound glared at him but let it go.

"Have you two had a chance to go over the dossier yet?"

"Yeah," Hound said. "Watch the video on the flash drive first."

They sat in silence as Amaro played the video on a large-screen TV. It started when the patrol car pulled into the alley and ended with Maliha leaving the scene.

"I like the extra touch of blood all over you," Hound said.

"Somebody made a copy before I had a chance to wipe out the video," Amaro said.

"Well, duh," said Hound.

"That somebody wants me to kill the man in the dossier. Can you give me a rundown on him?" Maliha said.

"You mean you're actually considering doing this assassination?" Amaro said.

"If we don't want Yanmeng to meet up with a chain saw, it seems like a good direction," Hound said.

Maliha felt her frustration about the danger Yanmeng was in boiling over. She lashed out with a pink-slippered foot and snapped the leg of the coffee table. Amaro, his feet jarred loose from the table, stood up in surprise.

"Sorry about the chain saw," Hound said.

"What he means is that we need to find Yanmeng fast so you don't have to do this," Amaro said.

"Damn, kid, when I need you to translate for me I'll fucking well ask for it," Hound said.

We've been having too much "together" time.

"Listen, I know we're all tense about this, but arguing among ourselves plays into the kidnapper's hands. We're supposed to have a truce, remember?" She lowered her eyes. "I've been meaning to buy a new coffee table."

"He started it," Hound said. He folded his arms on his chest and frowned.

She ignored him. "I haven't decided what to do yet. I resent someone trying to use me for personal gain, but let's face it, if I refuse, the next package could contain Yanmeng's head. So right now, I'm playing this as I would any assignment from good old Rabishu. I want to learn as much as possible about the target."

"Nathan Presser, forty-three, divorced from his second wife, no kids with her or his first wife. Presser might be shooting blanks, because he and his second wife Janice were in the process of adopting a baby when he sprung the divorce on her. He's a political fund-raiser now, formerly a real estate developer, and before that owned some food franchises."

"Successful? I've never heard of him before," Maliha said.

"Not particularly, at his former jobs. He'd make some money, then make bad investments and lose it. When he hit on fund-raising, though, he really took off. Current net worth approximately sixty-seven million. You wouldn't hear of him. He's a back-room kind of guy."

"So he's got a knack for squeezing money out of people for worthless causes. Is he strictly local in our fair city?" Hound said.

"In the past couple of years, he's moved up to national-level fund drives. He's getting a good rep."

"My guess is that he stumbled on something he wasn't

supposed to find out and has become a nuisance for the kidnapper. What should we call this kidnapper, anyway?" Maliha said.

"Mr. String Him Up by His Prick," Hound said.

Maliha laughed. It felt good to laugh. "Maybe something a little shorter than that."

"Shorter in what way?" Hound asked.

"Mr. X, the mystery man," Amaro said.

"Sold. Where does the target live?" Maliha said.

"Moved to Washington, D.C., right after the divorce," Amaro said.

"Any ideas at all on where Yanmeng is being held?" Maliha asked. "We think he's heavily sedated, remember? Has anyone checked medical clinics?"

"I'm on that next," Hound said.

Eliu came out of her room. The conversation stopped. She stared at the broken table leg, started to say something, and thought better of it. "Anybody hungry?" she said.

There was a soft knock at the door. Everyone in the room froze. Then Amaro hurried over to the computer he'd dedicated to receiving the input of his newly installed hall cameras. The screen was divided into four rectangles, one for each camera, and they were all showing nothing but static. Amaro slammed his hand down on the table in frustration.

"What about your reliable assistant investigators?" Amaro said.

"The best that minimum wage could buy. Fuck." Hound's scar stood out as anger flooded his face. "Christ, haven't we just done this knock-at-the-door thing?"

Maliha headed to the door, with Hound at her heels. When they got there, he drew a gun and motioned for her to open the door quickly. She did so, but no one was there.

There was a box on the floor outside her door.

Hound went to the emergency stairs again, but came out in a minute. "Nobody there. Whoever it is must be using the elevator. I'll go talk to the doorman, and so help me, if my assistants are asleep, I'm gonna fry their balls in butter."

Maliha picked up the box, took it to the kitchen, and

opened it. Eliu stayed where she was in the chair in the living room. Yanmeng's bloodied thumb was inside, along with a note that said, *WHAT ARE YOU WAITING FOR?*

Eliu stood her ground this time. She compressed her lips into a line and her eyes narrowed into a fierce glare. She said nothing, and didn't cry. Anger was taking hold of her, and Maliha knew just what that felt like.

I wouldn't want to be Mr. X if Eliu gets hold of him. There's more than one martial artist in the Xia family.

"I need more on Nathan Presser. I need his whole background, who his friends are, what he's been up to lately, his routines."

Hound and Amaro nodded.

She moved closer to Hound and spoke for his ears only. "Be sure Eliu stays here. Don't let her go out looking for Mr. X. Keep the body parts on ice."

"Aye, aye, Captain. Agreed." He hadn't missed the look on Eliu's face.

I haven't thought this through. But there's no time.

Chapter Fifteen

Maliha took her private jet to Dulles International Airport in Virginia. She rented a silver Nissan Sentra under a false identity, Ginger Wade, and headed out to D.C. on a half-hour drive that took her an hour and a half due to traffic. She checked into a boutique hotel in the business district on Capitol Hill. For a walk-in at 6 P.M., all the hotel had left was a suite with a whirlpool tub and two large-screen TVs. It wasn't her idea of staying under the radar, but she liked the location. She sent Amaro a text to let him know where she was.

If Mr. X is watching me, he knows I've gone to D.C. to do the job. There shouldn't be any more parts arriving at the condo. I'm cooperating, at least so far.

Maliha unpacked her weapons. She didn't know what the situation would require, so she brought everything, from her CheyTac M200 Intervention long-range rifle system to swords and knives. It was depressing to see them all laid out on the bed.

Just like old times, with someone else jerking my strings.

There was more snow on the ground here than in Chicago, an odd reversal for the time of year. Fresh snowfall made the view out her window, all the way from the back of the Capitol to the Lincoln Memorial, a postcard scene. What remained on the ground of Chicago's snow was piled in dirty mounds, recently glazed with ice by the rainfall and drop in temperature.

Why is it I live in Chicago, anyway? I guess it's because I love the place, filthy snow and all.

Maliha flipped through the dossier on Presser again, looking for clues for why someone wanted this man dead. From the scanty information provided, he seemed to be an all-around good citizen.

Either this is a test to see if I'll follow orders or this guy has a big secret. What if he is some random man? Do I trade his life for Yanmeng's?

Her mind was whirling with alternatives, none of them good. She decided she'd try to relax in the tub and then get some dinner. After that, she hoped, her team would have some news for her.

She started drawing water for the tub and tossed aside her travel clothes.

Come, wash off the dust of the journey. That's something I'll always have left of Abiyram.

Remembering Abiyram got her started on thinking about Jake, the blood gold, and his possible role in the assassination of her dear friend. She'd shoved aside the heartbreak and the whole subject of Jake when she was swept up in rescuing Yanmeng, but Jake kept making his presence known.

Jake is Ageless. He could speed right by Hound's surveillance crew at Harbor Point and disappear fast from in front of my door. I don't know about the static, but it's worth mentioning to Amaro and Hound. He wouldn't need me to kill someone for him, though, unless this is some kind of crazy control scheme.

There was a knock at the door. "Room service."

She walked back toward the door and considered what to do. She hadn't ordered any room service.

"I didn't order any room service."

"Compliments of the hotel, ma'am."

She thought about ignoring it or telling the man to leave the tray outside her door, but then thought it could be an opportunity to get more information about Mr. X.

Could even be Mr. X.

"Just a minute."

She went into the bedroom and selected a pistol from the weapons on the bed, picked the right magazine from her supply, and loaded it. Standing off to the side of the entry door, she undid the chain and twisted the deadbolt lock open. The waiter opened the door and began to push his cart into the room. She quickly checked his aura and found that he had some tendrils of black, an imprint of something he'd done that wouldn't make his mother proud. He wasn't Mr. X. Still, that twinge of black made her uneasy.

She pointed the gun at him. "Hold it right there."

Being confronted by a naked guest pointing a gun at him wasn't in the waiter's job description. His eyes were round and his jaw dropped. He raised his hands.

"I . . . I don't have any money," he said.

"Just do as you're told and you won't have a problem. Step inside and close the door."

The young man was in his mid-twenties. He did as he was told and started to tremble.

"Tell me where Yanmeng is," she said.

"I don't know anybody like that, please don't kill me—"

Maliha stepped closer and planted the tip of the barrel on his forehead. "I said, tell me where Yanmeng is."

"Please . . ."

She stepped back but kept the weapon pointed at him. "Uncover the plate."

He did so, but his hand shook so much he dropped the metal cover on the floor. It was a plate of sliced fruit and cheese with a bowl of chocolate-covered cherries in the center.

"I'll take it back if you don't want it," he said.

She lowered her gun. "Okay. Thanks. I'll keep it. And don't say anything about this." She signed the bill to give him a generous tip. It was the least she could do after the scare she'd given him. He backed out of the room with the cart, his head bobbing nervously.

She plucked a cherry from the bowl and headed back to the tub. Muscles relaxed but mind still worried, she went out for pizza from Matchbox on Capitol Hill. She called ahead and lucked out getting someone else's cancelled reservation for one, probably due to the weather. She walked there, with snow falling gently, leaving footprints on the sidewalk. Walking back to the hotel, hers were still the only footprints, and they were filling in with snow.

Later she placed an encrypted phone call to Amaro and waited for the authentication to complete. "What's up?" she said. "I just had pizza."

"We had Chinese delivered. If we're through discussing our dinners, we do have some news for you," Amaro said.

Maliha heard Hound's voice in the background. "Gimmee that phone."

It sounded like there was a brief scuffle for the phone, and then Hound came on. "It's me."

"You're reverting to boyhood, both of you. Couldn't you just put me on speaker?"

"Oh yeah. Hold on. Okay, we're both here. You know, this is a lot of stress on all of us. You might cut us a little slack."

"Sorry."

"We have what I think you wanted to hear. Nathan Presser is no angel. Remember he was a real estate developer?" Hound said. Without waiting for her to answer, he went on. "He was buying up property in Florida for a high-end condo building with some retail stores on the ground floor. The land was mostly undeveloped but it had great highway access to Naples. A gem in the rough. Once he got the building through, he was planning a whole village of homes, schools, and shopping."

"Okay so far," Maliha said.

"The only problem was that there was an old mobile-home park in the way," Amaro said. "You can probably guess where things are going from here. Nathan pressured and intimidated the residents to leave. The last two holdouts turned up dead."

"Convenient for him. Was anything ever proven?"

"No. The police screwed up the investigation. Evidence was lost, witnesses changed their minds. Some say money changed hands, but no one was able to prove that, so Nathan got off," Amaro said.

"He did the killings himself?"

"He was overheard talking to one of his partners about blasting two people in the face, said he wished he'd done it sooner because of all the trouble they'd caused him," Hound said. "The project went through. His partners bought him out during the first phase of construction, so he's not associated with it anymore. That was the last time he worked in real estate. Even though he wasn't convicted, somebody powerful might have scared him out of the business, and out of the state."

"How sure are you of all this?" Maliha said.

"Absolutely sure. Your target's a killer. Does that make it any easier for you?" Hound said.

"I don't like being given orders, regardless of how bad the target is."

"Does that mean you're not going to do it?" Amaro said.

Maliha knew exactly what he was asking. Was she going to compromise her morals and give them more time to search for Yanmeng?

"I'll talk to you tomorrow."

"Wait!" Hound said. "You asked about routines. This scumbag lives in Alexandria and runs every morning in Potomac Overlook Park. Seven fifteen A.M."

"Give me his address." She copied it down. "Every morning? It's snowing here."

"Says here he's a dedicated runner, enters marathons, comes in among the top ten."

Yes, he'd be out in the snow. The question is, will I?

At 7 A.M. the next morning, Maliha was on the rooftop of a four-story medical building about two blocks from Nathan Presser's home, with a perfect line of sight to his front door. The snow had stopped. It was the gray, still time right before dawn. She was leaning against an air-conditioning unit, staying in its shadow. Her long-range rifle transit case was at her feet, soft-sided with a backpack sling. She didn't have a spotter to work with her, but then again she never did. She'd already determined the distance—at 750 yards, not much of a challenge.

The challenge is pulling the trigger.

At about five minutes after seven, she took her place looking through the CheyTac's sight, her gloves removed for a better feel on the trigger. The sun's rays were leaking over the horizon, touching a few clouds with gold. A moment later—early—the door opened and Presser stepped out. He was dressed in layers of running clothes. There was a woman in the doorway, wearing a nightgown. He had a lover who'd stayed overnight. She hadn't expected that. Presser took the woman in his arms and gave her a lingering kiss. Words were spoken, and then the woman crossed her arms over her chest and shivered.

That's right. It's cold out here. Close the door, woman.

As if she'd heard Maliha, the woman closed the door. Although Maliha didn't expect overpenetration of the bullet, she waited a few seconds for the woman to move away from the door. Presser obligingly delayed by bending over to tighten his shoelaces. When he stood up, she held her breath and . . .

For Yanmeng.

. . . pulled the trigger.

The rifle's suppressor masked much of the noise. She remained in place to see if a second shot was necessary. Through the scope, she could see the man slumped back against the door, a hole in his forehead and a streak of red tracking where his head slid. She picked up the shell casing and obscured her footprints so that no clear impression remained. Repacking her case, she slung it over her shoulder.

A few blocks away, she was gripped with the pain of the scale on her body moving. It seemed that Anu didn't mind Nathan Presser's dispatch from the Great Above. She didn't think Hound or Amaro lost any sleep over it either. To them, it was like any other case. Investigate, determine badness, bang bang—especially in this case with Yanmeng's life in the balance.

Back in her hotel room, she called Hound.

"It's done," she said, and hung up.

Chapter Sixteen

Maliha was back in Chicago. It had been nearly twenty-four hours since she'd shot a man on his front porch, the kiss of his woman warm on his lips. There was no news about Yanmeng.

"Do you want to talk about it?" Hound asked. He sat next to her at the kitchen table. They were having a cup of coffee, her favorite, Kopi Luwak. It was distinctive and rare. The beans were eaten by civets in Sumatra and passed through their digestive system. Afterward, they were hand-collected from the floor of the forest. Amaro was asleep. He'd refused to drink the coffee once he found out where it came from.

"No." She understood he was talking about her feelings on the killing. *If I did, it would be with Yanmeng. Don't think I'm going to get any answers out of his fingers.*

She missed the touch of her friend's mind as he remote-viewed her. He checked in with her daily, and she hadn't realized how reassuring that had been.

I can only imagine how Eliu feels. Their bond was so close. Shit. Not was, is.

Hound shrugged, a move that sent one of his shoulders up higher than the other due to his war injuries. "I know you're unhappy. We're all unhappy, but we're each doing our part. Yours happens to be worse."

"What was the story with your surveillance people?"

"They swear they weren't asleep, drunk, or drugged,

and that nobody with a package got past them. No word on Yanmeng's location. I've been visiting some medical facilities in person, and Amaro has been hacking in, looking for sedation orders. Are we assuming he's still in the city?"

"In it or close. Those severed fingers were very fresh. They haven't traveled far from Yanmeng, not hundreds of miles or anything."

"Within, say, a drive of an hour or two?" Hound said.

"That's likely. They hadn't been refrigerated before delivery."

"How do you know?"

"I just do. What about getting a look at who's bringing the packages to the door? The cameras don't seem to do any good."

"Amaro is worked up about that, but it looks like we need eyeball surveillance."

Maliha nodded. "From the emergency stairs at the end of the hall."

Jake watched me from there when he figured out how to get into my haven.

That incident, coming home and finding Jake in her secure sanctuary, had rattled Maliha so much that she'd increased security at the doorway. Instead of having a switch on the wall to abort the launch of deadly darts, there was now a number panel to enter an eight-digit code, her fingers moving in a blur. While nearly blinded, after lunging across the vacant space of the entry chamber—tasks with split-second timing piled on top of each other.

As if reading her mind, Hound said, "Jake phoned while you were in D.C. Again. He's back from his assignment. What about involving him? He has a lot of resources . . ."

"Not yet."

"Not yet? You planning to wait until Yanmeng's nothing but a stubby torso?" He narrowed his eyes. "What's the deal with you two? Trouble in Happy Town?"

"I have new information about him. I don't know if I can trust him."

"Tell me . . ."

Maliha held up her hand to stop him.

"So now you don't trust me, either," he said. "What do you think I'm doing on those missions we go on? Looking to shoot you in the back?"

It stung to hear Hound talk like that. She trusted him with her life, and knew the feeling was mutual.

"Hound, it's all too much right now. I'll talk to you soon, I promise. I love you, you know that."

"I love you, too. Always have, since you carried my sorry ass out of that killing field in Nam." He put his hand over hers on the table.

"You know about that?" Maliha thought his rescue was a secret.

Maliha sped into the firefight and crouched over Hound to make sure he was still alive. To her astonishment, the man was conscious enough to react to her, and lifted his arm to her face, touching her tenderly. His fingers left a trail of blood across her cheek.

He must think I am the angel of death come to claim him, yet he reaches out for me.

Then his head lolled to the side. She gathered him up and took him to his platoon, leaving him on the ground so that one of the men tripped over him. She went back to the clearing, but the man Hound had been working on was dead.

"Damn straight. You were my angel."

"I . . ."

"You don't have to say anything. It's between us."

"Let me decompress a little. I'll take a shift watching in the stairwell. I'll tell you about Jake when I'm done."

"Fine. I have something I need to do anyway. I need to have a talk with Chick."

"You think he's involved?"

"With the timing of his coming on board as doorman, maybe."

Maliha picked out two knives for close-up work and her current choice of pistols, a Sig Sauer P266 in a waist holster. Full sized, with a reassuring heft and fifteen rounds, it was usually her last-ditch weapon. She was trained early in her life with edged weapons and usually turned to them for both attack and defense. There were times, though, when blowing someone away was the best move. Mr. X fell into that category.

Hound woke up Amaro so that someone in the condo was awake and staying with Eliu.

"What's building security going to think when their stairway cams get a look at me?" Maliha said.

Hound waved his hand in dismissal. "Nothing. Those guys have selective blindness if the bribe is high enough."

"That's nice to know. I feel so much more secure."

Hound headed down the hall toward the elevators. Maliha went in the opposite direction. On the landing of the staircase, she was pleased to find Hound's viewer exactly as he'd described it: a small hole in the wall a little below waist height. Inside was a wide-angle lens that gave her a view of the corridor. She couldn't miss anyone coming to her door. She settled down on her knees, blanked out all thoughts about Jake and being a puppet killer again long after she'd left Rabishu's control, and looked through the lens. She knew that a few people in her building took the stairs for exercise. If she heard one of them coming, she'd step into the hall for a moment.

Six hours later, she stood up and stretched. She'd seen nothing.

Back in the condo, Eliu was fixing dinner. She'd insisted—it gave her something to do. Amaro was ready to take his turn in the stairwell, but Eliu put down a steaming bowl of rice and stir-fried vegetables in front of him.

"You have to eat sometime, and you might as well eat while it's hot," Eliu said.

They all sat at the table as she served the food. Maliha was pleased to see her active and contributing in her way. Amaro shoveled in the food with his chopsticks, the bowl held in one hand. He was hungry, but rushed.

"Nothing to report," Maliha said. "Three people came into the hallway. I know them as neighbors and they each went into their condos."

"I talked to Chick," Hound said. "After a little persuasion, he admitted that he receives illegal packages of prescription pills from a car that pulls up in the cab zone outside the building. Three different people in the building pick them up from him. They have pain-pill addictions. He told me the names and I broke into their condos on the off chance that the pain pills are for Yanmeng, but I couldn't find any evidence of that. I'm not interested in a little personal medication abuse."

"I'm surprised Chick only has three customers," Amaro said.

"Told me he's just getting started. Give him a few more months and he'll have an extensive client list."

Eliu said, "When will we hear something about Yanmeng? Shouldn't he be released now?"

"That's what we're hoping, but we can't count on it," Amaro said. "Once a blackmailer gets started, there's no way to compel him to stick to his terms."

My thoughts exactly.

Amaro stood up. "Sorry to eat and run, but I have an appointment with a spyhole."

He opened the door and nearly tripped over the box at his feet.

Chapter Seventeen

Fred Smith's lovemaking was not to her liking, but it didn't matter. After a few centuries, it was all insert tab A into slot B, unless Elizabeth was free to indulge her whims. That wasn't possible with Fred—she needed him among the living to be useful.

Elizabeth arrived early at the hotel he'd picked out for their late-night delight and installed a video camera with a view of the room. The security guard who came with Fred was on her payroll, so the place was declared bug-free in spite of the presence of the camera. Recording sex with each new man was standard until she had at least three recordings to establish a pattern. Then she didn't bother with it anymore.

You never know when the leverage will come in handy.

She was on her side on the bed, her face away from the camera, but giving the lens a nice view of her curvaceous ass. Fred was still flopped on the pillow beside her. She pulled him toward her, and he began sucking on her breast. She tilted her body and he followed, so his profile was on camera.

Left side—not his better one.

She pushed his shoulder away. "I'd like to get cleaned up. Would you like to join me in the shower?"

A half hour later, Elizabeth needed another shower. But she was satisfied that she could lead Fred around by his dick.

Of course, I have to make him think he's going where he *wants.*

On his way out, she slammed him against the door, rubbed her body against his, kissed him insistently, and gave him a blow job. To her surprise, little Freddie was up to it. She'd figured it was about a 30 percent chance.

"Let's do this again," he said.

Uh-huh.

When Elizabeth got home, she went into the basement to check on the hub of her intelligence network. Although her home was a traditional redbrick on the outside, the basement was bright, ultramodern, and packed with computers and other communication equipment. She had a staff of hundreds, twelve of whom worked in this room keeping track of items around the world that might be of interest to her. The rest of her staff were field operatives. All of them were highly skilled and highly paid, and knew that quitting their jobs wasn't an option. They signed on for life. Their lifetimes—not hers. When they weren't able to work anymore, they retired in luxury, and in the meantime, they enjoyed the finer things. Intense loyalty to her, protection by her, and generous rewards. Betrayal was punished by a gruesome death, but that was rarely necessary. It had been a couple of hundred years since the last punishment, and the details of that one were enough to keep modern recruits in line. The system worked for her long before computers.

She sat down at a desk on a dais that overlooked the room. That extra height had cost her. The basement ceiling wasn't high enough, so she had the concrete floor and all the substructure lowered. But she thought it was important that she sit on a higher level than her staff. She flipped through some routine reports, with some items highlighted. She took note of them but didn't see anything worth following up. Nevertheless, she remained in the room for another two hours, keeping her staff on edge and liking it.

Chapter Eighteen

A maro picked up the box at the door and brought it in. Eliu saw him first. Her shoulders fell, but she said nothing.

"Christ, how can this be happening?" Hound said. He jumped up so quickly that his chair fell over backward. "That door was unguarded for all of fifteen minutes. We think we're watching him, fuck, he's watching us!"

He flung open the door, angrily pumped his fist, and yelled, "I'll get you, you bastard!"

Maliha felt her stomach ball up into a hard knot. "Does he have his own cameras in the hallway?"

Hound closed the door. "Probably watched me install the damn spyhole," he said. "Shit, shit, shit!"

"Why can't we get in front of this? We've tackled some of the worst problems in the world and now we're being jerked around," Amaro said. "What are we up against?"

Learn humility, Master Liu said. All right, I'm humble already. Yanmeng!

"We need to stop moping around and think like an Ageless. At least I do. If I wanted to deliver that box and knew no one was surveilling the door, I could easily dash in here from miles away, plant the box, and be gone without being seen," Maliha said.

"With some kind of device that's jamming our cameras," Amaro said.

"Sure. The Ageless have plenty of resources at hand.

There might be a secret lab somewhere churning out jammers and other useful things," Maliha said.

"You mean like Q in the James Bond movies?" Amaro said.

"Why not?"

"Then why the hell don't we have our own secret lab?" Hound said. He hadn't simmered down yet.

None of them wanted to open the box.

"Because I've always handled my needs individually, by finding talented people and paying them gobs of money."

Hound's mind tracked in a different direction. "You mean Ageless like Jake?"

Maliha shook her head. "This isn't a good time."

"You said you'd tell me everything after your surveillance shift," Hound said.

"What's this about Jake? Something I should know?" Amaro said.

"Wait," Maliha said. She nodded toward Eliu, who was sitting at the table listening to their Ping-Pong conversation. "Let's open the box. Then we'll talk."

"I got it," Hound said. He went over to the box, slit the packing tape, and lifted the lid. After unwrapping the contents, he said, "He's not dead."

Eliu appeared at his elbow. She looked, and her hand flew to her mouth. "It's skin," she said. "Skin from his arm. I know that tattoo."

Maliha checked the box. In it was a strip of skin, rolled like a belt. She gently unrolled it and found it to be about two inches wide and a foot long. "Are you certain this is his?" she said.

"Yes," Eliu said. "Oh, my God. They are skinning my husband alive."

"We'll put a stop to it. We'll get him back," Maliha said. *We have to. It's killing all of us.*

Maliha and Hound went off to pack the skin in ice. They were keeping the ice for the other body parts refreshed. Once out of Eliu's hearing, Hound gestured at the two other Styrofoam coolers.

"You know it's too late for replantation," he said.

"Maybe, maybe not," Maliha said. "It doesn't matter. We're keeping them here for Eliu, too. What do you want us to do, put the parts down the garbage disposal in front of her?"

"I see your point."

"The skin can be replaced, by the new artificial skin if necessary, but I'm worried about infection. If he's not being cared for by professionals in a sterile environment, when we find him, it could be too late."

"What fucking professional would do this to him?"

"Maybe one whose life is threatened."

They rejoined the others. The note inside the box said, MRS. PAGE'S DINER, 9 A.M. THE GRILLED CHEESE WITH HAM AND ONIONS IS TO DIE FOR.

"I don't think we need to watch the hall overnight," Amaro said.

"You're just saying that to get out of your shift," Maliha said. Her attempt to lighten things up fell flat.

All four of them settled in the living room and looked at Maliha expectantly. She filled them in on everything she'd learned recently about Jake, including her suspicion that he could have been the one who killed Abiyram.

"It seems to me that we're talking about Jake's missing years one minute and the next, Abiyram's killed by a sniper. I know Jake's an expert shot, and he was traveling and out of touch with me at the time. Come on, guys, tell me I'm being paranoid," Maliha said.

"I thought you loved Jake," Amaro said. "How does that fit in?"

"I don't know. There's always been something about him. He keeps me at arm's length with these secrets of his. I don't expect a perfect past—how could I? But he's so slippery about this moral code of his."

"Jake's back in Chicago. Why don't you confront him with what you learned and see where that gets you? If he's not one of the bad guys, we could use his help," Hound said. "I have to say, though, you seem too easily swayed by Jake.

When you're away from him, you think more rationally. But the minute he, well, you know, you lose your perspective."

House in the mountains. Kids. He's all my dreams in one very nice basket.

"You have a lot of nerve," Maliha said. Her voice started to rise. "That's not true."

"Yeah, it is," Amaro said. "That's the thing. You can't see it like we can from the outside. Is the sex that—"

"Stop it! You don't know him the way I do. How could you? He's Ageless. I have some . . . issues to resolve, that's all."

"As long as you've got your eyes wide open," Hound said. "Why aren't you bringing up the things you're doubtful about? That's what people in love do. They talk things over honestly."

Maliha sighed. "You're right. I desperately need to clear the air with him. I'll put that on the schedule—right after breakfast at Mrs. Page's."

The diner was on the southwest side, in Garfield Ridge. It was a family place, with lots of booths, coloring books for the kiddies, and a counter complete with chrome stools. There was a lot of all-American décor, from flags to signed baseballs. It was full of sunshine from sparkling-clean windows and nearly deserted at this hour. The working-class patrons, many of whom had jobs at Midway Airport, had already come and gone.

Maliha chose a booth near the back, close to the rear exit and with a good view of the front door. She was well armed, but no weapons showed. She didn't want to alarm Mrs. Page and have the police called. She arrived fifteen minutes early and ordered the recommended grilled cheese sandwich with orange juice.

Why not? I'm cooperating.

At nine, three men came in the door. Two took seats at the counter, and the third slid into the booth with her. He made a point of taking a photo out of his pocket and comparing it to her face. She smiled for his approval.

A waitress came over to take the man's order, but he waved her away. Each of the men at the counter ordered coffee.

"I hear the last guy who met up with you didn't end up so good," he said.

"You heard right."

"That's why I got Curly and Larry over there. I'm Moe. All I have to do is give you this envelope"—he put an envelope on the table in front of him—"and leave. We don't want any trouble in this nice family establishment."

"I don't want trouble either, Moe."

What I'd like to do is behead all three of you with one sword strike.

"Good girl." He left the booth and the three men walked out together.

"Hound," Maliha said. Hound was parked across the street, listening to everything.

"Here."

"The main one is wearing a dark green jacket."

"You heard her. I'll take green jacket. Don't lose them." He had investigators waiting to tail anyone who met with Maliha.

Maliha took the Orange Line back downtown and stretched her legs with a jog to her home. Inside her condo, everything was quiet. Eliu and Amaro were probably sleeping, or at least resting in their rooms. Maliha sat at the kitchen table and spread the contents of the folder out in front of her.

It was another assignment, as she'd feared. The dossier was extensive.

Maliha's second target—she had to think of someone she was forced to assassinate as a target, as in the time when she was a demon's slave—was not a black-and-white situation. A Kentucky senator, Carlton Plait, had had an affair and a child out of wedlock early in his career but had since been a loving husband and family man. Floating around him were rumors of accepting monetary bribes for pushing legislation, but the rumors hadn't crystallized into facts yet, and possibly never would.

An investigative journalist, Camila Reyes, was hot on the senator's trail and had uncovered hush money that the senator was still paying to the mother of his bastard son. If the information was released, plus if the pay-to-play story gathered steam, either the senator would resign or his political strength would be severely damaged in his conservative state. He probably wouldn't be reelected. If the story was published, the journalist stood to gain in prestige and promotions. It would be a turning point in her career.

It wasn't the kind of case Maliha would consider taking on.

Besides, who is the villain here? A journalist prepared to rake a man's career and private life over the coals because "the public must know the truth" or just for a juicy byline? Or a senator who, cynically speaking, is no worse than many of his colleagues?

Her designated target was Camila Reyes, the journalist.

Chapter Nineteen

Maliha speed-dialed Jake's work phone number and he answered immediately.

"I missed you," he said. "Did you like the flowers?"

"Yes, they were great. I'd like to get together as soon as we can, Jake, away from your office."

"Whoa, woman, you must have *really* missed me. How about this evening?"

"What about in an hour at your apartment?"

"See you then."

She took a cab to McKinley Park and walked a couple of blocks. He lived on the second floor of a building with four apartments. She'd arrived early, so she kept walking past his building. Watching his arrival from half a block away, she noted nothing unusual about it or about him. He looked as handsome as ever, lean, broad-shouldered, curly black hair falling over his forehead. She gave him a few minutes, and then buzzed his doorbell. He told her to come up.

When he opened the door, his blue eyes caught and held hers. She saw only love and desire in them.

He couldn't be involved. No way. Maybe . . .

Jake had changed into a T-shirt and sweatpants, and there was a fire going that looked inviting. He swept her into his arms and kissed her, then nuzzled her neck.

"You're beautiful," he said. "I can't get enough of you."

She pushed him back, smiling. "Are we going to do this in the hall, or do I get to come in and take off my coat?"

"Of course. Please come in." He stood aside and waved her in with a bow.

His place was decorated with antiques mixed with modern furniture. The antiques blended right in and had a comfortable, worn look to them—they hadn't been refinished, and they were meant to be used. No velvet ropes to keep them on display.

He bought them new.

Jake settled her on the couch and brought out a package of Oreo Double Stuf cookies and two glasses of milk.

"You remembered," she said.

"Yeah." He gave her a big smile that warmed her and released a smile of her own. "After you said they were your favorites, I started keeping a package in case you came over. Of course, I couldn't have them get stale, so I started eating them." He patted his hard abdomen. "Gotta watch my waistline, so I stopped. These might be stale."

They weren't. She ate two, twisting their tops off and licking the icing from the middle.

"Okay, I've had my comfort food and I'm a pliable ball of emotions."

"You're never a pliable anything."

Not with you. I need some answers.

"Hey, I brought back something for you." He disappeared into his bedroom and came out with a small crystal jar, just an inch high. He handed it to her and she looked at it, puzzled. "Any guesses?"

"Looks like beach sand."

"Close, but off by six point eight miles straight down. It's diatomaceous sediment from Challenger Deep, the lowest part of the Mariana Trench. I wanted you to know I was thinking about you even when I was working."

So much for the candy.

"Uh, thanks. How did you get your hands on it?"

"Friends in low places?"

She smiled, but wondered what a Drug Enforcement

Administration agent had to do with deep-sea exploration.
I'll never know.

She examined the sediment in the jar. "It's fabulous. I'll treasure it."

He took the jar out of her hands and moved closer on the couch. His hands began roaming her body. It was time to act, or he'd find her hardware. She slid against him, rotated one of his shoulders, and in a fraction of a second had his back to her and a knife at his throat. Her leg wrapped around his, pinning them in place. This was the riskiest moment. He was Ageless and the situation wasn't going to be in her favor for long. Only surprise had made it possible.

She sliced deeply into his throat.

He slumped on the couch. She leaped up and fastened his wrists and ankles in handcuffs. She ran to the kitchen, retrieved some clean towels, and pressed them to his throat. The bleeding was already beginning to stop on its own, due to the nearly instantaneous healing of the Ageless. Then she subdued him with an injection of curare.

It was a delicate balance to give enough to keep him immobile without paralyzing his diaphragm and stopping his breathing. It was a technique Maliha had learned at the feet of a shaman of the Piaroa Indians, natives of Venezuela living along the Orinoco River, long before most of them became Christian. They hunted with curare-tipped darts shot from blowguns and were experts in its effects. Chick had processed her rush custom order with true professionalism. She was starting to like the man.

The small dose she'd given Jake would last about fifteen minutes for an ordinary man. For Jake, she estimated it would be three to five minutes, so she didn't have any time to lose. She threw the rest of her glass of milk into his face, backed away, and pointed a gun at him. He sputtered and opened his eyes.

"Hey! Ouch! What . . ." His voice was synced with his breathing, like a person with a tracheotomy. He looked down at his body, which wasn't responding to his calls for action. "What did you do to me?" Then he glimpsed the blood.

"You tried to kill me!" he said. "You know that won't work unless . . ." He shut his mouth, not wanting to give her any ideas if she hadn't already thought of them. A sure way to kill the Ageless was decapitation, making sure that the head and body were far enough apart that they couldn't grow back together.

"Pay attention! I only have a few minutes," Maliha said. "Did you kill Abiyram Heber? Or Arnie Henshaw?"

"What? No!"

She viewed his aura. It was familiar to her. A black base hovered near his body and extended spikes inches farther. That reflected the evil he'd done in the service of his demon Idiptu. It wasn't surprising. Her aura was the same. There was no way to tell if the blackness was centuries old or acquired recently. Wisps of red indicated that he was angry but trying to control it, and she could understand that. Her behavior hadn't met his expectations, to put it mildly. Splotches of blue showed that he did have a desire to help others, and that fit with what he'd told her at the beginning of their relationship.

"I love my work. Remember the Justice League comics?" Without waiting for an answer, Jake went on. "I used to get them used. Never did get my hands on the 1960 debut. Anyway, I knew that's what I wanted to be part of. I couldn't be a superhero, but I could still bring the bad guys to justice. Sounds sappy, huh?"

She shook her head. "What's sappy about saving lives?"

He pointed at her. "See, you get it. Lots of women out there don't. Can't cope with a guy whose life doesn't revolve around them."

His aura showed no sign of deception. Maliha had never known anyone who could significantly alter an aura, only manage it a bit, and then she could usually detect the deception.

Yanmeng would know about altering auras. Too bad I can't ask him.

"What is your involvement with the secret blood gold program?"

He said nothing.

"I know where your swords are kept," she said, alluding to decapitation.

"All right. How did you find out about the gold program?" he said, with his voice in the odd cadence of puffs of breath.

"I'm asking. You're answering."

"It was during the years I haven't wanted to talk about. Everything I did, D.R. Congo, Venezuela, the Philippines, Sudan, Indonesia—all of them. I did it to save lives."

"You could twist it to see it that way. Makes you sound like a hero. Is gold from those countries smuggled out and used to support dictatorships?"

"I was . . ."

"Yes or no?" she said.

"Yes. But I didn't mean for that to happen and I've been working to dismantle it. It's not like I can just wave my hand and turn off the tap."

Jake's aura didn't waver. He was telling the truth. She had only a minute left. He was beginning to shuffle his feet. She remembered what Abiyram had told her about the blood gold. *At no time were Jake's actions unknown to a few in the U.S. government. A few at the top.* Jake could have done all the grunt work and then been betrayed by the people at the top.

Jake started moving his feet sooner than Maliha had expected. Keeping the gun pointed at his head, she moved in and gave him another injection.

"Damn. Stop that," he said.

Maliha didn't want to mention that she'd used her last injection. When he began to recover this time, there would be a serious problem.

"There's more," he said. "Abiyram got the basic facts right, but he made sure you thought I was responsible for the blood gold. I wasn't, I swear. Abiyram had another motive. Since you came back into his life, he wanted you for himself. He approached me and tried to bribe me to get me to leave you alone. When that didn't work, he sent an assassin after me. He doesn't know about the Ageless and how hard we are to kill. I sent his assassin back in pieces. He's left me alone since then. When that route didn't work, he made things up that he knew would alienate you from me."

"I can't believe what I'm hearing," she said. "I know Abiyram. He would never do anything like that!"

"How well can you know anyone like that? He was a man accustomed to a lifetime of lying and manipulation. You told your team you were considering him as a new member. He desperately wanted that, and wanted you. You slept with him, didn't you?"

Maliha sighed. "Yes. Once."

"He was old, Maliha, and he thought there was some secret process to make him young again. You showed up on his doorstep looking the same as you did thirty years ago and never explained it. He took you to bed and became obsessed with the idea of being young again—with you."

"I told him there was no process."

"He would think you were lying, because that's exactly what he would have done in your position."

"He was my friend. My old friend," Maliha said.

"Exactly. Your old friend from thirty years ago. Did you ever try to confirm a word he said about me?" Jake sounded bitter. He shifted his body so he was sitting up straight on the couch. Tensing his arms and shoulders, he snapped the chain of the handcuffs behind his back.

Right now, right this instant, I can still pull the trigger. A head wound would slow him enough for me to get out of here.

He pulled his hands forward, the metal bracelets still in place, then reached down and bent open one of the links of the chain on his ankles, freeing his feet to move.

Maliha's time was up. She kept the gun pointed at him but she knew that now, with his Ageless speed, he could disarm her and she wouldn't even see him do it.

He stayed on the couch, patting the towel against his neck. The knife wound was almost closed. "Did you confirm anything he said, or just take his word over mine? I'm the man who loves you." His breathing was back to normal, but there was a hurt tone in his voice.

"I . . . I trusted him."

"And you didn't trust me? Did you ever check his aura?"

Maliha thought back and then lowered her eyes. "No."

When humility hits, it's a knockout blow.

"Why didn't you tell me all of this?" she said.

"Abiyram was involved in the blood gold project, deeply involved. That's why he knew so much about it in the first place. I have that setup ready to tumble, and when I do, I'll be cleaning house. Abiyram would have been dead in a matter of weeks."

"So you wanted to spare me knowing about him."

"Yes, and I guess that was a bad idea. Look at what it's done to us." He pointed down to the pillows of the blood-soaked couch.

Maliha sat down on the couch across from him. She was defenseless, physically and emotionally. "I made a mistake."

"Put that gun down and get these cuffs off me. You have to remember that Abiyram was an expert at manipulation. It's not your fault."

She took the cuffs off. "I'm no babe in the woods, Jake. I've used men for my own purposes for centuries. I should have caught on."

"There's a difference this time. You're mostly human. You were blinded by friendship."

He moved over to sit next to her and lifted her chin with his fingers. Tears flowed down her cheeks and her eyes were closed. She couldn't face him. Jake kissed each eyelid gently and then kissed her on the lips. He picked her up in his arms and carried her toward the stairs.

"You owe me a new couch," he said.

Chapter Twenty

Maliha came out of the shower. Jake brushed her hair as she sat naked on the edge of the bed, talking to him.

"I have to get back home. There's a lot going on," she said.

"Chess game with Yanmeng?"

"Yanmeng's missing."

She heard a sharp intake of breath from Jake, and he stopped brushing. "Why didn't you tell me right away?"

"Because I thought there was a chance you might be involved in it."

"Do you still think so?"

"No. Yanmeng's in horrible trouble, Jake, and so am I, in a different way. He's being held captive and his fingers are being returned to us. The last package was a strip of skin. I'm being blackmailed to kill people that someone else is choosing."

"Oh no. Is Eliu safe?"

"She's with us."

The look he gave her let her know that if she didn't tell him everything immediately, she'd be the one with a knife to her neck.

"Come back to my condo with me and we'll fill you in."

"I take it I'm on the shit list with the rest of the team."

"Yes, but I'll explain. I need to leave now."

"Wait—Yanmeng is a remote viewer. Why hasn't he been in touch with you or his wife?"

"Presumably he's being kept sedated."

"An induced coma." He clasped her around the waist from the back, leaned forward, and kissed her neck tenderly. "I want to help. Let's go."

Maliha went through the door of her condo first. Both of her team members were armed, and Hound might shoot first and determine the merits of it later. All three in residence were at the kitchen table, eating pizza.

"Where have you been?" Amaro said. "Why weren't you answering your phone?"

Jake stepped in from the hall.

"Oh." Amaro lifted a large slice to his mouth, bit into it, and dragged cheese down over his chin.

Hound drew his weapon and aimed at Jake. "Over there, Maliha," he said, nodding toward the opposite side of the room. She took the look on his face seriously and moved.

"Now, do we want this guy in here or not?" he asked her. He wasn't acknowledging the fact that Jake could wipe all of them out in a few seconds and not be breathing hard.

"Yes," she said.

He raised his eyebrows at her and she knew he was thinking of their conversation about being easily swayed.

"I said yes."

"Okay, then." He put the gun down on the table next to the pizza box. Jake and Maliha sat down.

"I have a lot of catching up to do," Jake said. "Who wants to go first?"

An hour later, they were up to talking about that morning's meeting in Mrs. Page's Diner.

"Fingerprints?" Maliha said.

"The men at the counter ordered coffee but didn't touch it. They wiped the countertops with their jacket sleeves as they left. The booth you were in got the same treatment from Green Jacket. They've done this kind of thing before."

"I figured they were a step up from the first one I met in

the abandoned house," she said. "What about tailing them?"

"Took us all over the damn city and then they must have thought they lost us. All three ended up at the same place. A cemetery. They started digging a grave with a backhoe and a couple of shovels."

Maliha nodded. "Low-profile cover jobs. So we know names and addresses?"

"Nope," Amaro said. "We checked employment records later. They didn't have any gravediggers working that day. When we went back out, they were gone."

"Not my finest hour as a P.I.," Hound said.

"We all have our share," Maliha said.

"So now what?" Amaro said.

"Jake, I'd like you to do one of two things. Either stay here and patrol the hallways looking for another box delivery or start checking hospitals, clinics, and doctors' offices in person. Both of them are weak links for us. We can't cover as much ground as you can."

"I'll do hallway patrol. The most direct way to Yanmeng is to capture and question that messenger. I think he or she is more involved than just carrying around a box," Jake said.

"Why?" said Hound.

"Maliha said that the severed parts were very fresh when they arrived here. They didn't go through a long chain of custody and sit around in somebody's living room before getting here. There's no ice packed in the boxes. The messenger picks them up directly from the site. Or the messenger is the one doing the slice and dice."

Eliu winced. Jake glanced at her. "Sorry."

"They're keeping him sedated for one of two reasons. One, they know about the remote viewing," Hound said. "If he's allowed to regain consciousness, he could contact you and somehow give you his location. Two, the person doing this is concerned about not causing him pain."

"A compassionate kidnapper?" Amaro said.

"Someone comfortable in an operating room," Jake said.

Maliha said, "Amaro, look for surgeons, anesthetists, doctors, even residents or interns with gambling problems, addictions, lawsuits, psychological problems . . . anything that might tip them over the edge."

He frowned. "I can try, but that's one hell of a fishing net. You're probably talking about half the docs in this city," Amaro said.

Amaro headed off to his computer to get started and Hound joined him. Maliha walked Jake to the door. He spoke to her in a whisper.

"I know that this is tearing you up inside and you're thinking about going through with the assassination to buy time. Say the word and I'll do it," Jake said.

"I'm not your demon master. I don't give you assignments."

"I know that. Just keep it in mind if you can't pull the trigger. I'll carry this burden for you."

He vanished, and she knew he was running the hallways at top speed, something he could keep up for days.

"Eliu," Maliha said, "I'm heading for Washington, D.C., again. Let the others know, will you?" She had a strong feeling that the dossier was correct, and that it came down to the journalist or Yanmeng. She had her assignment. Her jet was waiting at the airport. She packed hurriedly and left, before her team could try to talk her out of it.

Chapter Twenty-One

Camila Reyes lived in a small apartment in the Adams Morgan neighborhood of Washington, D.C. During the day, there was a doorman, but at night there was controlled access with a video cam to each apartment so the occupant could see who was buzzing them.

A little research was all it took to locate a single man in his thirties living in an efficiency on the eighth floor. At midnight, Maliha went into the lobby and stepped in front of the video cam. She was wearing a blonde wig, heavy makeup, and a top and skirt that barely covered her body's erogenous zones. A skimpy jacket, not warm enough for the weather, hung around her shoulders. She pressed the buzzer.

A sleepy voice came on. "Yeah?"

"Mr. Hernandez, I'm here for you."

"Uh . . . what?"

"You will have the best night of your life, Mr. Hernandez. Ring me up."

"Just a minute." She pictured him shuffling to the door to get a look at the video screen. She smiled into the camera and waved, making sure that plenty of cleavage showed.

"I . . . I'm not Mr. Hernandez," he stammered.

"You are not?" She pouted and read him the address from a slip of paper. "Room 821?"

"No, you're at least ten miles away."

"I'm new in town. I guess Mr. Hernandez will be disappointed tonight." Her face brightened. "Who are you?"

"I'm Gil Ceja."

"Hi Gil, I'm . . . Trixy. I'm here already. Would you like some company, Gil? I'll give you a special deal. I promise you'll have fun."

There was a brief hesitation, and then the iron-barred doorway blocking access to the elevators clicked open.

"Oh, Gil," she said. "Get naked and wait for me by the door. I've got a surprise for you."

Maliha headed for Room 408, where the journalist lived. Using a torque and pick set, she opened the standard lock on the door. Easing into the room, she slipped off her heels and left them by the entrance. After letting her eyes adjust to the dark, she could see that there was a desk with a computer on it in the combination kitchen-living room. Checking it out, she could see that the computer was on, with a bouncing-ball screen saver.

Later.

She moved on to the bedroom, drawing a knife from a sheath that rested on her back, attached to the skirt's low-rise waistband. Maliha moved like the Black Ghost she once was. Soundless, a shadow, something glimpsed from the corner of the eye, followed by a rush of darkness and death.

She turned the doorknob and cracked open the bedroom door. In this room there was a night-light, a yellow starfish shape with a smile. Camila was asleep, her blanket slipped to one side and one leg exposed from the knee down. Maliha had an urge to cover the woman's leg. The heat was turned down for the night, and it was cold in the apartment.

She pushed the door open a little wider, revealing a dresser and mirror, a brush, makeup kit, and a tottering stack of books—the ordinary things of this woman's life that were about to become mute witnesses to her death. Camila was snoring softly. The double bed she slept in was shared with no lover, just a cat. The cat's eyes opened and looked at Maliha through narrow slits. Satisfied, it adjusted its position and went back to sleep.

Maliha could go in, slash Camila's throat, and be out in a few seconds without causing any noise.

Then what? Another body part, another target? I'm trapped. Give up on Yanmeng or go against what I believe in and deal with the fallout afterward?

Maliha pushed the door open further and stepped into the room.

She froze.

There was a crib against the wall that had been blocked from her view by the door. Maliha was drawn to it. She walked over, her knife still at the ready. In the crib was a baby boy, about six months old, wearing pajamas with feet. As she watched in the pale yellow light of the starfish, a bubble formed between his lips and gently popped. She put her hand on the baby's chest, feeling the rise and fall of his small rib cage as he breathed.

Maliha couldn't control the urge to push. With her back against the cold stone wall and her legs drawn up, she bore down. Her screams echoed in the room, again and again, as she strained and rested. One last mighty push and the infant slipped out onto the earthen floor.

She lay down next to the small body. In darkness as deep as a cave's, she could see nothing, but she could feel that her baby was flaccid, unmoving. Hope dying in her heart, she did what a midwife would do for a baby who appeared dead—try to share her own life with it. She placed her mouth over the baby's mouth and nose and breathed out in small puffs. Each time she lifted her head, she willed the baby to draw breath and begin crying.

After a while she stopped trying. The heat left the small body and the soft, perfect arms and legs locked into the stiffness of death.

Maliha closed her eyes at the painful memory. *Constanta, my daughter.*

She put away her knife. *There has to be another way.*

Back at the desk, she copied files from Camila's computer. She saw that there were physical files, too, folders of research color-coded and neatly stacked. She assumed there were backup files, too.

Destroy all this? Not yet. Too much to think about.

As she left the building, she wondered if Gil was still standing naked at his door waiting for his surprise.

Chapter Twenty-Two

Maliha had a video conference call from her hotel in D.C. to catch up on her team's activities.

"What the fuck got into you sneaking out like that?" Hound said. "We're supposed to be a team. Is Camila dead?"

"No. I got into her place and found out she has a baby, something conveniently left out of the dossier."

"I found that out when I was doing background work," Amaro said. "Too bad you weren't here to learn that. Or answering your phone. That's what these things are for"—he held up a cell phone—"to keep in touch when you're away."

"My cell was off. Does Jake have anything to report?"

"Jake? What Jake? We haven't seen him, either, since you left. We thought maybe the two of you eloped or something," Amaro said.

"Hey, that's uncalled for. Maliha would never run out on Yanmeng. You watch your tongue or I'll hand it to you in a pickle jar," Hound said.

"Pickle jar?" Amaro said.

"First thing I could think of. Sorry, Boss, you can see things are a bit tense here."

"Here too," Maliha said. "I have a copy of Camila's hard disk. Amaro, you can get it from my computer. I'd like to run an idea past you and see what you think."

"Downloading now."

"I'd hate like hell to kill Camila. The purpose of the assignment is to keep her from publishing her exposé about Senator Plait's philandering and the pay-to-play scheme. We should focus on that goal. My first approach is to offer her money. Lots of it. She's living small, and she has a son to support and put through college. My second idea is to destroy every bit of her research. The story will evaporate. If she tries to go to her sources again, I'll scare them off."

"I like Door Number One," Amaro said, "with one modification. By taking away this story, we might be derailing her career at an important point. What makes her career less valuable than the senator's? I say give her another story. A big scandal, even bigger than this one. Make her work for it. Give her some facts and some sources who'll talk to her and let her do her job."

"I like it," Maliha said. "One thing—where does this big scandal come from?"

"I might be helpful in that regard," Hound said. In his work as a private investigator, Hound worked for both the private sector and the public, including classified government projects.

"Remember we want scandal material, not government secret stuff," Amaro said.

At that moment, Jake appeared and sat down within camera range. "Am I missing anything?"

There was a brief recap. Jake liked the idea of the scandal approach.

"How fast can you put something together, Hound?" Maliha said.

"Two days?"

"Do it in one. I don't think Mr. X is very patient. Amaro, I could use your help here getting back into Camila's building. I'll send the jet for you."

"Wait! How do we get this across to Mr. X so he knows you satisfied the assignment?" Hound said.

"I think Mr. X is watching her closely. He'll know when she drops Senator Plait and begins working on an unrelated story. So we're going with Door Number One?"

They all nodded.

Maliha had some misgivings, but she kept them to herself. When she was still Ageless, she'd once tried what she was attempting now: satisfying the intent but not the literal order of the assignment, in order to save a man's life. It worked, but she suffered horribly at Rabishu's hands afterward for her creative defiance.

"What about looking for doctors who might be vulnerable to being forced to cooperate by working on Yanmeng?" Maliha asked.

"I decided to start close to home," Amaro said. "A person living in this building would have good access to your entrance door. All that would be needed is a jamming device for the cameras, and I think that's a given. There are one hundred and fifty-eight doctors living in all three wings of Harbor Point Towers."

Hound whistled. "I would never have guessed. I guess it's because these condos are so expensive."

"That's why most of them are surgeons or specialists, especially oncologists, cardiologists, and radiologists," Amaro said.

"Find any compromising situations?" Maliha said.

"Quite a few. This is not a group of people who live ho-hum lives."

"Pass the names along to Hound to check out," Maliha said, "but not until he comes up with a good scandal. That's top priority."

It was two in the morning. Wearing gloves, Amaro pressed the button for Gil Ceja's apartment, Number 821. There was no answer. Amaro leaned on the button. After several minutes of pressing, a gruff voice came on.

"Yeah, what do you want?"

Amaro held a badge up to the camera. "Detective Jeremy Weeks, Metro PD Homicide. I'd like to talk to you about Ms. Trixy Fox."

"Don't know her."

"Ms. Fox took a cab to this building and her fingerprint was on your call button. Open the door, Mr. Ceja. I need to ask you some questions."

"Is she . . . missing?"

"She's dead. Open the damn door."

"Shit."

The access door clicked open and Maliha, who'd been keeping out of camera range, walked through. She picked the lock on Room 408. Everything was the same as the last time she'd been there. She went to the bedroom and woke Camila up, first putting a gloved hand over the woman's mouth.

"I'm not going to hurt you," Maliha said. "Don't scream. I need to talk to you. Come out into the other room."

The woman cooperated. It was clear that she was anxious to get the intruder out of the room where her son was sleeping. In the kitchen, they sat opposite each other at a two-person table. With the high chair in the corner, there was barely room to move. Maliha put a gun on the table to impress Camila with the seriousness of her visit, keeping her hand on the pistol's grip. She wasn't worried about having the gun taken away from her.

Not unless Camila is Ageless—in which case I would already be on my ass with a knife at my neck, or in my neck.

"It's about the story on Senator Plait."

"Did Plait send you here? That son-of-a-bitch? You can tell him to go screw himself. Nothing's gonna stop this story from coming out and it'll be my byline he can ride to hell." Her voice was low and even, remarkable given the situation, except that she practically spit out the senator's name.

This may be a tougher sell than I thought.

"Everything you have on Plait is true?"

"Yeah. It's one-hundred-percent legit. I busted my butt for a year checking out all the shit."

"So you feel confident that the public has a need to know this, given that it's going to derail his career?"

"Don't kid yourself. He goes to some country-club jail for a while and when he gets out, he squirms his way back into politics like a worm. The public's got a short attention span. This is just a bump in the road for him."

"Even if that's possible, it could take years to get back on track."

Camila shrugged. "That's my concern because?"

"Are you doing this to make a name for yourself?"

"I wouldn't mind the extra money. Get a two-bedroom place, start saving a bit. But that's not the main reason. He killed my sister four years ago. I thought about hiring somebody to take him out, but it's too risky. My baby isn't going to Family Services. I'm getting some justice for Angelita the only way I can."

Maliha viewed Camila's aura. She detected some darkness there, which she guessed was due to her childhood experiences. She'd seen it before in the auras of abused children. There was no deception.

"What happened to Angelita?"

"I don't have to tell you my life story. I've told you too much already. Now it's time for you to answer some questions. Who the hell are you, and what gives you the right to come into my home with a gun? You're threatening my son and me. I want you out of my apartment."

"Calm down. I'm here to offer you a different story to investigate, a national scandal. And I can do something about your money anxieties. Give you and your son a secure life."

"What are you talking about? Haven't you been listening? I don't want *another* story. This is personal, with Carlton Plait. You're gonna bribe me out of getting justice? *No way.*" She pulled a string hanging around her neck and brought out an emergency call pendant that was hidden under her pajamas. "I pressed this when you put that gun on the table. How long has that been? Three minutes? The police will be here any second!" Camila stood up. "You are so out of your league, sister. You think I haven't been expecting something like this?" She upended the table, knocking the gun onto the floor. Grabbing a knife from a wooden block on the counter, she lunged at Maliha.

Maliha blocked the thrust easily and grabbed Camila's wrist. She twisted Camila's arm behind her back, hyperflexing the wrist and plucking the knife from her fingers. She kicked the back of Camila's knee and brought the woman down hard on both knees.

Maliha felt a rush of air. Viewing auras in the room, she saw the black streak left by an Ageless running at speed. When a person moved, his aura lagged a fraction of a second behind, a kind of inertia of the energy field. For a normal person, that slight delay wasn't enough to matter—his aura would appear to stay with him as he moved. At Ageless speed, it did matter, and was visible to Maliha as a black blur crossing her field of aura vision.

Puzzled, she said, "Jake?" Then she noticed that the gun on the floor was gone. "No, Jake, don't!"

She heard gunshots and Camila slumped in her grip. The woman had taken a bullet in the head and another in her chest. Maliha turned to leave and saw that the computer had been pulverized and flames were already leaping from the stacks of research folders to the nearby curtains. In a minute, the apartment would be engulfed.

The front door crashed in and a S.W.A.T. team rushed into the room. They stopped a few feet beyond the threshold. The carpet was on fire.

Maliha was already in motion. With the flames around her, she locked her fear of burning alive away and sped toward the bedroom, drawing on her Ageless speed. She pulled the baby from the crib and ran out the door, knocking into an officer holding a shield, who couldn't even see what had brushed him aside.

She spotted blood on the baby. Horrified, she checked him over and found no wound.

It's his mother's blood from my hands. I'm glad he'll never know it.

In the hallway she placed the baby on the floor and ran for the stairwell. She delayed long enough to make sure that someone noticed him, and then she bolted down the stairs.

She was running down the street, trying to distance herself physically and mentally from the horror of her plan gone wrong, when Anu's judgment hit her so sharply she stumbled and rolled. She grimaced in pain as a figure crawled from the lives saved side of her scale and made its way across her stomach in the wrong direction, burning its tiny footprints into her skin. Then the scale swung into motion as the pans readjusted their positions. The pull through time, since she aged every time the scale moved, was not great. The damage was already done to Maliha's heart.

The boy will die because I didn't save his mother. What on Earth went wrong in there?

Chapter Twenty-Three

J ake was here the whole time," Hound said. "He said he needed a couple of hours' rest. He was sleeping in your room at the time you were in Camila's apartment."

"How can you be so sure?" Amaro asked.

"I don't have a trusting nature. I pushed a piece of heavy furniture in front of the closed door. If he'd come out, I would have seen the furniture move."

"He could have jumped over it, genius," Amaro said.

"Shit."

"Could he have run to D.C. and back?" Amaro said. They both looked at Maliha.

"I couldn't have done that when I was Ageless. Not in two hours. It has to be some other Ageless who has taken an interest, protecting Mr. X. Or Mr. X is Ageless, and that was him in the room with me."

"Then why did you say that the first thought that entered your mind was Jake?" Hound said.

Maliha started to get irritated. "I was surprised. Can we move on?"

She didn't want to explain that she thought first of Jake because he'd offered to take over the assignment for her and in that instant, she'd thought that somehow he was doing just that.

"Looking at the practical side, that clone of Camila's disc came in handy. I found that she had an account for backing up her files on a cloud service. I wiped them out. We're sitting on that information about the good senator if we care to use it."

"If it's true, we'll use it, but not until we have Yanmeng back."

Maliha sat at a small table in Kelly's Pub later that night. She was on her second glass of orange juice. Hound was late. He'd wanted to talk with her in a private situation.

She was positioned so that she could see the front door and spot Hound when he came in. Ten minutes later, he entered, a fresh dusting of snow on his broad, uneven shoulders and his Indiana-Jones-style hat pulled down low over his face. The bar was full of students celebrating the end of the semester, but Hound stood head and shoulders above most of them. He acknowledged her with a quick upward nod of his head, and then went to the bar for a beer.

He sat down across from her and took a long swallow of beer. "Any booze in that O.J.?"

"No," Maliha said. "One of us has to stay sober, and it looks like I'm it."

"Hell, I've only had one, maybe two beers. Just to warm up. It's cold outside."

I'd say it was more to build up your courage.

"What did you want to tell me?"

"I've been thinking that when this is over, it's time to go our separate ways," Hound said.

"What? You argued against that when I suggested it. You said you'd spend the rest of your life looking for me if I disappeared."

"Things have changed. First, you're not the only one who has any say about it. The new democracy, remember?"

"Bullshit. This sounds more like a mutiny than a democracy."

"Hear me out." He took another swallow of beer. "Maliha, you've gone to pieces on this Yanmeng thing." He grimaced. "Poor choice of words."

"I have not—"

"Ah!" He held up one finger to stop her denial. His breath wafted across the table to her, and she was sure he'd had more than a couple of beers.

"My turn to talk," he said. "You said you were thinking of splitting the team because we were in danger due to our association with you. We"—he gestured as though Amaro were with them at the table—"think we're endangering you."

She frowned at him. "I can take care of myself. I've managed to survive a few tough spots. Explain."

"You're usually aggressive and confident of success. Now your confidence is eroded, which I think has been the point all along—breaking you down until you mindlessly follow directions like a good little assassin. When you take action, something goes wrong. Yanmeng is involved and your judgment has gone to hell."

"I swore to get him back and I will. If I don't, that means I'm dead."

"This is exactly what I'm talking about. Not everything is going to turn out your way because you said so. We come up against impossible circumstances sometimes and we lose our loved ones. You can't accept that. All that conflict going on in you is spilling out into just about everything you do. It's as clear to us as a mountain stream. You can't work rationally when one of us is in danger."

It was hard to hear, but Maliha knew he was striking close to the truth. She was treading on moral territory she'd rather not walk on, and she was forced to do it with the clock ticking on Yanmeng's life. The result had been mistakes and missed opportunities, which compounded and made her feel even worse. The frustration over not being able to find Yanmeng and put an end to the nightmare was turning her into a blindfolded woman with a loaded gun.

I'm playing right into Mr. X's hands.

A drunken man stumbled into their table. Hound rose from his seat. "Fuck off, jerk."

He was a happy drunk and didn't react to Hound's imposing presence. "Need to take a leak," he said, and smiled.

Hound gave him a shove toward the men's room. "The door with the stick figure of a man on it."

"Thanks." He moved off in that direction and Hound sat down.

"There's another thing. There's a worrisome pattern going here," Hound said. "The first target was a bad guy. The second target was gray, where it was hard to tell whose life or goals took priority, the journalist's or the senator's. Not the kind of decision I'd like to make without a big spotlight to point the way."

"Camila said the senator killed her sister. That's a sizeable spotlight."

"If it's true. Her sister Angelita died in a car accident. So far I haven't turned up anything suspicious about it. The whole thing might have been Camila's imagination. The next target might be a good guy. What then?"

"I don't know. You want me to let Yanmeng die? I don't want to do it, but I might take Jake up on his offer to kill the target."

"I didn't know he'd offered. Ain't love grand? What would you do if the kidnapped person wasn't Yanmeng?"

"I . . . don't know."

"Shit, Maliha, we're talking honestly here. If you're not going to start telling the truth, then you already have broken up this team."

"I'd refuse to do the killing. I'd try a bluff. Take a risk, something."

"There it is. You'd risk a kidnapped stranger's life so your moral compass doesn't go haywire. In this case, you don't feel you have freedom to act because one of us is involved. I rest my case."

Maliha shifted her feet and noticed something new: a box on the floor, right next to her ankles.

"Hound, the drunk—he left a box."

"Stay here!" Hound was up and running toward the men's room, plowing a path through the crowd.

Stay here? Why should I? I'll check the front.

Maliha started to rise and felt an insistent hand on her shoulder. Blood red fingernails walked down her arm and tapped the table.

"Sit down. Let your manservant do his job."

A woman slipped into the seat Hound had just vacated. She was tall, blonde, young, with skin as pale as if she lived underground and had lost all of her coloring. Her lips matched the color of her fingernails, and Maliha noticed that those nails were filed to a point. Her coat was drawn tightly around her body, but Maliha could tell that body was both fit and curvaceous.

Viewing the woman's aura, Maliha was shocked at its black intensity. She knew she had to be looking at one of the Ageless, a woman with more death and blood on her hands than Maliha could measure on her scale.

This woman had a good start on killing before she became a demon's slave and hasn't slacked off since. She is Mr. X or she is guarding Mr. X at her demon's command.

The woman tossed her hair. "Did you get a good look?"

She can tell when her aura's viewed! Never met anyone else sensitive to that except Yanmeng.

"Yes," Maliha said.

"I thought it was about time we met face-to-face. Speaking of faces, you really should do something about that skin of yours." She ran her fingers down her own perfect alabaster cheek. "I could give you some ideas on that."

"I'm not here for a beauty consultation. Let Yanmeng go."

"We're getting ahead of ourselves. Do you remember Xietai?"

Maliha couldn't figure out where the conversation was going. "Yes. He was a depraved snake."

"That may be, but he was my depraved snake. I reward depravity with advanced training. That training is now wasted."

That's why Xietai put up such a strong fight. He was trained by one of the Ageless. A nasty one.

"I have one of his knives. I'd be happy to return it to you, right between your eyes."

"I've heard so much about you, rogue, but up close you seem a bit unimpressive. I'll take you on though, and make the best of it."

Maliha blinked. "What?"

"You killed my top warrior. I expect you to take his place when Yanmeng's dead. Ooh, did I say that last part aloud?"

Fear and rage fought inside Maliha. She kept her voice as calm as the eye of a hurricane. "Who are you?"

"Countess Elizabeth. 'My Lady' will do." She stood and turned to leave.

Go!

Maliha rose from her seat, tugging on the grip of the whip sword wrapped around her waist as she did so. By the time she was standing, the two flexible blades were separated and whirling toward Elizabeth. They struck low, severing her legs below the knees. Blood spurted wildly. The crowd scrambled for the exits and the staff disappeared into a back room, heading for the loading door.

Maliha crouched over the figure on the floor. Elizabeth was losing a lot of blood. If she didn't act soon, she might become unconscious before she could put her lower legs back in place and let them reattach.

I could kill her now. But would I ever find Yanmeng?

She put a knife to Elizabeth's throat.

"Return Yanmeng or next time those blades will cut off your head, not your legs. You can forget about me becoming your warrior." She heard a siren approaching in the distance. "Better hurry up and put your legs back on or you'll have a lot of explaining to do to the paramedics."

Maliha picked up the box on the floor at her feet and walked out of the now-empty pub.

Hound came jogging down the block. He was breathing hard—he didn't have a lot of stamina due to the old injuries to his chest.

"The jerk who left the box is dead," he said between breaths. "Somebody killed him a few blocks away before I got there."

He glanced through the window of the pub and noticed

that the celebrating crowds were missing. "Where'd everybody go? What'd I miss?"

Then he noticed that Maliha was coiling the whip sword back into its sheath around her waist.

"Let's split up," she said.

He nodded and took off into the night.

Chapter Twenty-Four

.

Maliha took home the box from the pub. It contained Yanmeng's hand, the one that was already missing fingers. Eliu identified a small deformity of his little finger that Yanmeng acquired in prison during the Chinese Revolution.

Eliu had made one attempt to convince the team to go to the police, something Yanmeng would never have wanted. When that didn't work, she became withdrawn. She spent most of her time in a bedroom with the door closed, barely coming out to eat. No more treating them to fresh, hot meals as though they were her children.

She's already suffered the loss of her only son. If Yanmeng doesn't come back, she'll be alone in the world. She has us, but doesn't seem too keen on that idea right now.

Maliha was worried Eliu would give up and leave the condo, making her an easy kidnapping target if she went out on her own.

She thinks he's going to die. I can see it in her face.

"It's a very clean cut," Jake said. "Surgical."

Or a swing from Elizabeth's sword.

"We should confirm the identity with a DNA test, even though Eliu seems sure. I can take care of that," Jake said.

"A little late in the game for that," Amaro said.

"Excuse me, I got in the game late," Jake said, annoyed.

"Behave, children," Hound said.

The note containing Maliha's instructions for the next meeting was nothing but GPS coordinates and a time, 9 A.M. It was signed with Elizabeth's initial in a flowing script.

"I need information on someone who calls herself Countess Elizabeth. She's Ageless, so the title could be real. This woman is either the puppeteer jerking my strings or she's guarding the puppeteer." She gave a quick summary of the events in the pub, leaving out Elizabeth's plans to convert Maliha to her personal warrior.

She thinks I'll go into the human trafficking business at her command. Been there, done that. No way I'll do it again.

"I'll put together her background," Hound said.

"Where are we with the doctors in this building?" Maliha said. "You realize if nothing pans out we're starting from scratch with all the doctors in the city. I don't like those odds."

"That I've made some progress on while you've been out drinking," Amaro said. Hound shot him a warning look. "In all three wings of Harbor Point Towers, there are a total of seven hundred and forty-two units, minus any that have been cannibalized to enlarge other units. One hundred and fifty-eight docs in the house. Of those, one hundred and twenty-four check out clean."

"I'm impressed! How did you get all that work done in such a short time?" Maliha said.

"I recruited some hacker buddies from the old days. They thought it was a fun diversion from the usual."

"So we have thirty-four possibilities. How many are surgeons?"

"All but six."

"Okay, Jake and Amaro, will you work this list? We need to eliminate these people as fast as possible."

"That leaves you," Hound said. "What are your plans?"

"I . . . I need a break," Maliha said.

All three of them looked at her. "You're not running off somewhere again, are you?" Amaro said.

"No. Can't I just need a break?"

"Where will you be? In case we need to get in touch with you," Amaro said.

"She'll be in her haven, right, Maliha?" Jake said.

"Haven? What's that?" Hound said.

Jake looked at Maliha. "They didn't know?"

She sighed. "They do now."

"Sorry. I thought . . ."

"I have another condo in this building," Maliha said, to surprised looks. "I go there for privacy and I store some things there. No one's been in it except Jake, and that was only once."

"Yeah, and she stabbed me for it, too," Jake said.

"It's on the forty-eighth floor, Suite 4876. It's a secure place and the entrance is booby-trapped. If you manage to get as far as stepping inside the door, you'll be killed. So don't try it."

"You have a hidden getaway right in this building," Amaro said. "Amazing."

"For privacy, not exactly for hiding," Maliha said. She glared at Jake.

Suddenly she had a thought that gave her a chill. "What if Yanmeng is right here in this building? If I can have a secret condo, so could the doctor. These places are large enough for a complete medical suite if you only have one patient."

"Holy cow," Amaro said. There was silence for a minute.

"You don't use your real name for the haven, do you?" Hound said.

"I haven't used my real name in a long time. But I didn't use Marsha Winters, the name I used to purchase this condo, either."

"That's what I thought," Hound said. "The medical suite would be owned by someone not on our suspect list. A corporation, maybe."

She could see that they were growing excited about the idea. "You have to promise me something. If you come up with any suspicious condos, you will not break into them. It would be fatal to enter my haven, and I have no doubt there would be nasty security anywhere Yanmeng is being held.

Remember Countess Elizabeth is involved. I think we're talking about more than crushed potato chips on the floor. You have to promise that you'll back off and let me or Jake go in."

They both nodded. "Yes, ma'am, we'll call in the cavalry," Hound said.

She left them working and headed for her haven. Jake followed her.

"Thanks for blabbing about my haven," she said.

"I thought you were more open with your people."

She looked at him skeptically. "Don't you have a place you go for privacy besides your house? Do you tell everyone about it?"

"I do have places. It seems to come with the territory of having a long life. All this interacting with people. I'm not working with a team, so I haven't told anyone. There hasn't been a need."

"How about me?"

"I have one spot in Belize and one near here. It's an unused storage room in one of the museums. I'll take you to both of them, if you want."

"I have a second one, also," Maliha said. "It's an island in the Mediterranean."

He nodded. "Lucius's island. I know you inherited it."

It sounded odd to hear Lucius's name from his lips. They were at the door to her haven. Jake kissed her. "Want me to come in?"

"Then it wouldn't be private."

He left her in the hallway. She went in and lit some incense in a five-hundred-year-old burner from a Tibetan monastery. As the fragrant smoke spread throughout the room, she settled on the floor in a full lotus position. Her knees touched the floor and her spine aligned so that she could sit with minimal effort, enhancing the ability to sit perfectly still. Her hands rested loosely on her crossed knees. She leaned her head forward slightly, letting her tongue rest on the roof of her mouth. Shifting slightly, she nudged her body into a maximum comfort pose.

Closing her eyes, she concentrated on becoming aware of her breathing. Her thoughts gradually faded until all activity that was left was totally focused inward. She imagined slipping off her physical self and conscious mind and storing them in front of her, like coats on hangers. That left her subconscious mind and her life energy behind. It was similar to what she did when she experienced someone's death experience, without the death experience to focus on. She became very still.

Maliha was in her haven to try to contact Yanmeng. If he was unconscious, she might be able to reach his subconscious. Distance was no barrier, because she was moving to another plane of existence to do it. Yanmeng had told her that the planes were twisted and connected by what he described as ladders but that she visualized as wormholes.

She formed an image of herself in her subconscious and launched it with a single powerful message: *Yanmeng!*

Nothing happened. She was about to bring herself out of the meditation. Then she felt the faintest tug at her mind, and an image formed of Yanmeng. It wasn't the same as the way she saw him. He was younger, more vital. She was seeing him the way he saw himself. The link faded.

Maliha donned her body and conscious mind and came out of her meditation. She was ecstatic. She'd made a connection with him, she was certain. He was alive, and best of all, he knew that she was looking for him.

She unrolled her futon and fell into a restful sleep. Three hours later she awoke feeling deeply refreshed, her mind and purpose clearer than they had been for days. The stress and doubts that had been assailing her were alleviated. Whatever was coming, she knew she could handle it.

Watch out, Elizabeth. I'm baaack!

Chapter Twenty-Five

Elizabeth smiled into the webcam. She'd decided to go along with Fred Smith's request for a video call. She figured he was hoping she'd be in a hot negligee and they could mix business with pleasure. So she went one step further. She was naked, but submerged to just above her breasts in her tub.

"Good to see you, Fred."

"You look great, Liz."

She permitted the familiarity. He was the only man in her long life who had ever called her "Liz" and survived. She was looking forward to cutting out his tongue when the time came. She raised one of her legs from the water and turned it this way and that, as if inspecting it. Her lower leg, so recently separated from her body, showed no scars. Glancing at the monitor, she saw Fred staring with his mouth open when he thought she wasn't looking at him.

This is too easy.

"How's the plan coming?" he said.

"Excellent. The meeting is set up, as you insisted."

Idiot.

Fred had a smug look on his face. He'd wanted a face-to-face meeting with Maliha. Elizabeth had said no at first, then let him seem powerful and get his way.

It doesn't do any harm. Both of these people are under my thumb anyway. Or will be soon.

"Good. Uh, Liz, that isn't blood in your bathwater, is it?"

She gave him a puzzled look. "Why would you think that?"

"Just something that popped into my mind because of the color."

"Oh, silly. You mean this?" She held up a handful of water and dripped it between her breasts. "It's a special oil for my skin. I have it custom-made. If you were here, you'd know that it smells like roses." She stood up, with the red water streaming down her body. "It keeps my skin clear and soft all over. More pleasant for you to touch. I wish you were here. . . ."

The bath servant turned off the computer and then held a thick white robe for Elizabeth. She stepped out of the tub and wrapped up in the robe. There was a body hanging over the base of the tub like an upside-down doll, broken and battered, her throat wound hanging open like a bloody frown. Elizabeth caressed the girl's blood-spattered cheek.

You were sweet, little Katie, but ten-year-olds just don't have enough blood.

Chapter Twenty-Six

"Damn, when you pick 'em, you really pick 'em," Hound said. "This bitch Elizabeth is straight from hell."

"I couldn't agree more. Details?" Maliha said.

"Her name is Countess Elizabeth Báthory. She was born in 1560 and came by her title honestly, as a member of the Hungarian nobility. She had a political marriage at the age of fifteen to a man who spent a lot of time away as a commander in the military. She was left with the castle and the villages that came with it, and spent more time managing the home front than her husband did."

"She's used to getting her way. I can vouch for that," Maliha said.

"Now the bad news. Elizabeth is the world's most prolific female serial killer. She slaughtered over six hundred young girls and women, almost all virgins, most of them after her husband died. I guess her husband kept her in check while he was alive."

"I thought you said he was gone most of the time," Amaro said.

"Maybe he threatened her or hired someone to make sure she didn't express her murderous traits. She did have an outlet for violence, though. It was okay in those days to treat your peasant servants cruelly. The aristocracy didn't care and the peasants had no recourse."

"Basically slavery," Maliha said. Her cheeks burned. She

lived through slavery on the wrong side of freedom. As a demon's slave, she did things that were now abhorrent to her.

"Yup. Then when her husband died and the restraints were gone, Elizabeth started out by holding classes at her castle for daughters of the aristocracy, promising to give them all the skills to be proper young ladies. Only the young ladies didn't return to their families. They were beaten and tortured with everything a sadistic imagination could come up with. Razors, red-hot pokers, knives. The wellborn families became alarmed after too many 'accidents' at the castle and refused to send their daughters."

"I know they weren't big on autopsies then, but wouldn't the mutilated corpses give away what was going on?" Maliha said.

"The accidents were probably things like being mauled to death by a horse or burned, things that covered up the physical evidence of torture. Where there's a will, there's a way," Amaro said.

Hound continued. "Once the supply of daughters of her peers dried up, she enticed young peasant girls with the promise of high-paying positions as maidservants in the castle. Parents must have pushed their girls out the door for that. At least, until those girls started disappearing by the hundreds. Elizabeth had accomplices who helped her obtain girls by force if she couldn't get them by subterfuge."

"Didn't anyone speak up for the peasants?" Amaro said.

"It took a while for anyone with some power to notice. There was so much outcry that word finally reached the king, who was a relative of hers. I guess he didn't like a family member of his having the moniker of 'Blood Countess.' He sent a court representative to ferret out the truth—his cousin, I think. Essentially it was damage control. A small force of men invaded her castle at night and found the grisly proof. All of the accomplices were executed, naturally, but the king refused to even bring Elizabeth to trial."

"What? That's carrying nepotism a bit far!" Amaro said.

"One of the bennies of being king. He didn't want any more fuss, though, so he had her bricked into a room in her castle with a small hatch to take care of necessities. She died four years later."

"Except that she's Ageless now. I can see how a demon would be drawn to her! It's horrible to know what we're up against," Maliha said.

"All of that's historical fact," Hound said. "Now we get to the interesting legends. Elizabeth was a vain woman always concerned about her appearance. One day when she was beating a servant girl, the girl's blood landed on the back of Elizabeth's hand. She felt her skin was rejuvenated in that spot. Smoother, softer, whatever. So she decided that if a few drops worked well, a lot of blood would work even better. She began drinking and bathing in her victims' blood to preserve her youth and beauty."

"The demons must have been fighting over her," Maliha said.

"Besides being called the Blood Countess, she's also known as Lady Dracula," Hound said. "Did I mention she's from Transylvania?"

"Seriously?" Amaro said.

Hound nodded. "And she has her fangs in our friend."

Maliha hesitated. She didn't know what, if anything, to reveal about her contact with Yanmeng.

It brought happiness to me, so I should share it.

"I want to tell you something about Yanmeng," Maliha said. "He's alive. I know it for certain."

Hound sat down on the couch, put his elbows on his knees, and supported his head in his hands. Amaro's eyes flashed with hope that Maliha hadn't noticed was missing.

"How?" Amaro said.

"It was a brief mind contact, mostly Yanmeng's doing, I'm sure." She felt strange talking about an experience that was intensely private to her.

Hound looked up. "He can tell you where he is, then."

Maybe I shouldn't have mentioned this.

"No. All I got was an image of him, not where he is now or anything else helpful. It was the mental image of ourselves we all carry around. You know, years younger, no flaws, not the version of what we see in the mirror now. But there's no way I could have gotten that if he was . . ."

"Dead and refrigerated to keep the parts fresh?" Hound said.

Maliha nodded. "You thought of that too."

"Eliu has to hear this," Amaro said. He knocked at her door but she didn't answer.

"She could be asleep," Hound said. "I'll call her cell phone."

When there was no answer, Maliha was worried. She tried the doorknob and found the door locked.

"Stand back," Hound said. He was going to rush the door.

"Stop! This is my home. I don't need any smashed doors. Give me a minute."

She was back from her bedroom in a few seconds and picked the lock even faster. Maliha opened the door cautiously. "Eliu, it's Maliha. I'm coming in."

The room was dark. Light-blocking shades were pulled down. Hound and Amaro were crowding Maliha's back, wanting into the room. She flipped on the light switch, hoping she wasn't going to find Eliu's dead body.

The room was empty. The attached bathroom was empty.

It was a relief in one way, worrisome in another. Maliha rounded on her two companions. "Where did she go?"

Hound shook his head. Amaro shrugged his shoulders.

"You were here, right? When I took my break and went to the haven?"

"Of course we were," Amaro said.

"Then what the hell happened? Oh, I see, you were each in your rooms working."

"Damn," Hound said.

"Hall cameras," Amaro said. He rushed over to the laptop and played back the last hour at high speed. The door opened and Eliu walked out, wearing a long gray coat and a scarf over her hair.

"At least we know she left under her own free will. Get me a photo that shows her face," Maliha said. After tucking a ceramic knife in her hair, disguised as an ornament

at the top of her braid, she took the photo and went to talk
to Chick. He was standing right inside the front entrance,
taking a break from the cold.

"Have you seen . . ." Maliha said.

"This nice lady? Sure," Chick said. "She was here about
a half hour ago. I hailed her a cab."

"Do you know where . . ."

"The Art Institute. I told her it closed at five and she
should save her money and go tomorrow when there was
more time, but she didn't want to hear it."

It was 4:30 P.M. now. "Thanks, Chick. You've been very
helpful."

"You know, I could probably be even more helpful. You
and I should have a talk sometime."

"I agree, but this isn't the time." Maliha called Hound
and told him where she was going, then started to walk
outside.

"Call you a cab?" Chick said.

"No, I'm . . . going for a walk."

"You're gonna need something warm. Hold on a second."
He rummaged in the Lost and Found box at his station
and came up with a dark blue jacket with two pockets and
a hood. "This looks like it'll do the job. Keep your head
warm, too." He raised his eyes to the ornament in her hair
and winked at her. "See ya later."

She slipped on the jacket and walked out to the rear of
the building. The loading dock door was closed and there
was no one around. In privacy, she took off running at
Ageless speed so no one would see her vanish. The museum
was close, on South Michigan in Grant Park. She could get
there much faster on foot than in a cab in rush-hour traffic.
Weaving among the pedestrians and the cars in the street
slowed her down, but still Maliha was there in less than five
minutes. She raced up the steps between the bronze lion stat-
ues and headed for the stone arches of the entryway. Inside,
she failed to stop and show her membership card at the desk.

*Where would she go? Assuming the cab even brought her
here. Yanmeng likes the Asian collection.*

She headed for that gallery and slowed to a walk as she neared it. The space was beautiful, with lighted glass cases and other displays leading the visitor from one room to the next. Eliu sat on a bench in front of a case of thousand-year-old vases, and they had her rapt attention. One like them must have had some significance for her. Maliha looked around the room. There were three other people browsing and a guard in the doorway. It was near closing time and most visitors had left. None of the browsers looked threatening. Maliha walked through the room and checked the next one. It was empty. She put her head through the doorway to look into the room beyond. Her breath caught in her lungs and stayed there, and her heart pounded against her ribs. A chill climbed her spine like a ladder.

Moe, Curly, and Larry were in the room, and they were armed.

How did they get those weapons in here?

"Hey!" Larry said. He'd spotted her. She pulled her head back just in time. Automatic gunfire tore into the wall, gouging chunks from the corner where she'd been.

The museum guard, following the sound, came running into the room where Maliha was. His gun was drawn and he was running straight into an ambush. She ran toward him and put out her arm when he was right next to her. He wasn't expecting it and her arm slammed into him at chest height. She spun slightly with his momentum, or she would have crushed his chest. Instead, he crumpled to the floor with a few broken ribs. She snatched the gun from his hand and hit him with enough force to knock him out.

I hope Eliu gets out of here while they're distracted.

She yanked the guard by his arms, dragged him to the side of the room, and shoved him under a bench where he'd be out of the line of fire.

Best I can do, buddy. Why aren't the Stooges in here yet? I'm sure one look at me didn't scare them off.

Maliha flattened her body against the wall of the room and inched toward the door opening. There wasn't much time left before other guards arrived. She didn't want to be

holding the unconscious guard's gun when that happened—
she'd be mistaken for one of the bad guys. It looked like she
would have to take the fight to them.

Maliha changed her approach to the door so she'd be
going in at an angle. She ran through the door, assessed
the situation rapidly, and planted a bullet in Curly's forehead before diving to the floor and rolling. Automatic
fire screamed through the room. Glass cases shattered,
triggering security alarms. Two hot lines of pain streaked
across her shoulder. Still on the floor and in motion, Maliha
crashed into Larry's legs from behind, grabbed him and
pulled him down on his knees. She turned his gun on Moe
and squeezed his finger on the trigger. Moe went down in
a haze of red mist, a zipper stitched across his midsection.
Larry was struggling in her grip. She pulled the ceramic
knife from her hair and slit his throat. He slumped to the
floor. She slid the knife into a pocket of her jacket.

The whole thing was over in seconds. A glance at the
guard under the bench showed that there were four casualties in the room. The initial burst of gunfire must have
caused a few bullets to ricochet in his direction.

Maliha left the way she came, running so fast that she
passed several guards coming to the scene as a rush of air.

Maliha walked most of the way home. Her shoulder was
hurting but there was no one following her. The sun had
been setting when she left, and now it was nearly dark.
She stayed off the major streets and didn't linger under
streetlights. Her scale rewarded her for the deaths of Moe,
Curly, and Larry. Anu didn't penalize her for the death of
the innocent guard because he'd been killed by Moe or
Larry.

Chick opened the door for her. "Hey, are you all right?"

The jacket he'd lent her was torn and bloody where she'd
been hit.

"I kind of ripped it," she said, taking off the jacket. Chick
saw the knife and said nothing. She wiped it clean on the
jacket and tucked it back into her hair.

He stared at the blood on her shoulder. "Should I call an ambulance?"

She shook her head.

He took the jacket from her. "I'll take care of this. No problem. Here, put on this sweatshirt. You don't want to be scaring your neighbors. Go on home now."

"Thanks, Chick," she said, and meant it.

"You take care of yourself."

In the central core of the building, she waited at the bank of three elevators. With Arnie, her arrangement had been that she paid him thirty thousand dollars a month for his assistance and his confidence, plus a one-hundred-thousand-dollar end-of-year bonus. With the investment advice she'd shared, Arnie had become a multi-millionaire during the time Maliha lived at Harbor Point Towers.

Then he'd paid for his association with me with his life. Starting fresh with Chick, maybe I shouldn't get him involved. He's already proven himself useful, though, and I think he's already seen too much.

Eliu was home. Hound had followed Maliha in a cab, arriving a little before the shooting started. He intercepted Eliu as she fled the building.

She was crying. "I'm so sorry," she said between sobs. "I just wanted to be near something that reminded me of my husband." Hound was sitting next to her, one arm around her. Amaro stood off to the side with a tissue box in his hand. He might be the best hacker in the world, but confronted with a crying woman, he wavered. A piece of code wouldn't fix her.

Maliha went over and knelt in front of Eliu. She took the woman's hands in hers. "It's not your fault. You're here with us and safe now. Everything turned out all right."

Except for a guard who won't be going home to his family, but this isn't the time for brutal honesty.

"Oh no, you're bleeding," Eliu said. "You're injured! Is it bad? Let me see!"

Blood had seeped through the light tan sweatshirt. "I'll be okay. Just nicked by a bullet."

Eliu straightened up and wiped her eyes. "I did this with my stupidity. It won't happen again."

"It's no problem. . . ."

"Maliha, why don't you go get cleaned up?" Hound said.

She glanced down at the sweatshirt and saw that the bloodstain was large and growing as she watched. Blood trickled out from her sleeve onto her hand.

He's right, of course. The sooner I'm out of her sight, the better.

The bleeding stopped quickly with the application of pressure. Maliha took a shower and Amaro bandaged her shoulder. The wounds weren't deep and the pain was fading. She told Amaro that later that evening, she was going to take Eliu to her haven and tell her to stay there, making sure she didn't approach the entry foyer from inside. It would be a safe place for her to stay, and now that Eliu's life had nearly been lost, Maliha wasn't going to hear any argument about it. It made her a little sad that her private space would be used by someone else, but it would allow the rest of the team to keep Eliu close without having to guard her. Maliha hinted that Amaro and Hound could join her if they wished, but she had little hope that they would.

Maliha wanted to go out into the living room and show Eliu that the wounds were no big deal, but when she opened her bedroom door, Hound waved her off. He was sitting at the table, drinking tea with Eliu, and they were deep in conversation. She looked better than she had in days. Hound had probably told her that Yanmeng was alive.

Later, walking Eliu to the haven, Eliu had questions about that contact. She seemed disappointed that there was nothing more than an image.

"Tell me what he looked like."

"He was young," Maliha said. "No more than thirty years old. He had dark hair and was smiling as though looking at someone he loved. He was wearing a white robe that I think was silk. It came all the way to his ankles. The sleeves were very long and hung at his sides. He was so handsome."

Eliu gasped. "Was he wearing a blue sash?"

Maliha reformed the image in her mind. "Yes! How did you know?"

"That was an image of Yanmeng on our wedding day," Eliu said. She reached her hand out and touched Maliha's arm. "He was smiling at me, I know it. It was a message to let me know he's alive. It had to be."

"He knew I'd tell you. He gave me the image that would be most comforting to you," Maliha said.

Eliu's eyes were bright with tears. "Can you send him an image of me? I have our wedding picture, I can show you what I looked like. It would mean so much to me."

Maliha's shoulders sagged. "I can't do that. I was barely able to contact Yanmeng, and then he's the one who took over and responded."

"Do it again, then."

"I think he used everything he had to send that one image. He's sedated, and it's amazing he was able to gather enough strength for that."

She installed Eliu in the haven and gave her a run-through on how it operated, including warnings to keep out of the booby-trapped area near the entrance.

"What will happen if I don't?"

"Um, poison darts will rain down on you if you don't do everything just right."

"Got it."

"We'll keep in touch. There are secure communications between here and the thirty-ninth floor."

"It's beautiful here. So peaceful."

Low-voltage lights sparkled against the dark ceiling, looking like a starry night. Eliu nodded when Maliha showed her the tatami sleeping mat and the futon to be unrolled on it.

"From Japan," Eliu said about the tatami mat. "We use a mattress and down pillows. But I'm sure I will sleep well."

Eliu was looking at the displays of treasures collected by Maliha over her lifetime. Maliha thought about the most important of those, the shards and Tablet of the Overlord in the hidden floor safe.

"Thank you for bringing me here," Eliu said. "I will keep all of this secret." The look in her eyes said it all. She knew it was an imposition to be in the haven, but now that she knew Yanmeng was alive, she had reason to live—reason to be safe.

Maliha hugged her. "You'll enjoy the shower. Remember . . ."

Eliu nodded. She wasn't going to be making any more solitary excursions. While the haven was an elegant place to stay, it was also a prison cell for her. It would literally kill her to leave.

If I hadn't told Hound and Amaro about my contact with Yanmeng, we wouldn't have discovered Eliu was missing in time. She'd be dead now.

Chapter Twenty-Seven

LATITUDE 45° 23 58.12N, LONGITUDE 88° 39 59.52W.

The coordinates in the note that came with Yanmeng's severed hand turned out to be Lakeview Cemetery in Wisconsin. It was located in the Chequamegon-Nicolet National Forest on Forest Road 2358. Locals knew it as Eliot Road.

"I should head there tonight and stay in the closest motel. Looks like I'll be doing some cross-country skiing," Maliha said.

"Why not a snowmobile? I'm sure you can rent them around there," Amaro said.

"Skis are quieter. I'd rather not be heard coming," she said.

That night Maliha traveled to Wisconsin, rented a Jeep, and stayed in a bed-and-breakfast just outside the national forest, where she'd been summoned to a meeting. There was an eight-inch snowfall overnight, with the temperature around twenty below zero. She was on the road at dawn the next morning, in a white two-piece stretchable outfit that allowed her flexibility and blended in with the snowy surroundings.

I'm wearing more layers than an onion.

She had her whip sword in a sheath around her waist and a throwing knife strapped to each thigh. A Glock 26, the baby Glock specially designed for concealed carry, rested in a pocket holster, and a spare magazine was in her other pocket.

Why would the Blood Countess need an assassin? Can't she do her own kills?

She parked the Jeep a half mile away, pulling off the road behind some evergreen trees whose branches drooped with heavy snow. She put on her skis. Her shoulder was stiff, but after she warmed up from the skiing, it wasn't noticeable. Heading off into the forest, she paralleled Eliot Road until she reached the cemetery. She found a hidden spot where she could watch the cemetery entrance and waited. She was early. The day began with a cloudless sky and the sun sparkling on fresh snow, a bluebird day to enjoy, if Maliha hadn't been heading for a meeting with the Blood Countess. Her breath hung white in the air and the moisture in her nostrils crackled as it froze. When the air hit her lungs, it hadn't been prewarmed by her nostrils, so it cooled her chest from the inside. It felt like she had stuffed a peppermint patty in each lung. She pressed a button on her goggles and liquid crystal technology darkened the lenses for sunny conditions.

The roar of snowmobiles cut through the stillness of the forest. Elizabeth wasn't alone.

Her mind flashed to a long-ago assignment in Yakutia, a huge frozen land area in northern Siberia. Images of slashed bodies of men, women, and children—a small settlement subjected to a demon's revenge with her as the instrument of death. Hot blood spilled on the snow, melting down into it only briefly before freezing. Maliha's muscles tensed and her senses were hyper-alert. She was ready for anything.

There were four snowmobiles in all. Elizabeth led the way, hair flying in the wind, disdainful of the cold. She rode as if she were straddling a stallion, with a look of wild abandon on her face.

To look at her, you wouldn't think she'd ever had an evil thought in her head.

Two heavily armed men followed, and between them was a man who carried no weapon. He was confident in his escort.

They pulled into the cemetery, riding over the graves

until all four came to an abrupt halt, spewing powder into the air. They dismounted and huddled in a group. It was easy to pick out Elizabeth among them. There were two men with automatic rifles slung over their shoulders—bodyguards, and not the kind Maliha could dismiss. They carried themselves well and confidently, probably with military training in their background. A third man had his back to her. He wore a green parka with a hood. She skied over to meet them, stopped about ten feet away, then used her poles to disengage the heel locks on her ski bindings. She stepped out of the bindings into the snow, sinking a few inches.

If there's going to be any fighting going on, I can't maneuver on skis.

The bodyguards were leery of the knives she openly carried and asked her to remove them. She politely declined. They wanted to press the issue but Elizabeth told them to back off. With resentment in their faces, they did.

They don't like taking orders from her. They're not her people. I'm coming in late on whatever dynamic is going on here.

Elizabeth had her hand resting on Parka Man's arm. Her posture and the familiarity of the touch told Maliha they were probably lovers.

"Here she is," Elizabeth said, "as you requested. She's the vital element of Project Hammer. Meet Maliha Crayne."

The man turned toward her. He was wearing goggles, and the hood partially concealed his face, but she knew him right away. He pulled the goggles up on top of his head to get a good look at her, and that confirmed her identification.

"Hello, Maliha, I'm—" he said.

"Roger Cameron, vice president of the United States. We've met before, though I looked a bit different then." He was in his mid-fifties, fit, handsome but not a standout.

"You have me at a disadvantage," Cameron said.

You have no idea.

"At the president's first state dinner. I was with the son of the ambassador to India."

"I think it's coming back to me."

"Red dress."

"Oh, my God, that was you?" He scanned her from head to toe.

Elizabeth had had enough of old times. "Shall we get going? She's not going to give a show and tell."

"Are you cold, Liz? Jim, get her a blanket from the snowmobile."

"No, don't." It was said harshly. Elizabeth had let her annoyance show. Maliha saw the bodyguards smile at each other.

"I asked for this because I wanted to talk to the assassin. You just said she was a vital element of the project. Now that I'm here, I'm going to talk," Cameron said. The bodyguards' smiles got bigger.

"Maliha, I want you to understand what your role is and why it's so important."

"I'm listening," she said. *He's talking like I have a choice in the matter.*

"I'll be straight with you about what I want. I want the presidency. I've worked toward it all my adult life. You could say I was born to the task. Project Hammer began in 1955. Twelve couples—we call them the New Founders, because they are the originators of the new America—didn't like the way the country was going. They were wealthy, but even their wealth couldn't buy the kind of change they were looking for. They made a pact, each pledging a son or daughter to the cause." He paused with disdain. "Am I boring you, Liz?"

"No, no, I've just heard it all before," Elizabeth said.

"All twelve of us were raised as deep plants in the Democratic and Republican parties. We didn't have to believe the words we were mouthing, as long as we were convincing. I've risen through the ranks building an impeccable record as a moderate Democrat. I've made it this close to the Oval Office. The others are at the state-government level and aren't likely to advance. That makes me the only one who has a shot at it."

"You want me to assassinate the president," Maliha said.

"It's a shame. On a personal level, I like the guy. But gambling on him getting reelected in two years and then elected on my own as president in another four years is risky. Too risky."

"You know you're being used by the New Founders, don't you?" Maliha said. "Is this what you want to do?"

"Yes. I believe in this cause. You could think of me as a puppet, but I'm a willing one."

No way to put a dent in that. He's a true believer.

"Once I become president, Project Hammer goes into full effect. Simply put, we're tired of America being pushed around. America needs to be able to guide the rest of the world through these tumultuous times. That means a stronger military. A much stronger military. One that these terrorists won't dare challenge. I'd like you to join us in this noble cause. After all, what better way is there for you to save lives?"

Emergency. Emergency. Calling Homeland Security.

"My dear, you have seen the abuse America has suffered firsthand in your travels. All of those oil rich countries throttling back production of vital resources simply to manipulate prices? It's immoral. If the prices were something we could manage, we could pour the revenues into other sources of energy. We could even stop global warming, save the environment, feed all of the hungry children, if only I could be president. We could force the change that needs to happen by removing people's right to hesitate."

This guy is slick. He's got the patter down perfectly, as long as you don't examine what he says too closely.

"What about the Constitution and the Bill of Rights?"

"Not written for the twenty-first century. Once I get in office, I don't plan on leaving. Term limits need a bit of tweaking. It's going to take a lot more than eight years to convert this country into doing things the right way—the New Founders way." He unzipped his jacket and handed her an envelope. "Here's some information on the president's schedule."

A delusional ideologue. A very dangerous one, with

Elizabeth as his guardian. I can see why her demon set this plan in action.

"Did you have to reveal that much detail?" Elizabeth said.

"What, now that I've told Maliha, I have to kill her? She's part of the grand scheme, just like you. After I'm president, I'm going to need someone to eliminate people who get in the way. We don't want to have to deal with formalities like court hearings, let alone arbitrators without an understanding of the *real* world, like the Supreme Court."

Elizabeth did not like being equated with Maliha. She scowled but said nothing.

I don't think Cameron's getting lucky tonight.

Maliha rolled the facts over in her mind, trying to determine Cameron's chance of pulling this off. It seemed like he had a turnkey plan, no doubt with others on his payroll to step into new positions of authority. There was no certainty of success, but the consequences were unthinkable if Elizabeth managed to get him through this. Billions of lives could be at stake with Cameron's finger on the nuclear button, and what would the world look like after Cameron got through with it? Of course there would be rebellion against his plan, but rebellion could be quashed if he or Elizabeth had anything to say about it. Americans weren't used to martial law with a ruthless dictator calling the shots. She could contact Homeland Security, but who would they believe, the vice president of the United States or her?

Maliha was horrified to know the depth of the trap in which she was caught. With scheming at this level, and with so many years invested, it seemed unlikely that Yanmeng would ever be returned alive—Elizabeth had said as much in Kelly's Pub—and that her role as unwilling assassin would never let up.

Maliha's shoulders sagged with the weight of her decision. *Damn. I can't risk it. This just became a suicide mission.*

Project Hammer had to end here.

She took a step forward, alerting Elizabeth, but there was nothing Maliha could do about that. She dropped the envelope, pulled the whip sword from its sheath at her waist, and lashed out with it toward the two bodyguards. With her other hand, she launched a throwing knife at Cameron's heart.

The blades of the whip sword caught their targets, and heads rolled into the snow. The bodyguards slumped toward the ground, blood pumping from the severed arteries of their necks. Maliha had her second throwing knife in her hand.

The first one didn't land in Cameron's chest as she'd hoped. Elizabeth thrust out her arm, and the blade penetrated it near the elbow, the point emerging on the other side inches from Cameron. Maliha threw the second knife, hoping to slip it past Elizabeth. As soon as the knife left Maliha's fingers, she pulled her Glock from her jacket pocket.

Elizabeth already had a sword in hand, the same kind Xietai had used. She flicked it in the direction of the knife and as it straightened and formed a hard, deadly blade, it turned the knife aside to fall harmlessly in the snow.

"Get down, fool," Elizabeth shouted at Cameron. Not waiting for an answer, she swept his legs out from under him and he fell facedown in the snow.

Maliha fired a couple of rounds at Elizabeth in a desperate effort to slow her down, then aimed the weapon at Cameron's prone form. She got off one shot and hit him in the back.

Elizabeth yanked the knife from her arm and sent it whirling back toward Maliha. It struck the Glock, sending it tumbling from Maliha's grip. Elizabeth snatched the second knife from the snow and launched it in the air before the gun reached the ground.

The knife landed solidly in Maliha's right thigh. Pain exploded in her leg, sending shock waves down her leg and up her spine. She struggled to remain standing. Elizabeth moved toward her, the fox to the wounded rabbit.

Oh, shit. Here it comes.

Cameron groaned and tried to move forward weakly.

Elizabeth's orders from the demon took precedence. She shook her head. She was a guardian first, avenger second. She turned around and started dragging Cameron over the snow. With her strength, he glided as smoothly as a sled. She left with him on one of the snowmobiles.

Maliha leaned against one of the tombstones. The bloody scene in front of her looked eerily like the one in Siberia years ago, and she wondered if it had been more of a premonition than a memory.

After resting a little while, Maliha braced for a challenging journey. She retrieved the blood-spattered envelope and began moving toward the snowmobiles, putting as little weight on her injured leg as she could. She mounted a snowmobile, put her feet in the stirrups, pulled up the kill switch, and turned the key. The engine, still warm, fired up on the first pull of the start cord. She made the trip back to her car slowly, not wanting to lean into any high-speed turns. Noticing spots of blood along the road, she hoped that her single hurried shot had done the job on Cameron. She sighed with relief when she saw the Jeep untouched, and then again when it started.

Elizabeth could have disabled it on the way in. This hiding place didn't fool her.

When the Jeep was pumping warm air on her face and feet, Maliha considered her situation. She wasn't sure she could drive the manual transmission with her leg injury. There wasn't a lot of blood loss because the knife was plugging the wound, and she needed to keep it that way. There was a blizzard kit in the Jeep. Wrapping a blanket on either side of her wound, she steadied the knife to keep it from jarring loose and tied it securely with rope from the kit. She started driving on Eliot Road and found that it was barely manageable. She called Hound, gave him a brief explanation, and got directions to a nearby airport.

Maliha drove to the town of Rhinelander, Wisconsin. It would have been an hour's drive in good weather with a driver who didn't see black around the edges of her vision whenever she had to shift gears. As it was, it took her two hours before she had the airport in sight. Putting her trust in Hound, she sat back and tried to ignore the knife sticking out of her leg.

Hound came in by helicopter. He took Maliha to a doctor he knew in Green Bay. The doctor was curious about why Maliha's flesh had begun to heal around the knife. Hound doubled the pay, and the doctor sealed his lips and broke the still-delicate scar tissue formation to remove the knife. Maliha insisted on no sedation, and she shuddered when the doctor withdrew the knife. There was no massive spurting of blood from her leg, just a slow leakage.

"You're lucky," the doctor said. "It looks like the deep femoral artery is intact. A couple of centimeters over and you wouldn't have made it here."

Maliha let him stitch and bandage her wound. She'd take the stitches out later.

The doctor grunted when he was finished. "You need blood."

"No transfusions. I'll be okay. Give me IV fluids."

The doctor glanced at Hound, seeking affirmation that his patient knew what she was talking about. Hound nodded.

"Saline, not Ringer's or D5W," Maliha said.

"Antibiotics, then." He raised his eyebrows and set his mouth, prepared to stand firm on this one.

"In the drip," Maliha said. She saw Hound and the doctor conferring and money changing hands, then left in a wheelchair with a portable IV stand.

Hound and Maliha headed home to Chicago. Somewhere during the flight, Hound put something in her IV. When she woke, she was home in her bedroom. It was nighttime, and there was a single lamp on in the room. Hound sat in a chair watching her.

"Thanks for the lift," Maliha said. She smiled. It was good to see him.

"Christ, woman, you scared the shit out of us," Hound said. "I should've called a ranger to pick you up in the forest."

"I would have had some trouble explaining the two headless bodies."

"Beside the point. I'm sure you would have thought of something. When I got my first look at you . . ."

His unsaid words *I thought you were dead* hung between them.

"Just doing some meditation. It helped with the pain."

"You had the pulse rate of a hibernating bear."

"You're exaggerating. I did not have a pulse of ten beats per minute."

Hound crossed his arms across his chest and said nothing.

"Okay, I'm sorry I scared you," Maliha said. "I didn't want to bring in any outsiders. Even the doctor in Green Bay was a risk. Besides, as a medic you should be able to cope."

"Isn't that a backhanded apology."

"Come on, Hound. Let it go. I'm happy to be alive and thankful that you saved me. Is that better?"

He sighed, came over to the bed, and kissed her forehead. "We're hyped up, that's all. Yanmeng, the threat to Eliu, and then you."

"So am I, Hound. I'm—we're—in deep on this one and I'm not seeing a path out."

"We'll make it. We all will. And then I'm going on a vacation with Glass to someplace warm and fuck her brains out."

Maliha laughed. "Sounds good to me."

"Jake is here. You want to see him?"

"In a minute. How's Amaro holding up?"

"Well, you know he's not a field guy. All this is too much like stuff he sees in the movies. He's not trained for it."

"We need to have everybody able to handle fieldwork. Start training him whenever you get the chance. Tell him I ordered it because he's pathetic away from his computer."

"Ordered? Pathetic? That'll get him riled up."

"Exactly. Riled up to prove me *wrong*. That leaves him open to cooperating with you to learn. What's the news with the list of doctors?"

"We have three prospects. I feel like we're getting close."

"Okay. Let me know the names and I'll check them out." She swung her legs over the side of the bed and sat up. There was some pain, but she could deal with it. Keeping a grimace off her face was an old habit, one that Master Liu had cautioned her about on her recent visit, depending on the message she wanted to send.

Master Liu says that sometimes you should show pain as a strategy to make your opponent overconfident. He will strike toward pain, leaving an opening for your blade.

Hound left and Jake came in, striding over to the bed and pulling her up into his arms. "I was worried about you," he said, and kissed her.

"You know I have a leg wound, right?"

"Yes. Oh." He lowered her back to her seated position and sat down next to her. "Is it that bad?"

"No. I'd just like a little more rest before I hit the streets. Hound says there are places to go, doctors to check out."

"I can do that."

"I know, Jake, but this is personal. I have to be out there doing something. Have you been filled in about Elizabeth and the vice president?"

"Yeah. What a piece of shit."

"Which one?"

"Both. Elizabeth's got a reputation among the Ageless. You know we're not exactly warm and cuddly—excluding me, of course—but Elizabeth tops the charts. She doesn't just kill, she gets off on it, wallows in it. Her demon Tirid is considered crazy, which is a tough call when you're talking about demons. Elizabeth fears getting old and ugly, and the story is that's how Tirid keeps her in line. If she screws up, he punishes her by making her an old hag for a few decades. It makes her seriously toe the line."

"I understand something now. I wondered why Elizabeth needed me to be an assassin for Project Hammer when she could clearly do the work herself, and enjoy it. She's been ordered to stay close to Cameron whenever possible to make sure the plan succeeds. She doesn't dare disobey Tirid."

Jake nodded. "That makes sense. Cramps her style, too. Tirid likes to jerk her strings."

Another thought occurred to her. "It could be that when Cameron takes over as president, he's going to want to catch the assassin right away to impress the public. With Elizabeth staying in the background, he needs a visible assassin—me—he can put on trial. Something I haven't told the others is that Elizabeth expects me to become her chief warrior to replace a man I killed."

He cupped her chin with his hand. "Won't happen. I swear it."

I want to believe him, but how can he be sure?

"Jake, why don't you hunt down other Ageless and kill them? I know it's dangerous, but . . ."

"Believe me, I've considered it. The world just doesn't need Elizabeth in it. There are several problems, though. When the demons lose one of their slaves, they recruit another one. If I started popping off Ageless—were I to be so lucky—they'd be popping back up again as fresh recruits. They'd start to hunt me in packs, and I couldn't withstand that for long. Finally, there's my own demon, Idiptu. He ignores me now and no longer gives me any assignments. I'll stay that way as long as I don't do something that brings me back to his awareness. Killing the Ageless would definitely ring his bell. I'd be back under his thumb, forced to kill at his whim. I wouldn't be sitting here with you, I could be hunting you."

"You could turn rogue, like me."

Jake looked down at the floor. "We've been over that before. I feel I can be of most use to you and your goals the way I am. If I took the mortal path, I'd become . . ."

"Vulnerable, like me?"

Silence grew and stretched in the room.

"Yes. Vulnerable and less able to protect you. I love you, Maliha. I don't want to lose you."

He turned toward her with eyes overflowing with tears. She leaned forward and touched his cheek. "You don't have to explain your decision. I'm sorry I asked."

"There's something else I want to talk about," Jake said. His gaze went back to the floor. "I know about you and Lucius. I know you loved him very much. If he should ever make it back, I'll step aside for him if you ask me to."

Maliha felt a powerful sensation of barriers breaking down, barriers that she'd built around her heart in all the years she was Ageless, brick walls of defense that kept betrayal and love out and kept her able to function. The barriers tumbled and light flooded her body, the clear light of love. She could see it on the inside of her eyelids and feel it reaching out into her dark aura, the aura quivering and changing with its power.

She opened her eyes to find Jake staring at her.

"You look radiant," he said.

Maliha let out the breath she'd been holding. "I love you, Jake."

"Too bad you're in a fragile state right now."

Pain had fled from Maliha's mind. She smiled. "I'm not that fragile."

Chapter Twenty-Eight

Maliha got the suite numbers of the three doctors. From the hall outside each one, she used an infrared camera to search for heat signatures within. One suite was empty, one had a couple making love, and the third had a woman pacing back and forth. None of them had a bedridden figure.

No Yanmeng. Too much to hope for that he'd be in a condo owned under the real name of a doctor. Or we're off base with the whole doctor thing.

After she reported that none of the three doctors had a private medical suite with Yanmeng hooked up to sedatives, Jake took the camera from her and went out to check every condo in the building.

Maliha settled at the table and opened the envelope Cameron had given her. She tried to ignore the dried blood, a reminder that two men had died in the snow. They could have been Secret Service or on Cameron's private payroll. Either way it didn't make them evil just for that service. Yet Anu hadn't taken away any of her lives saved.

So many factors figure in Anu's decisions that I can't make any predictions. I just have to let my morals guide me. It seems like Jake got to this place way ahead of me.

The papers in the envelope detailed a choice of two venues for the assassination of President Randall Millhouse. The first was a speech in Phoenix and the second was an overseas trip to Pacific Rim countries. He'd be making an outdoor appearance in Wellington, the capital of New Zealand. In Phoenix, he'd be in a large auditorium.

Amaro told her to glance up at a TV news broadcast. The vice president had been reported injured on a Wisconsin hunting trip, and was expected to make a full and rapid recovery.

"Damn. That's one chance blown. Will the president leave the country while the VP is in the hospital?" she said. "His trip is scheduled a week from now."

"I think so. Cameron will probably be back at his desk by then, unless his condition is worse than they're saying," Amaro said. "I wouldn't expect the released medical condition to be completely truthful. There are appearances to keep up."

Amaro came over and sat with her. She shared the contents of the envelope. He said he'd start putting together complete information on the locations.

"Hound said you wanted me to get field training," Amaro said. "You didn't have to try to trick me into it. I want the training." He said it matter-of-factly, but she could tell he wasn't happy with her method.

Humility lesson number nine thousand nine hundred and ninety-nine.

"Sorry. I should have just asked you. I'd like to go over the details of why you and Hound picked those three doctors."

He narrowed his eyes at her.

She crossed her hands over her face to defend herself. "I trust you, I trust you. I want to know what the issues are. These doctors could still be involved, just keeping Yanmeng somewhere besides this building. A doctor who lives here would have an ideal way to bring in body parts from elsewhere and deliver them to my door. There would be no separate courier."

"It would have to be a doctor with a sophisticated device for turning digital recordings into digital mush."

"Agreed. Elizabeth should be capable of providing that. I've heard about some infrared LEDs you can wear on each side of eyeglasses, or on your collar. They're emitting infrared light, but your eyes don't respond to it, so it doesn't bother you. Cameras see IR, though, and they have filters to block it. All you need is emitters that generate IR radiation with enough power to overwhelm the camera's filters. The result is that on the recording, your head is a bright ball of light that blocks out your face. I've seen it in action. It's highly effective, at least until all commercial cameras get high-power filters. If you're concerned about your body or clothes revealing something about you on camera, you can put emitters all over. You'd look like a brilliant white ghost."

"Cool, and so simple. Do you think that's what our messenger is using?" Amaro said.

"I doubt it. The telltale white blobs weren't on the film, just overall static. I'm just saying that someone with Elizabeth's resources could do that. Now, about the three doctors?"

"One is selling drugs from her office, the next is in the throes of the world's nastiest divorce and had a breakdown, and the third has an active malpractice suit that looks rock solid against her. That doctor's attorney wants to settle out of court, the victim's family wants a full-blown trial and a sympathy award from a jury."

"Sounds promising. Tell me about it."

"Dr. Jill Bakkum is a pediatric neuro-oncologist. She cuts cancerous tumors out of little kids' brains. She has a profitable solo practice with an office in a medical building on Michigan Avenue."

"Her office isn't far away, then."

"She uses a car service to and from her office and to hospitals. I see that light in your eyes. You're thinking we could get the records from the car service and see where she's been going. She does have her own car, though, a gray Mercedes CL550, so the car service records wouldn't account for all of her movements."

"Get the car service records anyway. What did Dr. Bakkum do to earn the malpractice suit?"

"Basically, she was too aggressive in treating a cancer.

Weird. She removed a cancerous tumor from a delicate spot growing in the brainstem of a ten-year-old girl. So far, so good. Determined to remove a metastasized bit of the tumor that was beginning to spread into the girl's spinal cord, Dr. Bakkum damaged the spinal cord. The girl ended up a quadriplegic and the metastasized tumor was later treated successfully—nonsurgically—with radiation and chemotherapy. Dr. Bakkum should have tried the conservative, nonsurgical treatment first rather than gone digging further down past the brainstem trying to get the last bit of tumor. It was a major error in judgment by the doctor."

"Other specialists concur?"

Amaro nodded. "The hospital's protocols agree, too, leaving the doctor high and dry. Not only that, staff in the operating room stated that she was hyper or wired during the surgery, which turned out to be due to prescription drugs she was taking to keep up with her workaholic schedule."

"It seems hard to fault her for wanting to dig in and get all the cancerous tissue she could."

"Surgeons tend to think with their scalpels and sometimes discount the nonsurgical approaches. She could have been thinking at the time that radiation and chemo wouldn't do the job and the girl would lose her life to cancer," Amaro said. "Surgeon to the rescue. Besides, she was later proven to be making decisions with her self-confidence and focus boosted by Dexedrine. Maybe she recognized the risk and thought she could handle it."

"It's only a matter of time before Dr. Bakkum loses everything, including her ability to get malpractice insurance and suspension of her medical license while she undergoes drug rehab and stays verifiably clean for a long time. A person with a lot to lose will jump at any chance of preserving the status quo," Maliha said. "Cameron and Elizabeth could entice her with the prospect of making all her problems disappear."

"More likely they plan to make her disappear when they're done. There's plenty here to warrant surveillance on this doctor."

"Do you really think a doctor's oath would allow her to cut off body parts unnecessarily?" Amaro said.

"You'd think not, but the Dexedrine probably helped along the decision. At least Yanmeng's probably not in pain. Not even aware of what's going on, would be my guess. I have to get ready to go to Phoenix for the president's appearance. You and Hound can do the surveillance. Let me know right away if you come up with anything."

"Is Jake officially part of the team?"

Amaro agreed that I'm swayed too easily by Jake. What if it's true, and I'm letting the wolf in with the chickens?

Maliha hesitated just a moment. Amaro didn't notice. "Yes," she said.

"Good enough for me. So we can talk with him while you're gone. Are you really going to blow away the president?"

"Probably not."

"Probably?"

If Cameron ends up in power, many lives will be lost—so many that the resetting of my scales administered by Anu might be so bad that I can never rebalance. I could be expendable after the assassination. The world will not be a better place. With Elizabeth guarding him, I might not be able take out Cameron. On top of that, there's no clear way out for Yanmeng.

Maliha shrugged. "I'm making it up as I go."

Maliha had three days to get to Phoenix, so she decided to take her Zonda for another road trip. She'd driven it home from New York, but she'd been injured and barely paid attention to her new vehicle. This time, her knife wound was well on the mend, and she was determined to make the drive as enjoyable as she could under the circumstances. Eliu was safe. Amaro was helping with the advance work for the assassination attempt. Hound was surveilling Dr. Bakkum, and Maliha hoped there would be news about Yanmeng's location and Arnie's fate when she returned home. The Zonda's trunk was stuffed with weapons. She had a bag of jellybeans to snack on while on the road, and a lot of time to think, with eighteen hundred miles to go and six states to cross.

There was some snow on the first day, but when she got into southern Missouri, the highway was clean and dry. The Zonda was an effortless ride, quiet and powerful on the straightaways, tight and fast on the turns.

The night was cold and clear when she rose. The full moon lighted her way back to the McLaren. Moving from country road to country highway to interstate, Maliha headed home to Chicago, over eight hundred miles away. She intended to be in her condo before lunchtime. The McLaren was in its element, flying through the night. She rode with the windows down, drowning out her memories with the white noise of wind rushing past the car.

Pain streaked across the side of her neck, and then sliced across her left temple. She put a hand to her neck and it came away bloody. Maliha braked hard for an upcoming turn and struggled for control of the car. She felt the impact as the car scraped along the roadside barrier and then punched through it. When the tires left the road, there was a heart-stopping moment when the McLaren seemed to hang in midair before gravity took charge.

She stayed in a hotel in Springfield, Missouri, and left before dawn, heading for Amarillo. She hadn't been in the Texas Panhandle for a long time, and was surprised to see the huge wind farms bordering the highway. There was brown grass from horizon to horizon and lines of spinning windmills as far as she could see. The wind swept across these plains for miles, unbroken by tall buildings or mountains. Pulling over to the side of the road, she lowered the window. She could hear the *whoosh* of nearby blades turning. It seemed like an alien landscape with an army of giant beings marching.

Amarillo was bright lights, music, and steaks. Eating out, she was approached by friendly Texans who wanted her company for a meal and more. She turned them away with good humor, and it made her smile. There were people out there who were living lives that left them free to pursue pleasure, not dark, tangled lives like hers. She walked, sat, and ate among them, but her life would never be without deep issues. She had purpose, friends, and now love.

I am a lucky woman.

It had been a good idea to drive, and by the end of the second day she knew she was not going to kill the president in Phoenix.

Crossing New Mexico was like driving through an old western movie. Red rock formations, mesas, buttes, gulches. It was horse territory, and Maliha had traveled extensively here on horseback in the 1800s, sleeping under the stars.

I'd like to do that again someday with Jake. So many places I'd like to visit with him. I want to have time for everything.

Climbing in elevation to Flagstaff, she tried to design a plan that would allow her to look as though she'd made a good effort at the assassination, but put Millhouse in no danger.

Elizabeth is likely to have a backup, in case I don't take the opportunity when it presents. She's running her own agenda here, in addition to Project Hammer. What to do about a secondary shooter?

She let her mind work on the problem while her eyes appreciated the drive down from Flagstaff to Phoenix, a six-thousand-foot drop from ponderosa pine forest to the Sonoran Desert, from ski resorts to saguaro cacti, some of them a hundred and fifty years old.

After settling in her hotel, Maliha contacted Amaro.

"I have the perfect situation for you," he said. "A woman named Victoria Blake is attending the speech and the fundraiser dinner afterward by herself. Her husband, Norman, is in London and not returning until the morning after the event. They moved here from London just two weeks ago and don't have a network of friends yet, just Norman's business associates, and he's gone. She's not happy attending by herself but Norman thinks it's important. She's about your age—your apparent age—and build, though you're going to have to do an English accent if anyone talks with you."

"Flower girl or Professor Higgins?"

"Huh?"

"Never mind. I can handle it. How do you find these situations, Amaro?"

"It's better if you don't know the details. When the government goons interrogate you, I'll be safe."

"Hey!"

"Just kidding. I'll send you the details. The admission ticket has a photo on it. You can leave Victoria's on there and hope for the best or put your own photo on it."

"Thanks. I'll use my own photo."

"The venue is Comerica Theater, downtown. Victoria lives in Carefree, somewhere out in the desert. Homes blending in with nature. Sounds like hippie stuff."

"Hound?"

"Is planning to have a talk with the good Dr. Jill this evening. He also thought you might need some help and he wanted you to talk with a guy he knows in Phoenix."

"What's special about this guy?"

"He's a decorated Vietnam vet. He and Hound go way back. His name is Mickey Deer and he's a sniper."

"A sniper about sixty years old."

"I wouldn't raise the age issue with Hound if I were you. Hound says Mickey's sharp, in shape, and bored with sitting around. He wants to see some action."

"I can't bring him in as a sniper. I'd have to get to know him a lot better." An idea occurred to her. "Since Hound trusts him, though, I might have a role for him. Can you get him a ticket to the president's appearance?"

"Sold out way in advance. That's why you need Victoria Blake's ticket. She's got a reserved seat in the first row near the fire exit."

"Nice. Most of the tickets aren't reserved seating, though, right?"

"Only the ones that include the fund-raiser dinner afterward. Five thousand dollars a plate."

"The tickets probably have bar codes on them," Maliha said, "so they can be swiped, keeping track of who's there.

What happens if you make a duplicate ticket for Mickey with the same bar code as an existing ticket?"

"It would give an error when swiped . . . unless . . ." Amaro was quiet for a minute. "Unless the database record for that ticket ID is overwritten by the second swipe. Yeah, I can do that. Ninety percent chance, at least. The real ticket holder would have to get there first."

The delights of having a world-class hacker on your team.

"Good enough for me. That should put some excitement in Mickey's life right there."

"You're going to put me out of business if you keep thinking up this stuff."

"Thinking and doing are far apart. Your job's secure. Send me everything you have on Victoria, the theater, and whatever you can learn about the security arrangements. I need Mickey's phone number, too."

Maliha spent the evening planning and having a long talk with Mickey. She liked him, but there was no substitute for an aura check that told her things people didn't put into words. She went to bed with the full moon shining through her sheer curtains, painting the room in a ghostly light.

Nothing like a home invasion to start tomorrow off right.

Chapter Twenty-Nine

D r. Jill Bakkum had rounds at the hospital, her second time that day seeing her small patients. She was good with the kids and their parents, striking the right balance of infusing hope and determination yet remaining honest.

A hard thing to do when you're talking to a bald eight-year-old with brown eyes the size of saucers.

Hound thought she was an excellent doctor who'd stepped into quicksand of her own creation, a step that would soon prevent her from doing the work she loved. He didn't detect any definite signs of Dexedrine usage, although the doctor was a little irritable and it seemed like she'd lost weight lately. The loss on her small frame made her look almost gaunt. Both of those were possible side effects of Dexedrine abuse, but they could also have been caused by stress, something the doctor had in abundance on a daily basis.

I can't imagine her taking a saw to an innocent man's limbs. There could be some hidden mental problem here.

When she left the hospital, a Mercedes from the car service picked her up and took her home. Hound followed her to Harbor Point Towers, keeping his distance at first, closing in when she walked down the hallway to her condo door. When she opened her door, he rushed her and pushed her inside. Slamming the door behind them, he grabbed both of her hands and held them in one of his large ones, careful not to break any bones. She looked fragile. The next thing he knew, he was flat on his back, his gun was missing from his shoulder holster, and he was looking down the barrel of it.

Fuck. I've just been taken down by a woman half my size.

"Appearances can be deceptive," she said. "I hold black belts in several forms of martial arts. Why have you been following me all day? Or shall I just pull the trigger and not bother with any questions?"

Hound sat up and stretched his legs out in front of him as she watched closely. "I'd prefer we go with the questions," he said.

"Who are you?"

"Good start. I'm a private investigator, hired to find a man named Xia Yanmeng. He also happens to be a very good friend of mine. You wouldn't know where he is, would you?"

She ignored his question. "Who hired you?"

"Not at liberty to say."

Her foot hit his chin and he toppled backward onto the floor again.

I've had enough of this. And I want my damn gun back.

"Who hired you?" she said again. Her voice was calm, as though she held a gun on large men on a regular basis.

"The woman who has been on the receiving end of those body parts belonging to Yanmeng."

"Oh. Miss Winters. Get up into the chair, please." She gestured with his gun.

She'd gotten close, too close for a man with a good reach. He just had to make sure she didn't use his weight against him.

Stay on the ground. No leverage with fancy-schmancy martial arts.

He sat up again, as if to follow her order to get on the chair, then lunged at her feet instead, pulling her ankles toward him. She went over backward and he threw himself on top of her like a wrestler going for the pin. She gasped with the pressure of his weight. He locked her hands over her head and spread her legs wide with his so she couldn't flip him. He knew that in this position, rape would be screaming in her mind and he hoped it would scream a little while longer. Pounding her wrist into the floor, he made her release the gun. He grabbed it and rolled away fast, ending up ten feet across the room pointing the gun at her.

"Get up into the chair, doctor," he said. "Don't try anything dumb. I have a black belt in shooting."

For the first time, a bit of fear showed in the doctor's face. Her eyes darted around the room, no doubt trying to figure out if she could get to him or a hidden weapon before he could fire. Giving up on that, she sat in the chair and gripped the wooden arms tightly. Hound was careful to stay far enough away from her. He sat in a chair across the room.

"We use the advantages we have, Doc," Hound said. "I'm not here to hurt you. I'm sorry I frightened you. . . ."

"You didn't frighten me," she said with her chin up. It would have made a good show, but the chin was trembling a little. "What do you want? I don't keep drugs here." She stared at him closely. "I know I saw you at the hospital today. Are you stalking me?"

"Stalking? No. Following? Yes. I already told you that I'm a private investigator." He pulled out his pocket ID card with his photo and licensing information and held it up.

"Come closer, I can't read that," she said.

"Nice try." He put away the ID. "My name's Hound. We were talking about Xia Yanmeng and what you've been doing to him. I'll show you mine, and then you can show me yours." He gave her a brief description of what he knew about the malpractice suit. "Did a woman named Elizabeth approach you? Tall, blonde, never been in a tanning bed, red fingernails. You'd remember the fingernails."

Like little vampire teeth, Maliha said.

Dr. Bakkum hesitated.

"I'd hate to have to shoot you," Hound said. "Starting with those talented surgeon's hands of yours."

She looked down at her hands in alarm. Shattering them would end her career without even a trial.

"It wasn't the woman you described. I've only dealt with a man. An attorney, he said, but he didn't give me his name.

He said he could make the lawsuit go away if I did some custom surgery. I thought he meant something like changing a person's appearance so he could pass as someone else. You know, *Mission Impossible* stuff."

"Could you identify this man?"

"Absolutely. It turned out that he wanted horrible things done. A man kept in a drug-induced coma and submitted to operations where I had to cut off . . . extremities. I did everything in an operating room. Amputation isn't my specialty, but I use a Gigli saw on the skull at times, and it works well for cutting bone elsewhere."

"Two handles with a wire band between them, pulled back and forth?"

She nodded. "Surgical-grade stainless steel. Blood transfusions. I was provided with whatever I asked for. Mr. Xia's alive and pain-free, for now. If the drugs are discontinued, since he has no brain injury, he should recover consciousness with no problem."

"No problem except for his missing pieces. Is his memory intact?" Hound said.

"Almost certainly."

"Almost? Not what I want to hear."

"There are no guarantees in medicine, Mr. Hound. To add to the horror, I had to make deliveries to a condo in this building. The attorney gave me a device he said would prevent the hall cameras from seeing me. If I'd known it was going to be so medically and morally repugnant, I would have said no and taken my lumps from the malpractice suit. At least I was told I wouldn't have to kill the patient."

"More like the victim, not the patient. Why didn't you stop when you found out what you had to do?"

The doctor sighed. "I have a son."

"Your son's life was threatened?"

She squeezed her eyelids together, but that didn't stop the tears from escaping. That was all the answer that Hound needed.

How the hell do I get this woman to help me without jeopardizing her son?

"Where is Yanmeng?"

"In a secure facility where I do research."

"Cancer research needs a secure lab?" Hound said.

"I didn't say it was cancer research."

"Then what the hell is it?"

"Research in emergency techniques that can be programmed into battlefield robo-surgeons."

Well, damn. I guess medics are gonna look a lot different.

"I can't bring him out of there," she said. "I can't let you in, either."

"What's the name of this place?"

She hesitated.

"I'm not after your secret robot project. I just want to help my friend."

"Qixotic Labs," she said.

"Where is Yanmeng located inside the building?"

"I don't know."

"What the fuck? You've been chopping on him for days and you don't know where he is? Try again." Hound waved the gun as a reminder.

"I really don't. When I go to see him, I'm seated in a wheelchair and a black hood is put over my head. Someone takes me all around the building, up and down in the elevator, and spins the wheelchair a few times. By the time I get inside the surgical suite, I have no idea where I am. Before I got involved in this, I had seen other people being wheeled through the halls and thought it was strange. Now I'm one of the hooded ones. And before you ask, there aren't any windows in the room."

Hound whistled. "There's some weird shit going on in there, Dr. Bakkum."

She nodded. "Please, call me Jill. When I go to my usual work area for robotics, I know where that is and I walk there by myself. I only have an escort when I go to visit Yanmeng. My research is challenging, pays very well, and has the chance to save injured soldiers. When this malpractice suit came up, I thought that if it all goes bad for me, I'd disappear into my research and not do clinical work. Even if I lose my license, I don't think it would matter to them. But God only knows what goes on in the rest of the building."

"Jill, has it occurred to you that you were told you wouldn't have to kill Yanmeng because someone else was going to do it? When they don't need any more parts from him."

"I didn't want to think about that."

"Here's something else to think about. When they're done with him, they're done with you, and you know too much to live," Hound said.

Jill lapsed into deep thought. Finally she said, "It makes sense. It's hopeless for both of us. I can only hope my son survives. I've done something terrible and others are paying for it."

"I have an idea, but it's going to take your cooperation."

"Tell me what to do. If I can do it without killing my son, I will."

Chapter Thirty

Maliha went about the home invasion the easy way. She was invited in.

She rented a car for the drive—the Zonda would stand out too much in a back-to-nature area. Victoria's credit-card records showed regular purchases of a premium dog food. Maliha wore a business suit with a jacket and skirt, carried a briefcase, and bought a bag of the food on her way to Carefree. The homes weren't what she expected. There were large, expensive homes on acreage, many of them built into a hillside with a great view of Phoenix in the distance. True, they were made of adobe and had natural landscaping, but Maliha had already formed an image of earth homes with cacti growing on the roof. It was a tough image to shake, even when she pulled up in front of the Blakes' three- or four-million-dollar home at the end of a long private driveway.

I didn't have to rent a car. The Zonda would feel at home here.

She rang the bell. Looking up at the security camera, she put a big grin on her face and said, "Congratulations, Mrs. Blake! You've won a year's supply of Tail Waggin' Supreme Balance Kibble!"

When the woman opened the door, Maliha stepped inside, holding out the bag of dog food. When Victoria reached to take it from her, Maliha calmly shut the door behind her. Victoria's hand reached out for a security alarm button on the wall, but Maliha caught it and twisted, then brought the woman's arm up high behind her back. Painfully high.

"Anyone else in the house?" Maliha said.

"My husband, three of his friends and my vicious dog."

Maliha shoved the arm higher.

"Ow! You're hurting me!"

"Anyone in the house?"

"Just me and Barlett, but he's a wimp."

Bartlett chose that moment to wander in, demonstrating his tail-waggin' outlook on life. He was a young golden retriever with a smile on his face and love in his heart for all.

"Stupid dog," Victoria said. "We should have gotten a pit bull like I wanted."

Maliha reached down and patted Bartlett on the head. He licked her bare ankle, after rejecting the leather glove on her outstretched hand.

Just the kind of guard dog I like.

"Good doggie." The tail went wild. Victoria rolled her eyes. "Listen, Victoria, I need to borrow a couple of things from you. All you have to do is go along and you won't get hurt. When I leave I'm going to give you an injection to make you sleep for eight hours or more. You'll wake up feeling fine."

"I'm supposed to go to a fund-raiser tonight. When I don't show up, the police will come here."

"Are you meeting anyone?"

"Yes . . ." Maliha wrenched Victoria's arm. "No. Bugger off!"

Victoria struggled and Maliha waited her out. Bartlett danced at their feet, excited by the play. Finally, Maliha pulled a pair of handcuffs from her pocket, yanked Victoria's other arm back, and fastened the cuffs. Tugging on the cuffs, she walked Victoria over to the security control panel. Without too much persuasion, Victoria told her the correct password and Maliha disabled the alarm.

"Okay. Let's go up to the bedroom," Maliha said.

Victoria's eyes grew wide. "No you don't. Not with me, you . . . you pervert."

Maliha sighed and knocked her unconscious. Throwing the limp body over her shoulder, she went upstairs to the master bedroom, briefcase in one hand. She put Victoria on the bed. Barlett followed the two up the steps and jumped up on the bed. He circled a couple of times and settled down, his head resting on Victoria's leg, happily watching Maliha poke through his owner's possessions.

There were his and hers closets, so Maliha opened up hers. She was here to pick something to wear that belonged to Victoria in case someone who'd seen her before was at the speech or dinner.

Maliha chose a long black dress with a low neckline and a slit skirt, but one that covered her back completely. It was unlikely that Victoria had a hawk tattoo spanning her shoulders. There were sparkling crystals at the waistline of the dress, and a short jacket and matching high heels with the same crystals. She added a black silk scarf from a drawer in the closet. The jewelry box yielded a pair of diamond drop earrings. Maliha loved them, but set them aside.

Too expensive. These studs will do, since they're not going to make their way back into the jewelry box.

Maliha set everything out on a dressing table in the corner of the bedroom. Then she went looking for Victoria's admission ticket, and spent the next hour taking a photo of herself in the same outfit Victoria wore, same makeup, and delicately substituting her photo on the ticket. The photo was a good match, but her substitution job wasn't perfect using just the items she brought in her briefcase. She put the ticket on the bed and sat on it. The slight curve and wrinkle distracted the eye and made the ticket seem more authentic.

Victoria was coming around. Maliha waited with her and helped her sit up on the bed.

"You didn't . . ." Victoria said.

"No." Maliha thought about the last time she'd been with Jake, the exquisite and gentle union of bodies and hearts.

He's the man who broke through the barrier to my heart, but it was Lucius who created the cracks in that barrier.

"I did lie earlier, though. I'm not borrowing a few of your

things. I won't be able to return them." She pointed at the outfit on the dressing table.

Victoria glanced over at it, then looked Maliha up and down. "You're going in my place. Are you sure that dress fits? It looks like it would be a little tight through the waist. I don't want to look bad."

"Of course it will fit. My waist's no bigger than yours."

"Hmm. Prove it."

Mumbling under her breath, Maliha stripped to her underwear, keeping her back to Victoria. The dress slipped on easily. "There. In fact, it's a bit too big." She pinched the material out at the waistline, illustrating.

"Good. If anyone notices, they'll think I lost weight."

I pity Norman. I'm not sure this woman has grasped the situation.

"You're not going to do anything that will hurt my reputation, will you? Norman wouldn't like that."

"No." *Assuming you have a reputation as an assassin.*

"Would you mind turning on the telly? I watch some shows about this time."

Maliha searched the room and Victoria for cell phones, confiscating two from atop a dresser. She unplugged the landline phone and set it out in the hall, along with the cell phones and a laptop. There were no weapons in the room Maliha was worried about except a straight razor, which went out into the hall. She propped Victoria up with a couple of pillows and turned on the TV for her. Pushing a chair in front of the bedroom door, Maliha sat in it so the woman couldn't get to any of the items in the hall without going through her.

Maliha spent the next couple of hours going over the plans of the Comerica Theater that Amaro had provided and studying the map of its location in Phoenix. The theater wasn't ideal for her purpose. It was primarily a venue for band appearances and was a large open space with a stage. No fancy seating, just chairs on a concrete floor. If she had a seat on the main floor, as Victoria's ticket specified, Maliha wouldn't have any height to provide a good view for a shot.

For a clear line of sight, she'd have to be up in the catwalks of the theater, where the stage lighting was. Checking the plans, she saw that the stairs to the catwalks were behind doors backstage, as is typical for such places. With high security backstage for the president's appearance, access might be tough, especially if she had to pick the lock. A digital lock would be worse, slowing her down too much.

Elizabeth's sniper will likely have a government pass. Can't rule out anything.

The dinner after the speech was in a hotel banquet room, the same situation—everyone on one level—minus the catwalks. For a sniper to get a high, unobstructed view in the banquet room, he'd have to swing from a chandelier.

Shooting isn't the way to go for my attempt. Keep it simple. Elizabeth will probably have someone in the audience watching me, who will report to her—I would. Goal one: try but don't succeed to kill the president. Goal two: eliminate the backup.

It was nearly time to leave. Maliha turned off the television and removed the prepared syringe from her briefcase. As she approached, Victoria eyed the needle.

"My arms hurt and I'm hungry," she said. "I have to pee. You can't leave me like this."

Maliha considered. Victoria wouldn't like to be found in a wet bed. Norman wouldn't like it.

And I should care?

She looked at Victoria, who had a pleading look on her face. Bartlett was flapping his tail against the bed.

I'll do it for Bartlett. He wouldn't like a wet bed either— might get blamed for it. I can't believe I'm doing this. If anybody ever finds out, I swear I will die of embarrassment.

"Stand up," Maliha said. Victoria, who'd been lying down for several hours, stumbled to her feet. "Hold still. I'm going to put the cuffs on in front."

Victoria swayed a bit but offered no resistance. With her hands cuffed in front, she could manage in the bathroom.

"Potty break," Maliha said, walking her over to the door. She pushed Victoria into the room and politely turned her back near the door. She could see the woman in a mirror, so she'd have plenty of warning if Victoria decided to attack her. "Hurry up."

"You're making me nervous."

"Five seconds."

Ah. Success.

With Victoria back on the bed, Maliha injected her.

"Am I going to get high?"

"No. Just relax."

When Victoria was sound asleep, Maliha uncuffed her and went downstairs. Bartlett padded along with her.

"Hey, you're supposed to stay upstairs."

He sat down and looked at her expectantly.

"You too?" she said. There was a leash hanging up by the back door. She took Bartlett outside, and when they came in, she opened the bag of dog food she'd brought and filled his bowl.

"Can I leave now?" In answer, the dog went back to the stairs. He was heading up to the bedroom to keep Victoria company.

Out in the car, Maliha slipped off the high heels for more comfortable driving and went to the theater. She didn't use the theater's parking lot. Instead, she parked several blocks away. She took a zirconia knife from her briefcase and fastened it high on her left thigh, where the dress wasn't split, in a slim matching sheath. Zirconia, or ceramic, knives were usually detectable by security metal detectors because the manufacturers of the knives voluntarily put in a percentage of metal. Hers was custom-made, black, light in weight, and invisible to regular walk-through detectors. The knife was a superb weapon made for one thing only—killing.

If she were to go through the type of airport scanner that produced a full-body image, the knife would be visible under her clothing just like her breasts and butt. She didn't expect to encounter airport scanners at the theater. She put the heels back on and wrapped the scarf around her neck, pulling it up over her chin. With her hair in loose curls that tumbled down to her shoulders, she pulled the curls forward, partially blocking the view of her face and eyes.

Who is that mysterious woman in black?

Maliha walked to the theater and breezed through the metal detector. She was escorted to her front-row seat. Mickey planned to arrive at the last minute, right before the entrances closed. Once the speech started, people were supposed to remain in their seats and not leave the theater.

Like a high-school lock-in, except run by the Secret Service.

There were two speakers before the president, local politicians basking in the glow. The audience listened politely and applauded at the right spots, but curbed their enthusiasm. They were there to see and hear Randall Millhouse. When he appeared on stage, the crowd gave him a long and vigorous standing ovation. Few probably noticed the increased presence of agents on the stage and in front of it. Maliha noticed that an agent was posted at each of the fire exits. Although locked from the outside, the doors were considered weak spots because they led straight into the theater, bypassing the metal detectors.

Maliha waited for her cue to act. She hoped that Mickey had made it into the building and was up to the job, which was spotting the backup assassin. That was crucial to her plan to blame Elizabeth as the reason Maliha's attempt failed. She would be able to say that Elizabeth had brought in the backup and screwed everything up.

Just as she thought that the speech seemed to be winding down, a man in the audience stood up and yelled. It was Mickey. He was pointing up at the catwalk.

"Sniper! Up there!"

Maliha took a deep breath. The agents followed Mickey's accusing finger. Although the sniper snatched back the barrel of his rifle quickly, the damage was done. He'd been spotted.

The agents on the stage crowded in close around the president. Maliha pulled the scarf up, leaving only her eyes exposed, and vaulted onto the stage—not an easy task in heels. She approached the president. She'd debated using

Ageless speed, but it was a recording of her running at that speed that had resulted in Arnie's death and Yanmeng's kidnapping. Up on the stage, there were both security and TV cameras recording everything, and cameras sweeping the audience, too. She ducked her head a bit further, trying to look like a woman with no face.

Gunfire erupted. Two agents were firing on the sniper. Hands were pushing Millhouse down behind the podium, and she would have to go over or through the cluster of agents to reach him.

Just what she was counting on.

She ran at the group, yelling, "You've got to save the president!" and hoping they wouldn't be too fast on the trigger. When she got close enough, she kicked aside two agents who were blocking her way, and out came the knife. She let one of the remaining agents get in front of her, and stabbed him in the shoulder with a blow that was meant for Millhouse. At least, the watcher in the audience would report it that way. Maliha had made her good faith effort to kill the president.

She pulled the knife out and retreated fast, heading for the fire exit, mingling with the panicked people trying to get out the door. She ran in a semi-squatted position, hell on her knees but a trick that had let her escape before. With her head below the crowd's shoulder height, it looked as though she'd vanished. The Secret Service agents were reluctant to fire into a fleeing crowd with no target identified. The agent at the fire door propped the door open rather than have people get trampled underfoot and die in their eagerness to get outside the building.

Seconds after the stabbing onstage, Maliha was out into the night. She was running in cool, fresh air, a pleasant change from the theater space heated by five thousand bodies. People were taking off in different directions, but almost all of them were heading for nearby parking. Very soon there would be major jams in the blocks surrounding the theater. Maliha sprinted to her car, jumped in, and sped away from downtown before the jam had a chance to build.

She had no time to lose. There was the possibility of roadblocks and searches at airports, bus, and train stations. She'd be considered an accomplice to the sniper, who was too dead to deny it, and her photo would be taken from the theater's cameras and passed around. It had been a high-risk operation, another reason why Elizabeth hadn't wanted to take part directly.

An hour later, Maliha was on her way to Flagstaff. She stopped there in a darkened parking lot, waiting for Mickey to catch up to her. She wanted to meet him. She figured he'd been caught in the traffic jam and she might be there over half an hour, but was surprised when he pulled up next to her in about five minutes. He slipped out of his car and into the passenger seat of hers.

"Pleased to meet you in person, miss," he said. Mickey was of average height and muscular. His long gray hair was fashioned into two heavy braids that he wore in front, coming down to his chest. His face had prominent cheekbones, strong angles, and the wrinkled appearance of a man who'd spent a lot of time in the sun in his youth.

"How did you get here so fast?" Maliha said.

"I parked a few blocks away. When I got out of one of the fire exits, I ran for my car. It's a rental."

Sounds familiar.

"Good thinking. Hound didn't tell me you were a Native American," Maliha said. If they were to work together, even occasionally, she had to learn about this man.

"Hopi tribe."

"It's okay to call you Mickey?" She assumed that was a nickname.

"Sure. I picked that up in Vietnam and it stuck."

"Your service was as a long-range shooter."

"I guess that's what they're calling a sniper these days."

"I thought the Hopi tribe were farmers. How does that fit with shooting people?" She relaxed her eyes, focused beyond him, and let his aura come into view. His aura was clean and beautiful. He had a wide band of vibrant yellow surrounding him, indicating success and wisdom, and a light blue band, meaning that he was looking for a higher purpose in his life—a path to fulfillment. Maliha could certainly relate to that. There were a few flares of white that added a special element to his aura. He was a guardian. Interestingly, there were no traces of violence from the war. When he'd killed, he'd had no regrets and the deaths hadn't permanently marked him.

I like this man. A lot. I can see why Hound would too.

"We don't all have to be farmers because it's in our tribal history. I'm an attorney. I specialize in child abuse and rape cases. Much of my work is pro bono. I don't have a grand lifestyle, but that doesn't concern me. The problem is that I see cases in the courtroom after the damage or death has already taken place. I want to get out there and confront injustice as it happens and save lives."

"You're not concerned that you'd be breaking the law?"

"I've been an attorney for nearly thirty years. I could tell you horror stories you wouldn't believe."

I doubt that.

"The law has failed me enough times to make me cynical, I guess. I'll do my best in the courtroom, but I want another arena to fight in too. Hound . . . well, Hound didn't tell me a whole lot, but he hinted that you had some people who feel the same way. The work I did tonight, spotting the sniper. Piece of cake—I knew exactly what to look for, and where. But I think I helped save the president's life, and that feels damned good. Damned good. I did see you stab an agent, but I know I'm not in on the whole plan."

"You were a great help, Mickey. I want you to take this." She handed him an envelope containing twenty thousand dollars.

"Whoa! I can't take this. I don't even know your name."

"My name's Maliha, and consider the gift something to help you in your pro bono cases. Hire some experts or something." He started to object, and she raised a finger to stop him. "I think we're going to work well together. We still need to have a long talk, but it will have to wait until the case I'm working on is resolved. I'll contact you then."

He was silent for a minute. "I've just been recruited into something, haven't I?"

"Not if you don't want to be. We'll talk about it later. I can have Hound give you a little more information." *Without all the supernatural stuff.*

"Okay. See you later, then, Maliha." He left the car, moving with the agility of a much younger man, and drove off in his rental.

Maliha started the car and sat for a moment before leaving the parking lot.

Have I just recruited Yanmeng's replacement? Have I given up?

Chapter Thirty-One

Hound tailed Jill as she drove to the building where Yanmeng was held. The doctor had waited for this particular night for her risky move. The nurse on duty that night, Donna, used the opportunity when the doctor was present to take a nap, figuring that nothing was going to happen to the patient while he was in the doctor's presence. She wasn't supposed to, but Jill never complained about the naps because she knew that the nurse had two jobs. Now that time was going to be put to good use.

The doctor headed west on I–80 toward Joliet. She passed through an area of modern office buildings and turned off at one of the exits that led into an office park. At 7 P.M. most of the buildings were dark except for security lighting and widely spaced lights in the parking lot. Hound expected the doctor to turn in at one of the buildings, but she kept going. The office park ended abruptly and farmers' fields took over. There would be corn growing in the summer, but now there was cornstalk stubble sticking up through the snow. He topped a hill and knew immediately he'd reached the place.

Spread out in the valley below him was a compound containing a *U*-shaped five-story building lit up like the landing site in *Close Encounters of the Third Kind.*

Holy cow. That's some research lab.

He used binoculars to inspect the scene, snapping pictures with the built-in digital camera as he looked around. The building was surrounded by a doughnut of buffer space—outer perimeter fencing topped with razor wire, a dead man's zone, and then inner perimeter fencing with more razor wire. The outer fence was electrified. There were five guard towers and no part of the building's exterior was hidden. Halogen floodlights illuminated the sides of the building. There were two security checkpoints, one outside each fence.

I'm going to need help getting into this place. Stealth on this level isn't my style, but it's Maliha's. Jake might want to go with her instead, and that's logical, but damn it, that's Yanmeng in there. I'm going in even if I have to crash the party.

He watched as Jill's gray Mercedes went through the checkpoints, had its trunk and interior searched, and was sniffed by a bomb detection dog. The second checkpoint had a gadget he hadn't seen before, a retinal scanner built into a cup placed over the eye while the driver remained in the car.

Looks like ringing the front doorbell isn't a good idea. Too many details to get right.

Once the Mercedes was parked and the doctor had entered the building, Hound didn't have anything to do for the next several hours. Parking on the edge of the road wouldn't work—he had no doubt that there were routine patrols and that getting caught taking pictures of the facility wouldn't be good for his health. He went back out to the interstate and found a nearby motel. He didn't think he'd be able to sleep, but was awakened by the doctor's call at about four in the morning.

"I'm done. Everything went okay. I . . ." she said.

"Let's not talk now. I'll meet you where we agreed."

Hound met the doctor at a corner within the office park and she followed him back to his motel. He was eager for news.

"You weren't kidding when you said the lab has a lot of security. It's as welcoming as a porcupine on steroids. Tell me everything," Hound said.

"First of all, I was right. That tracking device you suggested would have been caught right away. I'm sure the body scan would have detected it."

"Even if you swallowed it?"

"Give me credit for knowing *something*. I do work there, after all. Anyway, I wasn't about to have that thing in my stomach."

"Okay, okay."

"The lab I work in is only a small part of that building, on the third floor on the west side of the *U*. I tried hard to pay attention to where I was taken this time in the wheelchair, and if I had to take a guess, I'd say it was underground at the back of the *U* shape. I could be completely wrong."

"Underground?"

"I'm not sure, but I think part of the basement is for utilities and the rest is finished space."

"I guess the right nurse was on duty?"

She nodded. "Donna was there. She was pleased with the chance to catch some serious sleep on the cot in the storage room and was asleep within minutes. I don't know how that woman handles it all." Jill stopped. Her cheeks colored. She was a workaholic by choice, not necessity, and had "handled it" with drugs.

Hound pretended he hadn't made the connection. "Go on."

"I examined Yanmeng thoroughly. His wounds are healing well and his basic level of health is excellent. I saw no problem why I couldn't lighten the sedation and let him emerge from his coma. The only questions were how long it would take and how he would act on awakening."

"Did he wake up?"

"Yes. You're getting ahead of the story. There was no brain or heart damage to begin with, and I didn't want to cause any with a rapid transition. I was pleased that he came awake after about five hours, with minimal confusion. He was in pain so he was given a painkiller."

Uh-oh. If Yanmeng wasn't mentally alert, I don't think he could do his remote viewing thing, which was the whole point of this.

"Was he drowsy from the painkiller?" Hound said.

"You said you wanted him alert and he was alert. I gave him just enough to dull the pain. He's a strong man. We're lucky, you know. Coming out of an induced coma isn't predictable as far as when it happens after drugs are reduced. The brain-injured can take days or weeks to emerge, there's memory loss, confusion, and a long-term recovery process, and that's if they're progressing well. You haven't explained to me why you wanted Yanmeng alert for a short time."

"Not at liberty to say. Did he talk to you?"

"He did. He asked to see his wife. I told him it wasn't possible yet, but that his friends were working to bring him home. He seemed content with that."

"He didn't ask about all of his injuries?"

"I don't think he had enough time to comprehend that. He didn't ask and I didn't volunteer. When he's awake longer, he'll probably need counseling. Most new amputees do."

"I'm thinking especially those whose situation is deliberate," Hound said. "We'll take care of Yanmeng as soon as we can bring him home. He'll get whatever he needs. How long was he awake?"

"About a half hour, but he was only clearheaded for about fifteen minutes. The nursing shift changes at four, and I had to have everything back in place by then. I explained I was putting him back in a coma, and that I didn't have a choice. He understood and said you'd better hurry up and get him out of there. It was a smooth induction."

"Did you remember about the EEG machine?" The electroencephalogram reading would leave a record of brain wave activity that wasn't consistent with a coma. Looking at the activity would show that Yanmeng had had an interesting night.

"I brought the printout with me, and I erased the last twelve hours on the hard drive."

"Any cameras or voice bugs?" Hound had given her a lesson in what to look for, but there were so many variations it would take an expert to be sure.

"I looked carefully. I don't think there's any record of

what goes on in that suite. I doubt that the man who employed me wants a record made, because it's clearly illegal."

Hound didn't bother to explain to her that the only one caught doing illegal things on camera would be her. *There might be a camera in spite of her search. What happened in there would make good blackmail material to keep Jill quiet.*

"Will you do what you promised now?" the doctor said.

Hound nodded. She'd held up her end of the deal. He'd told her that if a settlement of her malpractice suit out of court was possible at all, he and his friends could get it for her. They'd even pay off the fine that resulted, in return for her promise never to use drugs while practicing medicine.

Now all I have to do is convince Maliha to go along with the plan. Paying a multimillion-dollar fine would put a serious dent in my . . . everything.

"We'll get to work on it. Remember, I'll be watching you. Don't think you're getting a free pass for all you've done."

Chapter Thirty-Two

Maliha was passing through the wind farms on her way back to Chicago in the middle of the night when something astonishing happened. She felt Yanmeng's sweet touch on her shoulder. He was remote viewing her.

She was so unprepared for it, and so overwhelmed with emotion, that she swerved the Zonda onto the shoulder of the highway at ninety miles per hour. She fought to keep the car under control as she slowed down enough to pull back into her lane without flipping. The nearest vehicle behind her was a semi, about a quarter mile back. She put on her emergency flashers and pulled over in a controlled fashion.

The touch came again, a little stronger, as tears rolled down her cheeks.

Alive, alive, alive! Oh, my friend . . .

There was a knock on her window. Glancing in her rearview mirror, she noticed the truck's headlights. The driver had pulled off on the shoulder behind her.

"Somethin' I can do for ya, miss? You got car trouble?"

Maliha didn't roll down her window. She had to be cautious even though he seemed sincere. "No problem. Everything's okay. Thanks for stopping."

"Should I call the Highway Patrol?"

"No. Really."

"I seen you go off the road. I got some hot coffee if you want it."

She shook her head. "I appreciate what you're doing, but I'm fine. I'm going to ask you to leave now."

"Whatever you say. Just tryin' to help."

She watched him walk away and turned her attention back to Yanmeng. She had the feeling she was wasting precious time.

Yanmeng tapped her on the shoulder several times. It seemed clear he wanted to tell her something, but how? There was no exchange of thoughts. Maliha had a flash of inspiration. Yanmeng had been able to move his son Xietai's blade when it was descending on Maliha's back. If he could deflect that powerful blow, he could move Maliha's hand when she was cooperative.

She looked around for something to write on and spotted her briefcase. Turning on the car's interior light, she scrambled for something that would write boldly on the light tan leather. Nothing was available, so she propped her left arm on a jacket and cut a gash with a knife. Dipping her finger in the blood, she wrote the alphabet on the side of the briefcase, forming every third letter and leaving the rest as dashes to save time and blood. She wrote the numbers zero through nine, and made two circles, one with "yes" inside and the other with "no."

Maliha had drawn a basic Ouija board. Yanmeng, viewing her from above, would be able to see it. She moved her hand lightly over the "talking board" and spelled out the first question.

R u safe

For a minute nothing happened, and Maliha worried that her friend wasn't strong enough to move her hand. Her hand began to wobble and then moved in a smoother way, about an inch above the board, to one of the circles she'd drawn.

Yes

She spelled out another question.

where

Her hand, moving under his control, spelled out *3481*. She memorized it. It had to be a room number. Then Yanmeng asked a question of his own.

coma

She pointed at the "yes" circle. She knew he'd been in a coma.

eliu ok we get u

Her hand trembled with the relief he felt as he watched her spell out that message. It was his turn.

danger

In his desperate circumstances, he was worried about the danger involved in rescuing him. Maliha suppressed a groan.

get u

Her hand moved after he read the message, but it dragged slowly across the leather. He was at the limit of his strength.

go now
love u
lov

His touch moved to caress her cheek, and she leaned into it. Then it was gone.

The cut on Maliha's arm had stopped bleeding. She could see that the edges were smooth and would heal well. She wrapped her arm with strips torn from a T-shirt from her duffel bag.

She couldn't wait to share the good news. She phoned Amaro and told him. There was relief in his voice, and she wondered if all of them had been worried about the same thing—that it wasn't going to turn out well.

"We have a location and we're going in. Be sure to tell Eliu the good news. I'm going to get to an airport and fly home. This is going to take some planning."

"Hound told me the place has major security."

"Yanmeng implied as much. Then we need a major plan."

"Hey, what are you going to do with your new car if you fly home?"

"Long-term parking."

"What makes you think it'll still be there when you go back to pick it up?"

"The Zonda protects herself. She slaps the hand that tries any funny stuff."

"Oh, come on—you think an alarm is going to stop anyone?"

"No. I meant the flamethrowers and the electric shocks. I guess it would be safer to lock the beastie up. I'll rent a storage unit."

Back in her Chicago home, Maliha convened a planning session. She escorted Eliu from the secure haven to her public condo to join in and to learn the latest about her husband. Maliha had called her from the airplane and told her about the remote viewing contact. She'd been worried that Eliu would feel slighted because Yanmeng hadn't had time to view Eliu in the brief period that he was alert. She needn't have worried. Yanmeng had sent a message to his wife first. It was Maliha who came second.

Not practical as far as his rescue, but I would have done the same thing if I were him—go for my spouse. I like the sound of that.

Amaro rolled a large dry-erase board out from his bedroom. What he did with it, Maliha never knew, but he'd requested it and that was good enough for her. Now it came in handy. Hound displayed the pictures he'd taken of Qixotic

Labs on a large monitor, and then drew a diagram on the board. Eliu reacted with shock.

"I can't believe he's locked away in there. You'll never get him out," she said.

"We will. I told him so. There are no limits on this operation. We'll do whatever it takes." Maliha said it firmly. Eliu nodded, but hesitantly. Maliha didn't blame her. The woman didn't follow their activities closely, and she had no idea what they were capable of doing.

"Amaro, are there aerial photos available?"

"Only from military satellites. I know someone who has access," Amaro said.

"There's something the great Amaro can't do?" Hound said.

"I'd rather call in a specialist and not waste time. Lady Gray already has experience with milsat."

"I didn't think you hackers made nice with each other," Hound said.

Amaro glared at him. "I'll go set that up. Photos in ten."

"What's this Lady Gray like? Is she hot?"

"Cut it out, Hound. We have a lot of work to do," Maliha said.

"Just playing with the kid."

"Not helpful." Maliha looked over the drawing on the board. "Forget about going in the front, past those checkpoints. We don't have time to set up IDs, and we'd have to make it through the retinal scanner before even entering the building."

"Makes you wonder what the DOD is doing in there," Amaro said. He'd come back after making contact with his hacker friend.

"How about we blow the whole place up on the principle of 'There be Evil'? That is, after Yanmeng's out," Hound said.

Explosives. Good.

"We want to minimize casualties. Not everyone in the building is evil," Maliha said.

Tranquilizer guns.

"Matter of opinion," Hound said. "Blow holes in the

fences and go in with an armed force. I can have a team of mercs there in a few hours."

Holes in the fence—distraction.

"Automatic weapons in the guard towers would take out a ground-based assault," Maliha said. "Unless . . . unless we knock out the towers first. But if we do that on the way in, we're going to have an army of guards after us when we get into the building."

"Stealth entry, big-bang exit," Amaro said.

"That's what I'm talking about," Hound said. He slapped his fist into his palm.

"How will Yanmeng be safe during this exit?" Eliu said. "Don't get carried away with the logistics of it. You're there to get *him* out safely. Somebody has to carry him because he'll still be in a coma. Badly injured and needing special care, too. He won't be able to do his part in a firefight."

Get him out by air?

Amaro got a text message. "The aerial shots are ready." He brought in a computer and put them up on the monitor in a slide show. They all sat staring at the screen.

"I've got some ideas. Hound, call your mercenaries. We need support for the big bang. They won't be going into the building, just raising hell to help us get out. They have to be able to, um, exercise restraint in not blowing everybody away. Make it clear their mission is diversion."

"Got it. Equipment?" Hound said.

"A lot, and I have a source if you don't. We'll talk about that in a few minutes. I have something to get rolling, too. We're going to need air support."

"Damn. I wish Glass was here." Hound's fiancée was a helicopter pilot. "She's experienced under fire. Rock steady."

"No time for that," Maliha said. "I know of a rescue team with plenty of short-haul experience and sealed lips. They do extractions from hostiles."

Hound nodded.

"Who's going into the building?" Amaro asked.

Maliha noticed that Hound stiffened at the question. His mouth narrowed to a line.

What?

"Hound and I," she said. "Hound, you'll carry Yanmeng and I'll have your back."

The corners of Hound's mouth turned up almost imperceptibly.

Oh. He thought I was going to suggest Jake.

"What about Jake?" Amaro said. "He . . ."

"He's busy tracking down Dr. Bakkum's son. There's no one who could do a better job of protecting him, and we owe that to the doctor."

She walked over to the monitor and pointed at a fenced area separated from the main compound. There were several small buildings, some circular tanks, and a large rectangle of water-reflecting sunlight. "This is how we're getting in."

"What's that?" Amaro said.

"It's a water treatment plant for Qixotic. They must have a need for specialized treatment and they don't use regular sewers. The end of the road for the water is a constructed wetland—see those trees and tall grasses with what looks like streams running through them? That spot that's reflecting sunlight is a sewage settlement lagoon," Maliha said.

"Specialized treatment, like chemical removal?" Amaro said.

Maliha nodded. "In addition to the usual blackwater processing. The settlement lagoon is the first step. Raw sewage goes in there, scum like oil rises to the top and heavier wastes sink to the bottom as sludge. The water that's left in the middle is drained off and ready for further treatment. When you consider what kind of stuff Qixotic dumps down the drain, that lagoon should be toxic as hell. That's why the only security there would be a fence to keep the public from stumbling in and coming out as mutant superheroes."

"Seriously? We're going into that?" Hound said. "Shit."

"In twenty-four hours, if we can put it all together by then," Maliha said.

There was a knock on the door. Maliha dashed there and yanked open the door, expecting to see Dr. Bakkum depositing another box out in the hallway. There was no one in sight, but there was a box.

The doctor couldn't get away that fast. I was here in a couple of seconds. The messenger had to be Elizabeth.

Maliha had a sinking feeling. The box was fairly large and heavy.

Big enough to hold a head. Not now. Not when we're so close.

Maliha cut open the box. Eliu picked up on Maliha's sharply elevated level of worry and buried her face in Amaro's shoulder.

Inside the box was Yanmeng's severed foot, a note, and a picture. The picture showed Dr. Bakkum hanging upside down over a tub, her throat slit and blood drained.

Sickening. Damn Elizabeth.

Hound came over to look. "That's one nasty woman."

"We knew that already," Maliha said. "I hope Jake is successful in locating Dr. Bakkum's son, if he's still alive. He'll need a new identity."

"I'll work on that," Amaro said.

The note reminded Maliha that President Millhouse planned to leave for his Pacific Rim travel in five days, and warned her not to screw up again. The implication was clear. There was no need for a surgeon's skill anymore to keep Yanmeng alive. If another amputation was needed, it would be with Elizabeth's sword, and Yanmeng wouldn't survive it.

As with all the other body parts, Yanmeng's foot was carefully wrapped and placed on ice. The window of opportunity for replantation, roughly ten to twelve hours, had slipped by in all cases except for the new arrival.

There could be a chance.

She glanced at the time on the wall clock that used to grace a train station in Salzburg. It was almost 5 P.M. "Our timetable's been moved up. We go in eight hours," Maliha said.

Chapter Thirty-Three

It was 1 A.M. Maliha and Hound were at the fence around the lagoon. The water's surface wasn't frozen, even though there was no aeration and the outdoor temperature was 15 degrees.

"What do you suppose is in there that keeps ice from forming?" Hound said.

"I'd rather not know. Ever use a drysuit?"

"Nope. But I look damn good in a wetsuit."

"These drysuits are made for hazardous diving and they'll keep us warm, too," Maliha said. "The free-flow helmets keep a positive pressure inside the suit, just like in level-four labs where they have weaponized anthrax. Feeling any better about toxicity?"

"No. How the fuck do you get into these things?"

"First you pee. I didn't bring any diapers or condoms with catheters with me."

"Damn straight. I'm not wearing any of that shit." Hound wandered off a little and emptied his bladder. "How about you?" he said before he turned around.

"Done. You did wear that thermal underwear?"

"Thinsulate as requested. Wanna see?"

"I'll see soon enough. Take off your clothes and stuff them in the dry pack, then stick your feet in these boots."

After some tugging and swearing under his breath, Hound was in the suit. Maliha zipped the space-suit zipper and settled the attached helmet on his head.

A few minutes later, she had donned her suit and checked the contents of her dry pack. Everything they needed for the rest of the mission was crammed into two waterproof bags, one carried by each of them. She linked herself to Hound with a cable. Poor visibility was going to be a problem, as was working using the heavy gloves. Finally, she pressurized both of their suits.

There had been no patrols near the treatment plant. They had the place to themselves. The main building held the attention of the guards in the towers, not the dark surrounding fields. Maliha had already cut a hole in the chain-link fence around the lagoon. Inside, ready to take the risk of exposure in the water, she looked up at the sky for a last clear view. A waning gibbous moon rode high over a few clouds, reminding her that December was counting down to the new year.

Submerged in about eight feet of water, Maliha found that the view was even murkier than she'd anticipated. Her helmet light helped a little, but she had something much better to use. She touched a button at her waist. A green laser pointer beam shot out in front of her, programmed in advance to guide her to the inlet pipe for the lagoon. If she strayed from the correct direction, the beam changed to red, and then returned to green when she reoriented. Hound shuffled his feet, stirring up the sludge and making a thick cloud around them. She could only see the beam about a foot in front of her, and when she took a couple of steps, it turned red.

"Quit that," Maliha said into her helmet mike. "Raise your feet and set them down carefully. Besides not being able to see, think about what you're stirring up. You're putting us in a big swirling toilet."

"Can I vomit in this helmet?"

Maliha didn't answer. His flip attitude was starting to get to her, but she knew it was his way of dealing with stress on a mission. The next sound she heard was of him throwing up. He hadn't been kidding.

This man can plow his way through dead and dying

bodies without flinching—a medic even—and a little excrement does him in.

"Sorry," she said. "I shouldn't have been so explicit."

"It's okay. I'm just up to my chin in my own puke."

Maliha continued forward, correcting her path as needed, until her outstretched hands touched a wall. Halfway up was the inflow pipe that brought sewage from the compound. The water was turbulent in front of the pipe as a controlled flow entered the lagoon. There were also a filter, mechanical slats to control the flow, and a grill to prevent entry.

I hope this hazard suit is working.

"Torch man, you're on," Maliha said.

Hound came up, stepping with exaggerated care. He removed an insulated portable oxyacetylene cutter from his pack. It took up most of the room inside, but without it, their mission would come to an abrupt end. It was a two-tank machine, one tank holding the fuel, acetylene, and the other one holding the oxygen supply that permitted burning underwater. Hound put a shield over his helmet and started the burner. The cutting torch melted the iron grill, blowing away liquid iron that was trapped in globs on the metal slats, burning holes in them.

The intense light suffused the water, and from above, Maliha knew, a portion of the lagoon would be glowing. If the glow attracted attention, it would be checked out by security and they would be caught. She hoped the greenish-brown glow wouldn't compete with the floodlights in the compound.

Hound was done. He put the cutting machine back into his pack, leaving the hot torch hanging out in the water. A section of the grill lifted off in his hands. The slats that kept all the sewage from flowing in at once swung out on hinges for maintenance. The filter, a multilayered contraption filled with different media like sand and crushed glass, was removable. Water started pouring into the lagoon at a high rate, released under pressure from a deep septic tank that was their next destination.

Fighting against the current, they both went into the pipe.

Maliha tried to brace her hands and feet on the tunnel sides, but they were too slippery. At the end of the cable that connected them, Hound spun in the current and banged into the side of the pipe. When they were about to be flushed back out to the lagoon, she noticed overhead handholds in the pipe, probably for emergency use. They were slippery too, but better than nothing. Grabbing on, she pulled Hound into position behind her. He swung the slats closed and the water flow dropped to a point they could navigate.

Moving upward in the slanted pipe hand-over-hand on the emergency grab bars, Maliha didn't take long to arrive at the septic tank outflow. There was no security grill this time, but there were flow-control slats. The tank was a deep holding area for raw sewage, to make sure the waste released into the lagoon stayed there long enough to have time to settle out instead of being rushed through the system.

"Hang on, this is going to be a rough entrance."

"What, the other one was a joyride? You should have tried it from back here."

Maliha swung the control slats out of the way. Water under pressure from the forty-foot-deep tank flooded in on her. She gripped the sides of the pipe and struggled to push her body into the opening. As she'd hoped, there were more emergency grab bars, running vertically up the side of the tank. She pulled up on them and, when Hound slipped into the tank behind her, he closed the slats.

They couldn't see anything. The current had stirred the sewage into a thick brown liquid, as though they were swimming through mud. Maliha was startled when pieces of a dead pig came into view suddenly and smacked into her helmet.

Hey! That's supposed to be incinerated. They better not have dumped sharps in here too.

Sharps were needles and broken glass, which could cut the drysuits. Maliha was getting nervous about how long they'd been submerged, with unknown toxins in the water. She accelerated her climb, bumping Hound along behind her, until they both reached the surface.

"Damn, woman! There's not a spot on my body that isn't bruised."

"In a pressurized suit underwater? You had a cushion of air."

"You might have explained the conditions better. I could have worn a cup."

There was a dim light at the top of the tank. They were about ten feet down from the top. Across the tank, Maliha could see a pipe dumping in waste.

"There's the back door to the compound. It's a plain sewer walk from here."

"Yeah. A stroll on the beach."

"If you don't want to continue, you can go back the way we came in."

"Fuck you."

"I'm going to swim across. You can float behind me." She took off before he could voice any complaints. When she reached the other side, she levered herself up into the pipe. Hound refused her offered helping hand and pulled up on his own.

"Think I still need this cutting torch?" Hound said.

"Can't say for sure. We'd better take it."

Hound gave her a flashlight from his pack and Maliha took the lead. It was possible they'd encounter maintenance workers from here on. The drysuit wasn't as flexible as her usual fighting outfit, and the only weapon she had at hand was a knife. Surprise was on their side, though, and was all the advantage Maliha needed.

They made it to the spot where the sewer line connected to the building with no problems. Climbing up a ladder, Maliha pushed aside a manhole cover and emerged into a basement. Once inside, Hound started to take off his suit.

"Wait, let me help with that. I want as little contact with the suit as possible. We should be having a decontamination shower." She eased him out of the suit. The first thing he did was wipe his face with his undershirt.

"I've been wanting to do that for a while. I've been seeing everything through a film of barf."

He unzipped her suit zipper, which was across the back of her shoulders, with a gloved hand, and she took it from there. They changed into guard uniforms and dragged everything they were leaving behind into a maintenance closet. Maliha's pack was filled with weapons, things a guard wouldn't carry, but she didn't expect the guard deception to last long. They each had tranquilizer guns and a chest pack filled with additional darts. Maliha planned to use the darts as the front-line weapon, to make their attack as nonlethal as possible. Hound had complained a little—he was more of a bullet man—but he went along with the boss, with the proviso that lethal force was discretionary.

"You can always kill if you have to," she'd said when she explained it. "Just don't make it the default action."

"Is this the kinder, gentler Maliha?" Hound said.

"Not exactly. It's the morally ambivalent Maliha."

In addition to the dart gun, Maliha was bristling with other weapons: knives, a sword, her whip sword, throwing stars, and a semi-automatic S&W pistol with extra magazines. She fastened a watch on her wrist and checked the time. They were ahead of schedule in a plan that depended on perfect timing.

Hound was well armed with projectile weapons, including an automatic rifle, but he carried a knife for dirty fighting.

"Do I smell bad?" Hound wanted to know.

"No one's going to smell you coming, if that's what you mean. We're going to get a good scrub when we're done here."

"Naked?"

She nodded.

"Cool."

They headed for room 3481. Having nothing else to go on, Maliha assumed it was on the third floor. She was worried about Dr. Bakkum's statement that if she had to guess a location for the medical suite, it would be underground. Maliha didn't want to waste time romping all over the building, setting the two of them up with more opportunities for discovery.

They took the stairs to the third level on the cup of the *U*.

Looking out cautiously, she saw a long hallway lined with doors on either side. The lighting was dim, so she let her eyes adjust.

"Stay here," she whispered.

Hound tapped her on the butt in response.

I'm sure that's not an official special ops signal.

She slipped into the hallway, walking silently, staying close to one wall. The first door she encountered was numbered 6870.

What? We're on the sixth floor? Or is the numbering system not based on the floor?

She examined the next door and one across the hall, numbers 6880 and 6881.

At least it's not random.

She returned to the staircase and explained the problem to Hound.

"Simple," he said. "We're on the sixth floor, even though it's the first floor above ground. This is a ten-story building, with five floors above ground and five below. Dr. Bakkum was right, she just didn't know the extent of the underground development. We need to be three floors down."

"Three floors down is where we came from, and it looked like the basement. We can check, but I don't think we're going to find the medical suite right next to the boiler room. There must be hidden floors underground that have no connection to the stairs we came up." She looked at her watch. "We're good on time now, but won't be if we make bad choices."

"Then I suggest we find ourselves a guide pronto," Hound said.

"Okay. Wait—"

"I'll be right behind you."

They went out into the hall.

"Something odd here," Hound said. "No cameras, at least none I can spot."

"I guess these people like their activities private."

Still, it was eerie. No security guard patrolling, a low light level, and now no cameras.

Maybe I misjudged the security inside this building based on what's outside.

"Elevator," Hound said. She'd almost walked past it, wondering about the lack of bright lights and big guns. He pressed the DOWN button and they waited on either side of the door. When it opened, the car was empty. Inside, the button for the third floor was missing.

"What the fuck! This place is pissing me off," Hound said.

Maliha pointed out a slot that was the right size for an ID card. "I think all we need is the magic key."

"How are we going to get one when there aren't any warm bodies in here?"

That's when the robot came around the corner of the hall.

Chapter Thirty-Four

$\mathcal{E}$ ver killed a robot before?" Hound said.

"No. Maybe we don't need to."

The robot, about five feet tall and shaped like a hot-water heater, approached them on spidery legs.

First thought: get the hell out of here.

The robot had a face of sorts, probably to make it less threatening to the scientists who traveled these halls. Maliha had no doubt that the "arms" on either side were folded-up weapons. It stopped about six feet in front of them. The letters "Bruce" were painted across the front of it.

"Do you think that's its name?" Hound said.

"Your guess is as good as mine. If there are multiple robots, it makes sense that they'd have names."

"Christ, those legs creep me out. I wonder how fast it can move."

"Identification, please," Bruce said. His voice was not mechanical sounding at all, but low, male, and the kind of voice Maliha would like to hear on the other end of the phone.

"We're lost," Maliha said. "Take us to the third floor, Bruce."

"Identification, please."

"We left our identification on the third floor. Take us there now."

"Step forward for alternate identification." A panel opened on the top of the robot and an arm extended. On the end was a cup that would fit over one eye.

"Retinal scanner. Now what?" Hound said.

Maliha waved at him to be quiet. "I'm reporting you for inappropriate human interaction, Bruce. I order you to report to your maintenance station for diagnostics immediately."

Open the pod bay doors, Hal.

Bruce hesitated, considering the order. "Human interaction is consistent with procedures. Identify yourselves or I will take you into custody and summon security forces."

Maliha and Hound looked at each other. Hound gave a "why not?" shrug.

"We refuse to identify ourselves. Take us into custody," Maliha said.

A panel slid open below Bruce's mouth and Taser probes shot out, aimed at each of them. Maliha dodged hers but Hound was hit in the chest. He yelled and went down. The robot sensed that Maliha was still up and moving and one of its weapons unfolded and fired. The response had taken less than a second.

Yikes!

Maliha switched to Ageless speed and rammed into Bruce, attempting to put him off balance and send him over backward. Bruce was having none of that. A slit opened in his back, shooting out more spidery legs that caught him and levered him back into an upright position.

Hah! Try that again.

Maliha rammed into Bruce a second time, and when the stabilization legs came out, she lopped them off with her sword. Then she stabbed Bruce right in the middle of his smiling face.

Instead of sparking and smoking, Bruce was unaffected. A metal tentacle whipped out, wrapped around her legs, and brought her down to the floor right in front of the second arm. Now deployed, the arm looked like a flamethrower.

Maliha heard noises at the end of the hall. The summoned guards were on their way, and she was about to become flame broiled. She twisted away from the weapon moments before a stream of fire erupted from the nozzle.

Though aimed at her, the flames barely missed Hound, who was beginning to get to his feet.

"Stay down!" she shouted. Hound, no stranger to the smell or effects of napalm, threw himself flat, then began to inch forward toward the robot. "Don't move!"

Slicing with her sword through the tentacle holding her, Maliha was free. She leaped onto Bruce's back and tried to gain control of him, but found that he weighed much more than she'd thought and his center of gravity was low. She plunged her sword through the metal skin low on his back and yanked it sideways, nearly bisecting him. Then she switched to a vertical cut and pulled upward with all of her strength, slicing a two-foot-long path through his innards.

That's got to hit something important.

The flamethrower stopped spewing napalm and Bruce ceased his struggles under her grip. It reminded her of the old Japanese ritual *seppuku*, belly cutting, to commit suicide with honor. When a person showed bravery during the cutting, he would be mercifully dispatched by decapitation. If not, he died in slow anguish, holding his guts in his hands. She swung her sword a final time to complete the *seppuku*, slicing off Bruce's designated head portion, but leaving it hanging by a thin flap of metal. Leaving the head barely attached was the accomplishment of someone skilled with the sword, to keep the severed head from flying at the ritual's witnesses.

Napalm not only burns at more than 800 degrees, but it also consumes oxygen at a fast rate and produces carbon monoxide because of incomplete burning. The carbon monoxide level can be very high close to the source, especially in an enclosed area. Maliha and Hound struggled to breathe. If they became unconscious, they'd die, regardless of Maliha's victory over Bruce.

"Behind you!" Hound said. He was bent over almost double, choking, but managed to draw his tranq gun and fire down the hall.

Maliha turned and saw two guards go down, darts protruding from their chests. She drew and fired at the other two, and they joined their fellows on the floor. Maliha grabbed Hound's arm and tugged him down the hall, where the air hadn't been affected. After a short recovery, she ran back and collected all four ID cards from the unconscious guards.

"What are the chances no one else knows about us?" Hound said.

"Zero. Bruce blabbed and there must be more where these men came from. Let's hope one of these does the trick," she said, holding up the ID cards.

Back in the elevator, she tried inserting each guard's ID card. She went through three of them with no effect, but the last one lit up a small screen with the number three on it. She pressed it and the elevator car started moving. Maliha checked the time. It was a good thing they'd made fast progress earlier, because now they were behind by four minutes.

"We have to make up four minutes somehow," she said.

Hound nodded. "If we don't run into Bruce Two, we should be able to handle that."

"I killed my first robot."

"Don't get cocky. You never asked if I was okay from the Taser, you know."

"Are you?"

"Mostly. Every damned muscle hurts. That juice was set way too high."

The elevator came to a stop. Maliha and Hound took up positions on opposite sides of the door. When the door slid open, a robot named Wayne stood there on his spidery legs, resolutely blocking them.

"Identification . . ."

Hound moved forward and blasted the robot with automatic gunfire, raking the bullets up and down and across Wayne's cylindrical body. "Take that, you motherfucker!"

Wayne sparked, smoked, and died on the spot.

"I thought there might be one on each floor," Hound said. "Just a little revenge for that Taser. And the napalm. Bad memories."

The hallway looked just like the one on the sixth floor. Dim lighting, twin rows of doors. The nearest one was number 3463.

"We're close. Let's go." Maliha ran down the hallway. Hound could catch up while she opened the door.

She stopped in front of the door marked 3481 and blew away the lock with her S&W. There was no time to be subtle. Inside, she faced a startled nurse who'd come running at the sound—not the smartest move. Maliha tranquilized her. It was a relief to Maliha to see just a nurse. She'd been afraid she was going to encounter Elizabeth in this room.

Why isn't she here? This rescue must be a true surprise. If she'd suspected anything, she'd be here in person.

Moving further into the suite, she came upon Yanmeng.

The sight of him almost felled her. He was lying propped up in bed, connected to an IV, electrodes, and other equipment. He was breathing on his own, although there was a mechanical ventilator in the room. His eyes were closed and his face looked composed, as if he'd just settled down for a long winter's nap.

The rest of him was a different story. The two stumps bled through their dressings, a startling red contrast to the white sheets and white drawstring pants he wore. She wanted to comfort those wounds, but there was a difficult escape yet to go, one for which she was prepared to keep Yanmeng unconscious. If he became alert, pain would intrude on that peaceful face.

Hound came around the doorway into the room. She could see the sympathy in his face rapidly replaced by considerations of the escape. They had to make up time.

"Are you sure we can move him?" Hound said.

"Fine time to ask that."

"Then let's get those fucking tubes out of him."

"Hold on." Maliha injected a syringe from her pack into the connection hub of the IV tube. After a few seconds, she disconnected the tube from the bag and taped the tube to Yanmeng's arm.

"That's to keep him under until we get him to a doctor.

We can't keep jerking his brain around not knowing what the hell we're doing. Until then he's dead weight."

Hound nodded. His primary purpose on the mission was about to begin. The medic was going to carry another wounded man to safety. He pulled Yanmeng up into a seated position, then bent forward and picked him up in a fireman's carry. Hound's deformed body, with one shoulder lower than the other, made the position look precarious for Yanmeng.

"You okay with this?"

"Don't I look okay?" Hound said.

Maliha had nowhere to go from there. She couldn't carry Yanmeng and fight off security at the same time. She checked her watch. "On time."

She left the medical suite first and checked the hallway. Wayne was dead in front of the elevator and there was no sign of anyone else. The hall lighting was even dimmer, though, and she suspected a trap.

"Stay as close to the wall as you can. Move fast," she said. "We're expecting company in the hall or the elevator. Any slowdowns now and we'll miss the big bang."

"Gotcha."

She went out, gun drawn, Hound's automatic rifle slung over her shoulder. Hound moved rapidly toward the elevator, and she followed close behind him, running backward, watching their backs. It was up to Hound to spot anything coming at them from the front. About halfway to the elevator, one of the doors lining the hallway sprang open. From a darkened room, six guards ran out firing. They were so close to Maliha they couldn't miss. She took a bullet in the shoulder and another in her side.

"Go!" she yelled at Hound. He didn't need any encouragement.

Maliha pulled on the grip of her whip sword and snapped it into play as soon as it unwound from her waist. A twist of her wrist expertly separated the blades in midair and they bit into flesh, sawing two guards in half. With her other hand, she used her pistol to drop another two guards with

shots to the head. Whirling the whip sword around danger-
ously close to her body, she severed a man's head. The last
guard didn't like what he was seeing and took off running
down the hall. She planted a tranq dart in his back and he
toppled forward. Maliha ran after Hound, who was at the
elevator, punching the UP button frantically.

*That little bloodbath might catch Anu's attention. I hope
he's taking a nap. I don't need my scale slowing me down now.*

"Stairs?" he said when she arrived, dragging the bloody
whip sword behind her.

"I don't know a way off this floor without using the elevator. Stand away from the door."

*Too bad Amaro couldn't have gotten us plans for this
building. It would have saved some time and lives.*

Hound stepped away, planted his back against the wall,
and swiveled his head to check both ways in the hall. "Clear.
You're wounded."

The elevator door opened and Maliha snapped the whip
sword into the interior. Two heads rolled. "Get in!"

Hound went into the elevator car. "Damn, it's slippery in
here. What happened to kinder and gentler?"

"We get out any way we can. Any objections?"

"About damn time."

Maliha pushed the button for the top floor. She had to
kick one of the heads out of the way to let the door close.

During the brief ride, she felt Hound's eyes on her, trying
to evaluate her wounds. Two sources of fiery pain competed
in her body, left shoulder and right hip. She knew neither
of them was serious, but if they cut into her concentration,
they might as well be fatal. There was no time to meditate
to attempt to control the pain.

Her blood mingled with that of the guards on the floor
of the elevator car.

Been in worse before. Can't fail Yanmeng. And Hound.

The elevator opened on the top floor. Maliha was prepared for a robot, but none showed up.

Bad sign. They know where we're going.

She heard explosions from outside. The big bang had

started. The windows at the end of the hall lit up red and orange. All they had to do was get to the stairs to the roof.

Checking the hall, she didn't see any opposition, and that worried her. It was too easy. They were being channeled toward the stairs. A quick inspiration—she picked up one of the heads and hurled it down the hall in the direction away from the stairs, where she suspected guards were hiding. It worked. Startled, they showed themselves long enough to fill the hallway with rounds. Maliha, who'd ducked back into the elevator, waited until they stopped firing.

"You bring grenades?" she said.

"Damn straight." Hound turned his back to her. There were four grenades in holders on his belt. She took two of them.

Maliha changed the magazine in the automatic rifle and kept it slung within easy reach. With a grenade in each hand, she squeezed the striker levers and pulled out the safety pins with her teeth.

One, two, three.

Stepping out in the hall with Ageless speed, she threw the grenades toward the source of the gunfire, then laid down covering fire to keep the guards from retrieving the grenades and tossing them back at her.

The grenades exploded with a thunderous sound that reverberated in the confined space. With a kill radius of about fifteen feet each, they disposed of the guards at the end of the hall.

Anyone who isn't already dead is too busy dealing with frags to worry about us.

She edged her way out of the elevator and put Hound behind her, no longer worrying about an attack from that end of the hall. They reached the steel door to the roof stairway and found it full of bullet holes from the guards firing down the hall at Maliha.

A bonus. They cleared the stairway for us.

The door was locked, but the impact of the spray of bullets had almost knocked it off its hinges.

"Give me some room," Maliha said. She spun and delivered a powerful kick to the door. It fell into the stairway, on top of the bullet-riddled bodies of two guards. After checking that there was no one else in sight, she and Hound went in. She noticed that Hound's calf was bleeding.

"You take a bullet?"

"Just grazed," he said. "I'm okay."

Maliha considered taking Yanmeng from Hound to remove the extra weight on his leg, and letting him do the trail blazing instead. She rejected the idea and began moving up the stairs. She stepped out onto the roof and into the big bang in full swing. The mercenaries were delivering distraction in an attempt to keep all eyes focused on ground level. As she watched, a section of perimeter fence went up in a fireball and a couple of rocket-propelled grenades impacted the side of the building. Security forces on the ground had taken any available shelter and were firing in the direction of the attack. Their fire wasn't returned. It was all an elaborate and convincing show. The mercs weren't out to kill anybody, at least not on purpose.

The shock attack was only meant to last a few minutes. Maliha looked up expectantly. Right on time a helicopter appeared overhead. Down below, the mercenaries began firing machine guns aimed a few feet above the heads of the guards to discourage them from looking, or shooting, upward. Trailing down from the copter were two lines with bundles at the ends. Maliha ran to one of them and unfastened it. Opening the package, she called Hound over.

"This one has the double harness. It's yours."

She helped Hound get the harness on both himself and Yanmeng, so that Hound was hugging Yanmeng to his chest. She put on her own harness. This was to be a short-haul rescue. The copter was going up with them suspended below it from the ropes, and it would fly to a place where they could be safely delivered. They weren't going to be pulled aboard the copter. The short-haul was faster, and every second counted now.

She and Hound tugged on their ropes. The spotter watching them signaled the pilot to go. Maliha felt her feet lift off the roof and with a jerk of the harness, she was airborne.

We did it.

Looking down, she could see that guards were pouring onto the roof. The distraction gig was up. A spotlight caught her in its beam and she heard automatic fire.

Bullets shredded the rope holding her, and for a moment she was held by a few threads. Then, arms flailing, she tumbled downward, falling straight into the field of fire that the mercenaries were laying down. The copter rose higher and moved off into the night with her friends.

As she fell, pain stabbed her abdomen as her scale rebalanced, with figures moving to the lives saved side. Anu had judged her rescue of Yanmeng successful and a significant event, in spite of the casualty count.

Chapter Thirty-Five

A replantation team and a neurologist were standing by at the University of Chicago Medical Center. Amaro had taken Yanmeng's foot there, and all that was needed was Yanmeng.

He arrived by medical helicopter in stable condition although, gratefully, still unconscious. Hound was with him, and needed care, too. A couple of the bullets that had shot down Maliha were lodged in his legs, and one of them had chipped a bone, which would need a metal rod for support.

Hound, already a bit drowsy from the light pre-op sedation, was able to talk briefly with Amaro and Jake before going into surgery.

"She fell. I saw her. I couldn't do anything about it. What about Jill's son?"

"He's okay. I got to him just in time. Did Maliha fall inside the compound?" Jake said.

"Yes. We were barely off the roof. She could have even hit the side of the building on the way down. I loved her, I loved her, I can't believe this happened . . ." Hound's eyes overflowed with tears. His voice was so choked up he couldn't continue.

Amaro put his hand on Hound's arm. "You brought Yanmeng home. She would have been happy about that. They were so close. Yanmeng could try to remote view her, but he's already in surgery, and he's going to be there for about twelve hours."

"You guys are talking about Maliha in the past tense. What's the matter with you?" Jake said. "She's not dead for certain."

Hound looked at him as though Jake were crazy. "She fell five stories into the path of gunfire. You're saying Maliha can survive that?"

Jake's pain showed on his face, even though he was trying to be the voice of reason. "Depends on what gets damaged and how fast she can repair it. I'd be up and walking around in five minutes."

"Dammit, she's not *you*!" Amaro said. "She's human! Not some heartless freak like you!"

Jake lowered his eyes to the floor. A nurse headed in their direction to kick them out.

"I . . . shouldn't have said that," Amaro said. "I'm just really upset, you know."

"You can stay here and moan about it all you want," Jake said. "I'm leaving to go look for Maliha. I don't give up that easily." He walked away before he could be ordered to go.

The nurse came up. She said, "You'll have to go out into the waiting area now."

Amaro stood up and squeezed Hound's arm. "See you later."

Hound, left alone, gave in to the sadness and disappointment he felt. If he'd been alone instead of carrying Yanmeng, he might have cut his own rope and gone after her.

Idiot. You'd just smash your own head open on the ground like a ripe cantaloupe. Did she even have a chance? She said she could bleed out if she was unconscious and couldn't stop the bleeding. Oh God, she's dead. She might as well have just let me lie there and die in that field in Nam for all the good I've done her.

He closed his eyes. The next time he opened them, he was in the recovery room, woozy and in pain. A brief stay in intensive care melted away most of the pain and he awoke several floors up to a private room, where Amaro waited in a chair.

"Hiya, kid," Hound said, and fell asleep.

Chapter Thirty-Six

Maliha awoke from surgery, but kept her eyes closed as she listened to her surroundings. When she was sure she wasn't in hell, she opened her eyes as narrow slits to take in more information. She was in a windowless room, glass on all sides, filled with monitoring equipment managed remotely by several medical personnel outside her glass box. She was either inside the compound on the hidden third floor or had been whisked away to a different secret facility while sedated. Judging by the military uniforms on the doctors and nurses clustered outside, she was in the hands of the Department of Defense. She closed her eyes.

A nightmare come true. Alien Autopsy, here I come.

She took stock of her physical condition and found that she was in better shape than seemed possible.

No broken bones, no internal bleeding, bullets are gone. I feel pretty damn good for a woman who dropped sixty or seventy feet. Or I never hit the ground in the first place. Hound! Yanmeng! Did they escape?

Her eyes flew open and her arms jerked in distress when she thought about her friends, only to find that she was fastened down with leather straps.

A doctor came in. "She's awake," he said. After checking her vitals, he elevated the head of her bed slowly, so she could see around better. "Sorry about the straps. I hope we'll be able to get those off you soon. What's your name?"

She shook her head and felt dizzy.

"The dizziness will wear off fast." He adjusted the flow of the drug piggybacked on her IV. "Glad to see you awake. I'm Dr. Terry Seeton. You can call me Terry."

"How long have I been out?" Her mouth was dry and it was difficult to speak. Terry fed her ice with a spoon, and she melted the cubes in her mouth.

"Better," she said. "Thanks, Terry."

"You came into our care two days ago."

Couldn't have hit the ground, then. I wouldn't be this far along in healing. I might even have been killed.

"Now it's your turn," he said. "What's your name?"

Maliha tried to remember one of the fake identities Amaro had created for her, but her head was throbbing, and it didn't matter anyway. She wasn't wearing the fingerprints that went with the fake identity.

"Lola Carson." It was the first name that came to mind.

"Lola, how long have you known about your special healing ability?"

"Did my companions make it away from the building?" she said.

"I'm not authorized to tell you anything about that," Terry said. Then he winked.

Did he just tell me Hound and Yanmeng got away? Or is it a trick to make me talk?

"The last I knew I was falling from the roof of a building," Maliha said, lying a bit. "Why didn't I hit the ground?"

"We have robots here for numerous purposes. One purpose is fire safety. I don't know for certain, but I'd guess you were caught by a fire-safety robot."

"Caught?"

"In some kind of net or cushioning device. I know they were designed after unfortunate people jumped or fell from the windows of the World Trade Center towers on 9/11. Judging from your initial injuries, I'd say you didn't hit the ground."

She started to ask another question and he held up his hand. "That's all I know about it. Really. Now about your healing. We can learn so much from you. We're going to have questions about that. It would be best for you if you answered."

"What happens if I don't?" Maliha said.

"Not a good thing, Lola. As soon as I verify that you're healthy enough for interrogation, you'll be removed from my care. You're opening yourself up to be hurt very badly—over and over, since you'll recover."

Kinda what I thought.

"Then I should talk to you. Right now, I'm tired. Can we continue this after I get some rest?"

Terry hesitated. "Of course. If you need anything, just press the button." He dimmed the lights in the room and left. Outside the glass room, the lights also dimmed.

Maliha wasn't ready to sleep yet. She wanted time to figure out what to do. Her best opportunity for escape was while she was still being treated nicely on the assumption she was going to talk.

Suddenly she noticed that the brand on her left shoulder, the *shou* symbol of Master Liu's school, was growing hot. She was Ageless at the time she'd been branded, but her skin didn't heal. It had been there hundreds of years as a reminder of her pledge to Master Liu.

I swear to honor you as my grandfather, to do nothing to bring shame to you or the school, and to never stray from the teachings of this school.

Maliha pulled her hospital gown away from her shoulder as flames began to flicker along the outlines of the brand.

He's coming! How could he be here in this locked glass box?

A glowing shape shimmered into view, hovering over the foot of her bed. It focused into the form of Master Liu, in his young persona instead of as a blind old man, as he usually showed himself. Bare-chested, his long black hair streaming over his muscular shoulders, he wore loose white pants and was in a lotus position. He floated about a foot above her bed.

Master Liu's eyes lit up with golden light, and a beam of it pinned Maliha to her bed. A tingling sensation swept through her body. She felt there was nothing she could hide from him, so she took a deep breath and gave herself over to the warmth of the glow.

"Daughter," he said, "I have made your body whole."

I hope I'm wearing clean underwear.

Master Liu smiled. "You are."

"You read my thoughts?"

"Unless you take care to guard them."

She bowed her head to him. Pain had vanished from her wounds, and well-being thrummed in her blood.

What? He can heal me now, from the outside? Wait a minute . . .

"Are you here, Master, or am I dreaming?"

"I'm here with you."

Maliha looked at the medical staff. No one seemed alarmed or even curious.

"Don't worry about the others," he said. "Their minds are occupied."

"Your powers have grown."

"True, but not so much as you might think. It's your perception that is changing."

"Will you help me escape?"

"I play only this small part, but your rescue will come from another source. I'm here concerning other things. Yanmeng and Hound are safe."

Maliha's eyes closed and her head drooped toward her chest. "I'm content, then."

"Fool yourself if you wish. I see your heart clearly."

Good job. Offend the super-powerful being.

"This visit is not about me. I'm here to talk about two things. The first is Countess Báthory, Elizabeth. I did not train her."

"I thought you trained all the Ageless."

"I work with all who are sent to me. She came, but after a short time I turned her away. Her evil was like a black poison in my school. She was affecting other students. I paid a price for it."

Master Liu's form went out of focus for a moment and was

replaced by the old blind man. Across his chest were horrible scars that looked like the claw tracks of a tiger or some other large cat. They were raw and oozing blood, as though they'd just been inflicted. Elizabeth would have been in training about four hundred years ago. Master Liu had endured his punishment for sending her away for all that time.

"I've never seen those scars before."

Master Liu was a young man again. "I've never had reason to show them to you. Elizabeth is vain. Slash her face in a fight and it will distract her. I have observed her style. Don't let her get you down on the ground, or you won't be getting up."

Maliha inclined her head respectfully. "Thank you for these observations. Are you saying that I will definitely fight Elizabeth?"

"I don't see the future."

"You told me that I will be rescued by someone else."

"No precognition involved. I set up the rescue. You need to leave this building to do your part. The next thing I want to talk about is Jake."

Maliha's whole body tensed. She'd asked Master Liu a question the last time she saw him: *Why didn't Jake bear the symbol of his school?* Master Liu said at the time that Jake hadn't taken the pledge of loyalty that Maliha took.

"Why didn't he take the pledge?" She waited nervously for the answer.

Master Liu hesitated, then came to a decision. "Jake has a flaw. He will continue to kill."

"He explained to me about his moral code. Is that what you mean?"

"There is no moral code, daughter."

"You mean—"

"There are certain people, Ageless and human, in this world who love to kill. Elizabeth is one. Jake is another."

"Jake is like Elizabeth? But . . . I felt a breakthrough with him, real love. How could I love him?"

"What you felt is the opening of your heart to love. Jake just happened to be there."

Maliha tried to take it all in. "Did Jake kill Abiyram Heber in Tel Aviv?"

Master Liu nodded.

Then that story Jake told me about Abiyram being the evil one—all lies.

"Are my team members in danger from him?"

"Eventually. He will grow bored with them—and you. Immediate danger, surely not. He needs to continue a good relationship with them to keep your affection, and he's a long way from growing tired of you. But if you reveal to him what I've told you, I can't predict what he'll do. My advice would be to keep quiet until you have time to think about everything, including the safety of your friends. The worst thing you can do is confront him now, in anger."

Okay, I've thought about it long enough. I'm going to chop him into tiny bits. Lucius was gone and I wanted to believe Jake. He even made that remark about letting me go back to Lucius if Lucius somehow survived. Jake knew how that would affect me. It was all a ploy, a game to him.

Tears slid down Maliha's cheeks. "Why do you tell me this now when you refused earlier?" Maliha said.

"I have come to understand that our lives are linked, but in ways that I don't understand yet," he said. "The mortal path is hard, daughter, and you have stumbled into a trap along the way." He reached out and touched her face gently. "The Ageless can be deceptive, as you know, and rarely do they truly care for humans. You were an exception and it drove you to become rogue. Lucius is another and proved it by giving his Ageless life for you."

"What are you, then, Master?"

"A simple priest of Anu, god of the heavens and he who sits in judgment. Get some rest now."

His presence began to fade and was soon gone. The heat dissipated from the brand on Maliha's shoulder and her eyelids grew heavy.

I have trusted Master Liu with my life. Do I trust him now with the truth?

* * *

Maliha awoke several hours later, feeling rested and with a plan in mind. Master Liu had told her she had to get out of the building. She was about to alienate Dr. Terry, even though he was doing his best to stay on her good side. He'd ordered that she could be unstrapped from the bed to use the bathroom, as long as there was a guard in the room.

No one's briefed him on what I can really do, beyond what he's seen with his own eyes. "Need to know" screws up again.

He examined her and shook his head in amazement. "Astounding. You've made a giant leap in recovery. What is your pain level, one to ten?"

"Why should I tell you?"

"I explained that. The minute you leave here, you'll be subjected to rough interrogation. You can only stay as long as you cooperate."

"You'd love to have me all to yourself, wouldn't you? Nobel Prize, here we come."

Terry blushed and she knew she had him. He wanted to claim exclusive rights to the secret of her rapid healing—he didn't know about her long life yet—and make the grandest discovery in medicine since DNA.

"I have only altruistic motives," Terry said. "Imagine what the world can learn from you. If I can replicate the process, millions can be saved from disease and death."

"Haven't you figured out you work for the Department of Defense?" Maliha said. "Do you think they're going to be eager to share your great discovery? Not likely. What they want it for is to heal soldiers rapidly so they can send them back into battle. Over and over, like what you said would happen to me in interrogation."

"Don't be ridiculous. This is a chance to advance medicine decades into the future, maybe more," he said.

"With you getting all the credit. What do you think is going to happen to me? Whether you study me, or someone else in the DOD does, there will come a time of experimentation. 'Let's hurt her under controlled circumstances so we can have precise measurements.' Tell me you haven't thought of that down the road."

Terry was silent.

"What happens after experimentation? Dissection of the subject," Maliha said. "I think I'd rather deal with people who know what they want and have no illusions about how to get it, than with you and your sweet tongue."

"Really, Lola. You're letting your imagination get the best of you." He picked up a notepad and pen. "Let's talk about your medical history. When is the first time you noticed you were able to heal rapidly?"

"Okay. I was about twenty when I noticed that a side effect of rapid healing was extreme horniness."

Exasperated, Terry set down his pen. "You're not taking this seriously!"

"I have no intention of talking to you about my 'medical situation,' as you call it. Not now, not ever. No Nobel Prize for you, sorry. I'll take my chances with the torturers."

"I'll give you a shot of XP–110, our latest truth drug. You'll talk."

"So you do believe in torture. Anyway, truth drugs do nothing to me. My metabolism of barbiturates is different."

"Oh? How? Spell it out for me. "

"Different. D–i–f–f–e–r–e–n–t."

Terry grabbed his notepad and left the room, looking crestfallen. An hour later, a phlebotomist entered and drew vial after vial of Maliha's blood. It looked like when Terry had nothing solid to report, his project was being yanked from him and all he could do was keep some blood to study.

"Trying to drain me dry?" Maliha said.

The phlebotomist was in no mood to joke.

Jake sought out the mercenary team for a firsthand account. He came with money and with an intimate knowledge of the mission, and with news of what had happened to Hound. There was a little lack of trust to get over—he wasn't the one who hired them—but Jake was comfortable with these men. They recognized one of their own.

"You lose any men?" Jake said.

Bear nodded. He was their leader, and he'd come by his nickname honestly. "One. Three wounded. Not a bad mission except for the surprise ending."

"Tell me about it."

"Strangest thing I've ever seen and I've seen some unholy crap. We were laying down cover fire while the helicopter took off for the short haul. Some motherfucker on the roof got off some rounds before we landed an RPG in his lap. If he'd kept on firing, he would've taken down both of them. The woman's rope broke. We stopped firing and they did too. Man, it was a bad sight. She was lit up by the floodlights and dropping like a stone. I think we were all holding our breath. I signaled our two fastest men. They were going to run out and get her, what was left of her anyway."

Bear shook his head. "Fuck, I don't like female casualties, especially ones that aren't fighting back, like her. Just falling."

"Then the damnedest thing happened. These things—robots—came running out from the building. They caught her."

"What do you mean, caught? She didn't hit the ground?"

"They had this net between them and they scooped her up like soup in a ladle. You had to see it. We couldn't shoot at them—afraid we'd kill the woman. She was taken into that building. You planning to snatch her out of there, my men are ready to go. Half price. We're all fucking mad they stole her."

"I don't plan on letting those bastards keep her," Jake said.

A group of guards came in and transferred Maliha from the bed to a rolling gurney. She was strapped in solidly, with six parallel straps and separate ones for her wrists and ankles. She felt like Hannibal Lecter, minus the mask. She was loaded into a medical transport van with two armed guards riding in the rear with her and another up front with the driver. After that, she couldn't see anything from the windowless van, but assumed she was being taken to some secure, secret facility where she would vanish from the face of the Earth.

I hope Master Liu was right about a planned escape. If not, I just cranked up the pain and torture by being unco-operative.

A half hour into the trip, there was a commotion outside of tires squealing on the road and an abrupt halt for the van. Then gunfire erupted, and a few bullet holes opened up in the side of the van. The guards were trying to communicate with someone on the outside.

The van started moving again. It seemed like the escape had failed. Suddenly a fist burst through the top of the van.

"You okay?" It was Jake's voice. She'd almost expected Elizabeth to be her rescuer, so that Maliha could complete her mission of assassinating President Millhouse.

"Yes. Tied down," she shouted over the noise the guards were making.

"Hang on."

The guards shot at the hole he'd made and then sprayed the entire roof with rounds. Maliha felt the van start to tilt, then it was in the air, rolling and bouncing down a hillside. Maliha, strapped in the latched-down gurney, was secure. The guards, free to move, rolled around like clothing in a dryer. They screamed at first, until the van became streaked with blood.

The van shuddered to rest on its side against something hard, trees or large rocks. Maliha was dizzy, bruised, and splashed with blood, but not seriously hurt. Jake appeared again at the hole in the roof, and enlarged it with his hands. When it was big enough, he slipped inside and unfastened Maliha.

"Some ride, huh?" he said.

It was hard to let him put his hands on her, but she kept reminding herself that Master Liu said it wasn't the right time for confrontation. Besides, though her first reaction had been to believe Master Liu, she should think more about it before assuming the worst about Jake. She plastered a smile on her face.

"About time you got here," she said.

"Are you all right to move?"

"I'm banged up a little. Bruises from the straps, but I can walk."

He lifted her away from the interior wreckage and pushed her toward the hole. She got out under her own power. They walked back up the hill to the road. She was shocked to see that the van had had an escort of four security cars, two in front and two in back, and they were all devastated. The cars were still in flames and there were some body parts visible on the ground.

Rocket-propelled grenades. Effective but overkill. Or am I just being critical because it's Jake?

"Let's get you home," he said. "I'll take care of you."

Even coming from Jake, it sounded wonderful.

Chapter Thirty-Seven

$\mathcal{E}$verything digital about you in the DOD files has been destroyed," Amaro said, "including the blood test results and DNA findings. The problem is, there can be paper copies, plus the original physical samples still exist and can be retested. Now I've set it up so that those results will be automatically erased whenever they're reentered. But eventually they'll find the code that's doing the monitoring and erasing, and remove it. In the meantime, paper copies can shoot all over the world."

"Meaning I'll be in a DNA database," Maliha said.

"Nope," said Amaro. "Well, you will. Entry into the database is accurate, but once entered, no one goes back to check against source material. I can slip in, alter your record, and cover my tracks. So any genetic material you leave at a scene won't come up as a match."

"I don't know what identifiable weird stuff will show up in my blood," Maliha said. "It's about time I knew, though. I have a place I can find out."

Maliha made plans to transfer both Hound and Yanmeng to the Clinique des Montagnes, a private medical clinic located in a valley in the Swiss Alps. Ringed with snowcapped mountains, the valley was serene, a perfect place to recover, with mountain views from every window. Patients were the wealthy of the world seeking privacy, security, and outstanding medical care—those who, if they even had them, could afford to leave their insurance cards at home. An application in advance established that someone could afford the exclusive Clinique des Montagnes. Maliha, under her "Marsha Winters" pen name, had carte blanche at the clinic.

Her private physician there was Dr. Ryman Corvernis. She supported his expensive research laboratory solo, plus she had some information on a family scandal that the doctor was desperate to keep hidden. He was in her pocket, and treated her with no questions asked about her rapid healing or how she acquired the wounds she brought to his care. When she expanded the care to include her team members, he didn't object.

It isn't secure against a concerted attack by Elizabeth, but I have something in mind for that.

She phoned the clinic and asked for admissions. After identifying herself, she said that she had four people who needed a pickup.

"Two are patients. Xia Yanmeng, reattached foot, other amputations, recent induced coma. Hound, recent pinned bone. One is Mr. Xia's wife, Eliu. The fourth is a . . . bodyguard, Jake Stackman. Do you have a four-bedroom medical suite so they can all stay together?"

"Yes. One is now reserved in your name. Current location or locations?"

"They'll all be at the University of Chicago Medical Center. I'm requesting fully secure medical transportation."

"We'll take care of it, Ms. Winters. Your physician is Dr. Corvernis. Do you want him to treat these patients?"

"Yes, though Mr. Xia will need specialists."

"Understood. Dr. Corvernis will assemble a treatment team. Will you be joining us as a guest?"

"Not at this time."

"Secure medical pickup for four scheduled in one hour, helicopter at the University of Chicago Medical Center to O'Hare International Airport, departure by private jet to Switzerland. Have passports available. The Clinique des Montagnes is pleased to be of service to you and your associates."

What a relief to be making these *plans instead of planning a funeral. The clinic was the easy part. Now for the tough task.*

She told Amaro to search out the passports for those traveling. They all carried passports at all times, so he would find them in Maliha's condo. Another contact, this time to Mickey Deer, and the only thing she had left to do was the task she'd been postponing.

She called Jake.

Her timing was perfect. He was already in the lobby of her building, getting on the elevator on his way up to her condo. She hung up and waited for him to arrive. The doorbell rang. She was prepared for a conversation that could go almost anywhere, and armed for it, too.

Could Jake possibly know that Master Liu has talked to me? I don't see how. From what Master told me, Jake is a sociopath who uses people for his own purposes and then disposes of them. Elizabeth is an open book compared to Jake. If it's all true. Master Liu might have his own reasons for wanting Jake out of the way. He did say our lives were linked somehow and wouldn't explain. Bride of Liu?

When she opened the door, Jake stood there with a smile on his handsome face. He moved inside the condo and took her into his arms. She pretended she was happy to see him. His embrace was so warm, it wasn't hard to pretend.

"Hey, what's with the weapons? Expecting Jack the Ripper?" he said.

Odd choice of words.

"I just don't feel secure with Elizabeth at large," Maliha said, "and mad at me for taking Yanmeng away from her."

"I have a better chance at fending off an attack by Elizabeth. How about I move in with you?"

Gulp.

"Uh . . ."

"Or let me take you away from all this. I can keep you safe."

Maliha blinked. *Have to admit that sounds great.*

He put his hands on her hips, drew her close, and put

his strong arms around her. She rested her head against his shoulder.

This feels so right. Maybe. . .

Jake whispered, "I love you. Marry me. I can make you very happy."

She jerked her head away. "Oh . . . Jake . . ."

"Say yes. Please say yes."

There was white noise buzzing in her head and she felt a bit dizzy. He led her to a couch and put his arm around her waist.

"Is that a yes?"

"No . . . I mean, I'm in the middle of something I have to finish. Can we talk about this later?"

Disappointment flashed in his eyes, so fast she almost missed it. Then he kissed her on the cheek. "Of course. Later. Is there anything I can do now?"

His response was so gracious that she felt guilty putting him off, but she needed more time to think and couldn't do it while planning her encounter with the president.

"I'm leaving the country in a little while," she said. "I would appreciate it if you could keep Yanmeng safe from being kidnapped again."

"Oh lovely one, you know I'm here to help. I'd be happy to do that. What hospital is he in?"

"He's at U of C Medical Center. I'm sending him to the Clinique des Montagnes. Do you know it?"

"Switzerland?" he said.

"Yes."

"Never been there, but I've heard of it."

"The clinic is picking up Hound, Yanmeng, and Eliu at the hospital. I'd like you to go with them. It would make me feel so much better knowing you're there to protect them."

"Are you coming?"

"No, I have to finish Elizabeth's demands," she said.

"Why? You have Yanmeng back. Screw Elizabeth."

"That sounds good to me and I'd do it, except for one thing. Didn't I explain Project Hammer to you?"

"Apparently not well enough."

Maliha went over in detail the plot to replace President Millhouse with Vice President Cameron, the deep plants of the New Founders organization in American politics, and what the goals of the New Founders were.

"Damn. They're doing the demons' jobs for them, or trying to. I understand why you need to see this through. Are you planning to kill Cameron?"

"If he's there, which I doubt, and if I get the chance," Maliha said. "Mainly I'm there to make sure the presidential assassination doesn't happen. Last time there was a backup. I can't see that this time would be any different."

"Think you can find the other deep plants after Cameron's out of the way?" he said.

"Not sure. Abiyram would have been good for that," she said.

Shit. Open mouth, insert both feet.

Jake said, "I guess he was a damn good agent, in his time."

Jets scrambling. Prepare for battle.

Maliha was nervous that she'd mentioned Abiyram. Jake had glossed it over, but there was no telling what connections he was making in his mind.

Whoa! Is it too dangerous to send him with the team?

Her thoughts raced. She had nothing but what Master Liu had said to go on, that Jake was using her team to keep her, and that he wasn't through with her yet.

The more interested in me he stays the better. Time for some manipulation of my own.

She put her arms around him and rested her head against his chest. "I've missed you so much." Using her body to protect her friends didn't even ring a muted alarm bell.

"I love you, Maliha," he said.

"You don't have to be at the hospital for another forty-five minutes," she said.

He caressed her hair. "You okay? Green light?"

"Burning bright."

He swept her up in his arms and headed for the bedroom.

Chapter Thirty-Eight

Maliha slept aboard her private jet on the way to Wellington, New Zealand. President Millhouse was making the same trip on Air Force One. His journey would be shorter, due to the longer flying range of Air Force One and its ability to refuel in flight, a luxury not shared by Maliha's much smaller Cessna Citation XLS+.

The Citation's range was about 2,100 miles, meaning it had to refuel three times en route for the 8,000-mile-plus trip. With nineteen hours of flight time, Maliha needed refreshed pilots and copilots, since one crew couldn't go the distance. All of that was handled smoothly for her, so she could sleep through refueling and piloting shifts.

Mickey Deer was on board, and she talked with him about her background. Everything this time, including her age, her past occupation, and her current goals. He asked a few questions for clarification, but overall absorbed it well.

"I've believed in the supernatural for a long time," he said, "ever since I saw my father's ghost right after he died. I'm open to the fact that we don't know everything. That there's a larger world out there."

I've experienced the last minutes of hundreds of lives and allowed their spirits to move on whole instead of fragmented and trapped. So Mickey sees a ghost? Why not?

"I believe you," she said. "I've seen a few ghosts over the centuries."

"You don't think I'm a freak or something?"

You're asking me *that?*

"No."

"Good. I don't think you're a freak either."

Glad that's settled.

"Listen, I need to get some rest," Maliha said. "Feel free to explore the plane. There's a food-prep area forward, and a very nice bathroom aft. Ask the cockpit crew if you have any questions."

"Sure." He stared at her.

She settled in for some sleep but had the feeling she was being watched. Her eyes popped open and there he was, still staring at her.

"Uh, Mickey, I look totally normal when I'm asleep."

"Yeah, sorry."

Mickey sat in a recliner and started reading a book, glancing at her every now and then. He didn't seem to know what to do, but Maliha was sure that would wear off. He'd just never shared quarters with a three-hundred-year-old woman before. She used the time to get some deep rest and meditation, figuring that she was going to need to be in the best shape she could manage.

Maliha awoke in the last leg of the journey, looking out at puffy clouds over the Tasman Sea, between Australia and New Zealand. Famished, she went to the galley and checked out the available food. She had a large selection, but most of it had to be microwaved, so that took some of the fun out of dining. She went for pasta with mushrooms and sun-dried tomatoes. Pleased to find some fresh Italian bread, she poured some olive oil in a dish á la California for dipping.

She sat at a small conference table to eat and work on her laptop, going over the notes Amaro had sent about the Wellington venue with Mickey. She valued his expertise in sniper detection, although she wasn't ready to give him a weapon to do anything about it.

"Have you eaten yet?" she said.

"I had toast and eggs, but what you're having smells good."

She offered him some bread and they shared the dip.

The president was speaking outdoors in the Civic Square. It looked like a nightmare from a security standpoint, with flowing foot traffic, multiple points of access, and multi-story buildings on the perimeter. She looked at photos from various angles and the two of them tried to figure out where a sniper would choose as an ideal location.

"Not working," Mickey said as he put down the photos. "I have to be right in the location. See where the sun is, which way the wind's blowing, where the shadows are. Wind is going to be a significant contributor here, with the site so close to the water and this City to Sea Bridge." He tapped one of the pictures. "Going to make that space between the buildings like a wind tunnel, almost. Well, from a sniper's standpoint."

"So we have to wing it," Maliha said.

"Yup. One thing for certain, the security snipers are going to be ringed fairly close around the speakers' dais. They're not planning to shoot each other at rooftop height, just down into the square. All the nearby roofs will be inspected beforehand and the snipers planted. Then they'll use aerial surveillance to make sure no one unauthorized pops up on a roof. That means our guy has to be far away, yet with a line of sight and able to compensate for the wind and other conditions. He could be a mile and a quarter out, or a little more, and it would take quite a marksman."

"Could you make that shot, Mickey?"

"If I was having a good day and had that CheyTac Intervention system in that case over there. Depends a lot on the wind, since the city's known as Windy Wellington. The sniper could have to move in much closer than that. What about alerting the Secret Service or the New Zealand government to widen the perimeter for their surveillance?" Mickey said.

"I've thought about it. The only problem is that it will hinder our own movements. We'd have to pull out and trust that security can handle it. With a basic assassination plan, I'd probably take that chance. With someone like Elizabeth involved, I don't think we can leave everything to government security."

"I see your point. You don't mind me asking all these questions, do you?"

At one point, I would have.

"No. We're dealing with lives here. It's good to look at everything about an operation, including our motivation for being involved."

The pilot interrupted with an announcement. "Two hours out. Good weather and smooth flying ahead. Any change of plans?"

Maliha pressed an intercom button. "No change. Thanks for the update."

"Speaking of change of plans," Mickey said, "I know you have a sniper system on board. You told me to feel free to poke around while you were asleep, and I did. Are you sure you don't want me as a shooter?"

Something could be off here. This man might even be Elizabeth's backup sniper. Not that he's a bad guy, but if she's got his balls squeezed about something . . . Put him up on a roof and he might shoot Millhouse, and I wouldn't be able to do anything about it from where I am in the square. Sounds like Elizabeth's brand of irony. The fact that Hound knows Mickey means nothing if Mickey's being blackmailed.

"Let's stick to the plan. If you can spot a sniper who's suspect, I can take care of him."

Mickey shrugged. "Okay. Just trying to pull my weight."

"I'm going to get in some more sleep before we land." Maliha left him sitting at the conference table. She slept lightly this time, a warrior's sleep from which she could instantly awake. Since it occurred to her that Mickey might be working for Elizabeth, Maliha didn't want to give him any opportunities to scrub the mission before it started.

She checked his aura again and found it as before, clear and inspiring.

Does Elizabeth have a shield of some kind that can cast a false aura? Getting paranoid in my old age. He's already had chances to attack me and hasn't taken advantage of them.

New Zealand from the air looked as though someone had placed a green carpet over both islands. A lumpy one, because of the highland areas poking up underneath. South Island had a snowcapped mountain range running slightly off center, like a spine. The serene appearance covered disaster lurking underneath. New Zealand was part of the Pacific Ring of Fire. Lately, major earthquakes somewhere in the country had been regular events, including devastating ones in Christchurch, on South Island, two years in a row. Wellington had a major fault line running right through it.

Wellington was perched on the southern tip of North Island, surrounded by hills and the water of its attractive harbor. Spiraling down toward the airport, the jet took them over the harbor and the central business district—the CBD—where Civic Square was located.

Peering out the window, Mickey said, "I thought so. Wind tunnel. Look at those flags whipping around."

"Would the sniper give up or move closer?"

"Might have to move closer and stay off the roof. It might be an easier shot from a window if the location's sheltered from the wind, like in one of those right-angle corners of the buildings. Moving closer and inside is good for us."

Two hours later, Maliha had rented a car under a false name and they had checked into a hotel several miles away from the square, traveling as a married couple. Mickey actually blushed.

They spent some time checking out their equipment, including the wireless transmitters they were going to use to keep in touch. It was 4 P.M. and the speech was three hours away.

"Time to get down to the square," Maliha said. She drove them to within a mile of Civic Square and then they both got out to walk.

"Good luck," Mickey said, and left heading south, a

roundabout way he wanted to take to check the outskirts for good firing positions.

A gust of wind blew Maliha's hair in front of her face. Clouds were moving rapidly across the sky and it looked like rain could develop later in the evening. It was summer in Wellington, so heavy clothing to conceal weapons would only call attention to her. She'd ended up with a knock-off of a police uniform, dark blue pants, a light blue short-sleeve blouse, and a dark blue stab-resistant vest. The hat with the shiny black brim—*reminds me of Arnie*—gave her a bit of disguise, since the brim shaded most of her face. She had the rank insignia of a senior constable. Her duty belt had a few surprises that were nonstandard—including the fact that it covered her whip sword—and she carried a gear bag with, among other things, a sword.

Maliha made her way to the back entrance of one of the buildings that faced Civic Square. It was Sunday, and although the cafés and shops were bustling in the CBD, the office buildings were sparsely filled, mostly with security personnel. There were police patrolling the perimeter streets, but because off-duty officers were contributing as additional security, the police were seeing a lot of unfamiliar faces on law enforcement personnel. She fit right into a scenario like that. She picked a lock at a loading dock entrance and went inside. The building had little interior lighting, only security lighting in halls and specific rooms. She imagined Elizabeth and a sniper or two doing the same thing she'd just done.

The buildings had already been swept for weapons and bombs, and would be swept again closer to the time of the president's appearance. To compound the problem, there was underground parking beneath the square. The entrance had been closed the day before, but there were cars remaining inside that needed to be checked thoroughly.

I would not want to be location manager for security here.

Maliha wouldn't be inside any of the buildings when the last-minute sweep took place, unless Mickey had pointed out a target. Maliha walked out the front door and blended into the gathering crowd in the square. She still had an hour to go, but local politicians were already speaking from the dais, not wanting to miss the opportunity to address a crowd. She glanced up. Sunset wasn't until about 9 P.M. There was plenty of sunlight left, and she was worried that glare from the windows would prevent Mickey from spotting any snipers.

He's the expert, go with it. Besides, he has thermal imaging binoculars and he'll be looking for hot spots near windows. He was right about the wind here—unpredictable, with some strong gusts.

Maliha froze. She'd just caught a glimpse of Elizabeth across the square, coming down some steps near a sculpture. She wasn't wearing any visible weapons.

Go after her now?

As she watched, from one instant to the next, Elizabeth disappeared. Maliha knew she'd taken off running at Ageless speed.

She could be coming right at me.

Maliha let her eyes relax into aura viewing. It was tough to do in crowds. Auras overlapped, wavered, and some shone brightly among the others, distracting her. She forced herself to focus on only one thing: the black smear left behind by an Ageless moving at speed.

There she is!

Maliha pulled a knife from her vest pocket and concealed it in her hand. If Elizabeth kept on course, Maliha could slash her as she went by. Elizabeth came closer. She was going to brush past Maliha to let her know she was there, watching and judging Maliha's performance. Maliha raised her left arm to a 45 degree angle, the height of Elizabeth's thigh. As Elizabeth passed, a streak of blood formed in the air and held suspended there for a fraction of a second. Maliha immediately kicked out her leg and extracted the blood from the air, letting it fall along the length of her dark blue pants rather than hit the ground. She whisked the bloody knife into concealment.

First blood, Maliha.

Elizabeth's minor leg wound was probably already healed. It wasn't intended to be disabling, just enough to serve notice that Maliha had claws too. She didn't expect any retaliation from Elizabeth.

It's part of the game to her.

She looked around to see if anyone had observed her peculiar action of suddenly kicking her leg into the air. A girl about nine years old, bored with the speeches, was staring at her and tugging on her mother's shirt to get her to look at Maliha. Maliha pointed at her, then at herself and smiled a wide grin. Then she did a handstand and walked a few steps on her hands. The girl was giggling. Maliha drifted away, leaving the girl trying to do a handstand against her mother's back. By the time Maliha tried to detect the black smear of the moving Ageless aura again, she couldn't find it.

Her earpiece came alive with Mickey's voice. "Target sighted."

"Where?"

"Can you see the metal fern ball from where you are?"

There was a sculpture of silver fern leaves suspended in the square, over forty feet up in the air.

"Yes."

"Move toward it."

"Moving. Where are you?"

"Second floor of the City Gallery," Mickey said. "Very nice in here."

"What am I looking for?"

"The Town Hall building. Tan and brown with columns built into the front. Third floor, last window on the left as you face the building."

"Got it." There was a shadow visible in the window.

Maliha slung her gear bag over her shoulder and raced toward the building. She found a side entrance out of view of the crowd, but guarded by two Wellington constables. She walked up to them and asked to check that the door was locked. When they turned their backs on her, she kicked one of them into the side of the building, dropping him unconscious. The other spun around to confront her. She punched him in the stomach, and when he bent over, she kicked his chin, sending him back against the building. He hit his head and slumped down the wall, leaving a blood stripe on the surface. She checked his pulse. He was alive. The scalp wound was superficial. She opened the door and dragged both of them inside. There was a utility room nearby so she stored the bodies out of sight. She didn't want to take the chance of leaving someone behind who could report her activities, so she shot both of the officers with her tranquilizer gun.

Maliha took the stairs on the south end of the building. The first office facing the square was locked, and that's where she expected to find her target. Slipping a small mirror on a rod under the door, she twisted the rod and the mirror responded by moving from horizontal to vertical, allowing her a view around the room.

There!

She spotted him at the window, seated in a chair. His rifle was already set up but he was relaxing, smoking a cigarette. He knew there was some time to wait. Maliha gently withdrew the mirror. She had no qualms about doing away with a sniper working for Elizabeth and decided on a blitz attack.

She knocked the door down with a powerful kick. The sniper just had time to bolt up from a sitting position before two throwing stars struck him in the throat. Clutching his throat, he fell backward over the chair. Blood poured from his neck, soaking into the carpet. Maliha continued the momentum of breaking down the door and ran into the room to check her kill.

That's when she spotted the other man, sitting on a wooden chair in the corner of the room. He was either the sniper's spotter or bodyguard. The mirror hadn't revealed him. He'd been smoking, too, but had tossed the cigarette aside. Their eyes met and he fired his Israeli Tavor assault rifle at her. Maliha kept moving, diving at the floor and rolling behind a desk. Bullets tracked her across the room and smacked into the wooden desk, which for the moment protected her. The wood splintered as he fired again. Maliha reached up and grabbed a paperweight from the desk. Looking underneath, she could see the man's feet to locate him. Swinging her arm up, she threw the paperweight hard in his direction. She heard a thud when it hit and an exclamation of surprise and pain from him. That's all the incentive she needed.

Sliding out from the desk, staying low to the floor, she saw the man clutching at his chest. She'd struck him over his heart with the heavy brass paperweight, breaking ribs and delivering a stunning blow to the heart muscle. Maliha threw a knife and skewered his heart. He collapsed to the floor.

She walked over and picked up his Tavor, then unclipped several spare magazines from his belt. She snubbed out both cigarettes that were smoldering on the carpeted floor, leaving ugly black marks.

"You should have obeyed the ban on smoking," she admonished the bloody corpses. "Just look at the mess on this carpet."

Chapter Thirty-Nine

Maliha moved rapidly out of the building, because the sound of gunshots, even muffled by the suppressor on the Tavor, should draw a bevy of security forces. She was outside on Wakefield Street, doing her best to look like a patrolling officer in spite of the assault rifle.

Will they let Millhouse go on speaking after finding this room? I wouldn't.

"Threat eliminated," Maliha said into her communicator. "Did you hear anything over there?"

She didn't feel it necessary to explain to Mickey that there had been two men in the room. If he'd taken out one of them with a bullet and assumed the job was done, the spotter might have been able to squeeze off a shot at Millhouse. Both members of the sniper team could handle the rifle.

"No. The crowd's really wound up. Millhouse will speak in a couple of minutes and I found another sniper."

Maliha was alarmed. "Where the hell is he?"

"He is a she. She's in the Central Library—tan, fluted columns, second story, center."

She. Could be Elizabeth.

"There's not much time," Mickey said. "Want me to handle this one?"

"What?" Maliha said.

"You didn't think I left that beautiful rifle on the plane, did you? I went back for it."

Shit. Whose side is he on?

"Uh, no. If it's Elizabeth in the library, a bullet will just make her mad. I'll go check it out."

And to do that, I'll be in Mickey's gun sight. I don't even know he's really where he says he is.

"Okay. Be careful."

Maliha decided that her safest route would be to stay out of the interior of Civic Square and walk on the boundary streets. Time was pressing, so she found a spot out of sight of most and started running at Ageless speed. She hated vanishing in front of observers' eyes, especially observers packing cameras.

Maliha ran up Wakefield Street until it joined Victoria, and kept going until she reached the Central Library, which was closed for the day. It wasn't hard to find a side entrance, but there was an alarm system. As soon as she opened the door, there would be an audible alarm plus an alert at a police station. She checked some windows but it was likely the alarm system would detect the sound of breaking glass. That was the preferred method now, instead of having silver wires around the perimeter of each window.

Is this a wild goose chase to keep me away from Millhouse while Mickey finishes him off? No time to think . . .

She made her decision. Opening the gear bag, she picked out a piece of equipment she'd thought she probably wouldn't need, but had tossed it in anyway. It was a retractable grappling hook fired from a compressed air gun.

On the roof I'll be visible to the helicopters and they won't hesitate to fire. I'd better be moving fast up there.

Maliha shot the grappling hook onto the roof and tested to make sure the rope would hold her weight. She shinnied up the rope and reached to pull up onto the roof of the building.

Elizabeth peered down at her. She didn't say anything, just slashed both of Maliha's forearms with a knife.

Expecting her rope to be cut any second, Maliha ignored the pain and levered herself up onto the roof. Elizabeth was gone. There were no helicopters in her immediate vicinity, but she knew she had only seconds to get out of sight. With blood running down her arms, she gathered the rope and grappling hook and ran to the cover of a ventilation shaft. Lifting the heavy cover, she noticed that her arms had been weakened. She got inside the shaft, let the cover drop over her, and hung for a moment on an interior handle on the cover.

Then she let go.

Falling down the shaft, Maliha saw a side opening coming up. Her timing had to be perfect. As she fell past it, she thrust the grappling hook into the metal lining of the opening and felt the prongs bite. Grabbing the rope, she came to an abrupt stop in her fall and instead swung sideways against the metal of the main shaft.

Ow.

She climbed up the side of the shaft, using her feet and the rope. She reached the side opening where she'd snagged the grappling hook and crawled into it.

Once out of danger, the full impact of her wounds struck her. One of the cuts was nearly down to the bone. If Elizabeth had meant to handicap her, she'd done a good job. Maliha tore off the sleeves of her blouse, wrapped the cloth tightly around her wounds, and convinced herself that she felt better. She had to get moving.

She made her way through the ventilation shaft until she found a grill that allowed her entry into a room. After checking that no one was in the room, she kicked the grill with both feet and went through the open rectangle.

It took her a moment to get her bearings. She was on the first floor. She took the stairs, hoping she wouldn't run into any patrolling guards and for once, her luck held. The sniper was in a room that stored archived media. Maliha quietly picked the lock and planned her next moves. She had to assume there were two people in the room. Turning the doorknob, she eased into the room enough to see the situation.

There were two people near the window. One, a woman, was fingering the trigger of a rifle. The other, a man, crouched next to her with a laptop. He'd cut a small hole in the window and inserted a probe to take readings of outdoor conditions. They both had their backs to her and were intent on what they were doing. Millhouse must be on the stage.

Maliha considered the tranquilizer gun, but its results might not be instantaneous and could cause muscle spasms. The woman's finger was closing on the trigger. Maliha reached into a vest pocket, took out two throwing stars and sent them whirling through the air at an angle toward the man and woman with a twist of her wrist. The stars separated in midair and hit their targets: the backs of two skulls. Maliha burst into the room, reaching the duo in just a few steps. Taking the woman first, Maliha snapped her neck, then turned her attention to the man. He was on the floor and still alive.

"Don't . . . don't . . ." he said.

She saw that the throwing star was not deeply embedded. He might have a chance of survival. Something in her rebelled against killing a man pleading for his life, even if he did work for Elizabeth. He might have been coerced. She shot him with a tranquilizer dart.

He'll either make it until he's discovered here or die under sedation. Best I can do right now, since I'm not going to call for an ambulance. Elizabeth's out there. She's here to make sure I do the job, and since I've made it clear I'm not going to, she'll have to kill the president and find some way to blame it on me.

Outside, Maliha retrieved her gear bag. There was no pretense now. She discarded her duty belt and vest and strapped her sword on her back. Two gleaming sai were tucked in her remaining belt, the one that served as a sheath for the whip sword. The assault rifle was reluctantly left behind—too much opportunity for collateral damage where so many people were gathered. In the square, she felt vulnerable with Mickey able to spot her. She switched to Ageless speed to conceal her formidable-looking presence from security and from Mickey, in case he wasn't trustworthy. Dodging through the crowds, she scanned with her aura vision, looking for signs of Elizabeth.

There she is!

Elizabeth was in the clear space between the president and the barriers holding people back from getting too close. Maliha headed for her without daring to think about it. She already knew that her likelihood of stopping Elizabeth was small, especially given her weakened arms. And Maliha knew her chance of surviving a full-on confrontation with Ageless, cruel Elizabeth was even smaller. But if Maliha stopped to think about all those things, she wouldn't take action.

She leaped the barrier and joined Elizabeth in the open space. An invisible battle began at Ageless speed. Maliha, already weakened from the deep knife gashes, struggled to keep up, but Elizabeth wouldn't let her rest. Elizabeth fought two handed, a sword in one hand and a knife in the other, meaning that Maliha's defense had to be perfectly timed with her sword and a sai, or one of Elizabeth's two blades would break through it.

While their bodies were invisible to the crowd as long as they kept up Ageless speed, the clanging of their swords was audible. Maliha knew people would be running away in panic from the unexplained sounds of swordplay, and the president would be surrounded and taken away by the Secret Service. Elizabeth was so involved with Maliha in her face that the president was safe—at least for now.

Running out of time and life, Maliha remembered what Master Liu had told her. She began to taunt Elizabeth about her appearance. Bathing in the blood of young girls hadn't really kept her young and beautiful. It never did work, but Elizabeth's demon fostered that lie and kept her looking young.

Pulling back, trying to get a little relief from the hammering blows, Maliha said, "You know Tirid will punish you when you fail this assignment. You'll look like an old hag."

"I won't fail. When I'm finished with you, you'll look like puzzle pieces."

In spite of her words, Elizabeth faltered just a little at the thought of her demon's punishment. Maliha reached across her own body with her sword and sliced Elizabeth's face from her earlobe to her jaw.

"Oh!" Elizabeth said. It was a serious wound, an open flap of flesh baring the bones of her jaw on the left side. Elizabeth desperately wanted to hold it back in place so that it would heal quickly and return her to her beautiful state. To do so, she could fight with only one hand. In her rage and frustration, Elizabeth threw herself at Maliha with all the force an Ageless could muster, and pinned her to the ground. People still nearby were horrified at the sight of the two women suddenly visible in their midst, bleeding and slashing at each other.

This time it was Maliha who was desperate. Master Liu had told her not to let Elizabeth get her on the ground for infighting—that Maliha wouldn't survive it. Maliha felt the hot penetration of a knife in her side and her whole right side lit up with pain. Her right arm—her sword arm—and leg collapsed briefly, leaving Elizabeth with a solid opening for a fatal blow. Maliha did the only thing she could do. She dropped the sai she held in her left hand, grabbed the flap of skin from Elizabeth's face, and pulled as hard as she could.

Elizabeth screamed in pain and rolled off Maliha, leaving Maliha clutching a hunk of bloody flesh. Maliha rose to her knees, getting as much use from her numb right leg as she could. Clasping her belly in sudden agony, Maliha felt the acid trails of small footprints moving across her skin. She was being rewarded by Anu for taking out the snipers and saving the lives of their future victims.

Shit, not now!

Elizabeth, far quicker to recover, was on her feet and heading toward Maliha fast, with her sword ready. Suddenly Elizabeth was jolted forward once, and then again.

Shot from the back. Mickey!

Maliha struggled to her feet, pain screaming from her midsection as the pans of the scale began to shift and seek a new balance. She swung her sword one handed as Elizabeth fell toward her. Elizabeth's head and body crashed separately to the tiles of the square. Her eyes wide open in surprise, Elizabeth's head had a few moments to absorb what had happened to her before her brain shut down.

By that time, Maliha was gone, using the last of her energy and her greatest tolerance of pain for an invisible sprint from Civic Square.

Chapter Forty

Vice President Cameron was at work in his office on the first floor of the West Wing, the same floor as the Oval Office, the room he desperately sought. He was plowing through a budget bill in order to offer his suggestions to the president. His suggestions hadn't been solicited, but that never deterred Cameron. The site of his gunshot wound ached, but that was a private matter and he had to put up a good public front.

Between flipping one page and the next, he vanished.

Cameron found himself in an area of dense fog. Ice crystals formed on his skin, as though he were standing in a freezing rain. The cold affected his entire body, and he looked down to see that he was naked. The fog was so thick he couldn't see anything lower than his knees, and when he tried to move, he discovered he was stuck in place.

"What the fuck is going on here?" he shouted. There was no answer. He squirmed, but the fog might as well have been concrete. Cameron continued to shout until his indignation turned to fear and then to pleading. Tears poured from his eyes and froze on his cheeks.

I'm going to die here.

He had no idea how long he'd been in the fog when it started to thin. A shape approached, something that rang alarms of horror in his mind. The fog swirled as the creature moved, and the air movement brought a terrible stench Cameron's way. The odor was something unclean, born of the charnel house and the battlefield, of putrefaction in dark, hidden places. Streams of foul brown fog came toward him, and where they touched his skin, the ice crystals were displaced by slime that sickened him. He vomited and felt the spew cascade down his body, but couldn't move.

Finally the creature stood in front of him, and he couldn't avert his eyes. What he saw was over ten feet tall and spherical. In the center of the sphere was a cavity with rings of vicious, inward-pointing fangs. As Cameron watched, the muscular action around the mouth—for it had to be one—moved the fangs in waves. He stared. It was both hypnotic and terrifying. He felt a warm stream of urine on his legs. When he was able to take his eyes from the mouth, he noticed that the creature had four arms, each ending in four claws that dripped blood and flesh from its last victim. There were no eyes, at least none that Cameron could discern.

"I am the demon Tirid."

The sound was so loud that it burst both of Cameron's eardrums. Blood ran down his cheeks. Inner ear damage muffled the rest of the sounds he heard. He was too stunned to say anything in response to Tirid.

"My Ageless slave Elizabeth was advancing your plan at my direction. She no longer lives. A valuable asset has been lost because of you."

Cameron summoned what presence of mind he had left. "I . . . I had nothing to do with her death."

He'd only recently learned that she was dead. The information came as a shock to him, as the most promising path to the Oval Office had just crumbled beneath his feet.

Tirid roared with anger. Cameron was unable to cover his painful ears, unable to protect himself in any way. The demon's claws clacked together in a menacing way.

"It matters not what you did or did not do. You are at fault. I do not tolerate the loss of my slave from any hand but my own."

An odd calmness took hold of Cameron. He was doomed

and there was nothing he could do about it but silently curse the day Elizabeth had stepped into his life.

Tirid moved close and began to use his claws to rend the object of his anger.

I failed, Cameron thought, and then thought no more.

Chapter Forty-One

Amaro arranged Maliha's pickup for medical evacuation to the Clinic des Montagnes, where Dr. Corvernis tsk-tsked over her, asked no questions, and supported her recovery with his medical skill, his dry sense of humor, and the clinic's excellent cuisine. Mickey went back to the States.

Either Mickey was with me all along or he was forced to work for Elizabeth and took the opportunity to help eliminate his tormentor. Either way, he gets a passing grade with me.

The morning after she arrived, Hound came limping in holding a computer printout.

It was the headline of the *Chicago Tribune*: VICE PRESIDENT DIES IN ROOM PROTECTED BY SECRET SERVICE. Then he showed her the *Enquirer* version: VP GOES TO PIECES!!

"I think I know what happened," she said. "Elizabeth's demon blamed Cameron for her death. He was taken to the Midworld, ripped apart, and put back in his office."

"Gotta love those demons," Hound said.

Maliha glared at him.

"Well, you have to admit this saved us some trouble."

"I see your point," Maliha said. "But don't start admiring demons. Roger Cameron died a horrible death. A bullet to the head would have accomplished what I wanted without all that torture."

If I'd killed the bastard, I would have gotten a bonus from Anu. This way I didn't get any credit.

"You getting soft in your old age?" Hound said.

"Not at all. Just getting some perspective."

"The considerate assassin," he said.

"The considerate seeker of justice."

"Now we're getting politically correct. You can use that shit on the others. I'll stick with assassin."

She shrugged. She was happy Cameron was gone, and Hound was being Hound. He kept her company telling stories from his Vietnam days, all of which she'd heard before. He had a smile on his face these days, since Glass was back at his side, staying at the clinic. His injuries weren't severe, and soon he was complaining, impatient to get away from revealing hospital gowns and back to his work as a private investigator.

Yanmeng was mending, at least physically. He'd lost a hand, which would be fitted for a smart prosthetic when the time came—one that reacted to his thoughts. His foot replantation looked good so far and he was starting to regain some control, but it would be a long haul to full recovery—and there was no guarantee of that.

The missing strip of skin had been replaced with artificial skin, and it was taking well. The remaining lower layer of Yanmeng's skin was growing upward into the scaffolding of the artificial skin. Growing in the lab was a sheet of real epidermis, the outer layer of skin, started from Yanmeng's cells. At the right time, real skin and artificial would meet and marry.

Jake. He's going to visit me. What do I say?

She pushed the thought aside. She'd have to wing it when he arrived, depending on what he said and how he acted. She didn't have long to wait. He showed up the next morning with a huge bouquet of flowers. Hound was in the room with her, but he left immediately when Jake walked in.

"Hi, Jake," she said.

Hi, Jake—there's an impressive opener.

He kissed her on the forehead and pulled a chair up to

the bedside. An aide appeared with a vase already prepared for the flowers.

The efficiency of this place can get on my nerves.

"How are you feeling?" he said.

"I got my arms slashed and a knife in my side. I'm healing okay, though—just not as fast as you would." She smiled.

She searched Jake's face for signs of the monster Master Liu described, and then checked his aura. It was the same as the last time she'd viewed it, similar to hers. Black with the stain of killing, but streaked by a desire to see justice done and an urge to help people.

If this man is a sadistic killer, then I could be one myself. How is he hiding his cruelty and disregard for life?

"You'll be better soon. I thought we might take a vacation. Get away from work and go somewhere romantic, just the two of us."

"That sounds wonderful."

Alone with him for days? Not unless I call Master Liu a liar, and the jury's still out on that.

"Good. I'll make plans."

Maliha decided to test the waters and see what kind of reaction she got. After all, it was hard to believe Jake would pull anything at the clinic.

"Jake, can we talk about Abiyram again?"

"Sure."

"I had already told Abiyram that he might be able to join my team. He was optimistic about it, waiting to hear the details. Why would he, as you said, be plotting to get on the team when it was going to be freely offered to him?"

Logical question. Just a clarification needed. Certainly not offensive.

"I guess he wanted to be certain. His focus was that he wanted you and wasn't going to let anything stand in the way of having you to himself. Who knows what an old human like that thinks, anyway?"

It just didn't ring true. She'd worked with Abiyram a long time, and he'd never once let his heart rule his head. When they'd worked together, if she'd gotten caught, Abiyram would save her if he could, but not at the expense of success of the mission. It was his training and his personality mixed together, and it had nothing to do with having a woman as a partner.

I think Jake might be talking about himself, not Abiyram. There's a lot of disdain in that crack about old humans, too.

She hesitated with her answer.

"Is there a problem?" he said.

"Not really. Well, maybe. I just don't see it the way you do. From working with Abiyram, I don't think he'd let his attraction to me cause him to do anything stupid."

"So he was more important to you than I am?" Jake took her wrist and held it tightly enough to hurt a bit. There was an expression of concern on his face, concern with anger creeping in.

"I asked you before, is there a problem?" he said.

"The problem is you're hurting my wrist."

He didn't let go. "What is it with this Abiyram? You're going on about him and I can barely remember his name. He's not a problem anymore."

"What are you saying?"

His hand subtly tightened around her wrist. "I'm saying that the old man won't bother you anymore. Or try to take you away from me." Furrows formed on his brow. "Why don't you ask what you really want to know?"

Did you kill him? Did you kill my friend? Don't go there.

"I don't know what you mean," Maliha said.

Isn't it time for my blood pressure to be taken or something?

"I mean, is there a problem with Abiyram out of the picture? You love *me*, don't you? Not him? We're going to get married."

Hold on. I never agreed to that.

He twisted her wrist so hard that she thought it would snap. Anger got the best of her.

"Let go of my damn wrist or I'll scream." She pressed her lips together in a line and glared at him, daring him to take any action.

He eased up enough to take away the sensation that her wrist was about to break.

"Master Liu told me why you didn't take the pledge to his school," Maliha said.

I shouldn't have said that.

"He shouldn't have said that," Jake said. His voice was cold.

Maliha viewed his aura again. His voice might have been cold, but his aura was raging hot. Brilliant flares of red anger and violence nearly drowned out the black.

That's how he does it. He controls his aura somehow— until he gets angry and his control slips. Then his true colors show.

Maliha lifted her chin. Her eyes were bright with defiance. "He warned me about you. He said you'd kill me when you got tired of me. My friends, too."

A knife appeared in Jake's hand.

Call for help? Anyone who came in here now would be slashed to ribbons. He's my problem. I brought him in, I'm the one who has to take him out.

She sat up a little straighter in bed and kissed the hand that held the knife. "But Jake, we love each other. That's all that matters."

He smashed his hand up into her face, leaving her nose bleeding. "Cut it out, Maliha. I see you now for what you really are, a scheming whore. Are you really rogue or still working for Rabishu?"

He leaned over her on the bed and the knife went to her throat. He made an experimental slice on the side of her neck to see if she would heal instantly. It was all Maliha could do to hold still.

"What happened to 'I don't want to lose you'?" Maliha said. She struggled to keep her voice from trembling. She was stalling for the right moment, the correct position of her body relative to his, and she couldn't make any sudden moves until she was ready. She was only going to get one chance.

"Shut up."

He lifted the knife a fraction of an inch. A minute passed quietly as Jake waited for the cut on her neck to heal. It didn't.

"Son of a gun. You really are a rogue."

He started to sit up, and that's when she took the biggest risk of her life.

His hand still held her wrist, but not gripped as tightly as before. She stiffened her fingers and rammed them into his eye, then slid her fingers back through his encircling fist as he dealt with the pain of her surprise move.

Free!

She grabbed the wrist that held the knife, pulled it to her, and bit it as hard as she could. Tasting blood, she knew she'd severed the radial and ulnar arteries used to commit suicide. They were close to the surface of the skin on the inside of the wrist. It wouldn't be more than a distraction to Jake, but a distraction would be helpful.

They struggled in complete silence, neither one wanting to attract outside attention. Jake dropped the knife on the bed and Maliha lunged for it. It was slippery with his blood, but she grasped it and plunged it into his heart. Pulling out the knife, she bent her legs and kicked out at him, hitting him squarely in the chest. She felt her own wounds respond to the action with fresh bleeding, especially the wound Elizabeth had given Maliha in her side. There was no time to consider body damage. At this point, she held not only her own life in her hands, but also the lives of her friends.

She dove from the bed and landed atop Jake. To weaken him further she broke both of his arms. The cracking of bone sounded loud in the otherwise quiet room. She straddled Jake and put the knife to his throat.

How could things go this wrong? I was ready to marry this man—until he asked me.

"We've been through this before, you know," Jake said. His voice held only a tinge of pain.

"In my haven," Maliha said. "I was ready to kill you."

She stabbed his thigh as she went by, then she hit the wall of the weapons cache and spun around with a sword in her hand. She felt a little less naked.

Jake was down. Against the odds, she'd surprised him and landed a blow. She shoved off from the wall to press her advantage. Half a second later, she was on him, her sword balanced at his throat. Her chest pressed against his and she could feel his heart thudding. The edge of her weapon drew blood. All she had to do was lean her weight on the sword, sending the edge deeply into his flesh.

She'd delayed so long that by now he should have thrown her off. Instead, he went still beneath her.

She saw his lips move, forming the shape of her name with no sound.

Her hands weren't obeying her mind, they were taking orders from her heart. The blade broke the skin in a short line that welled with blood but went no further.

She rolled off him, kept going, and came to her knees a short distance away. Then she rose to her feet and dashed back toward the door.

"*I love you,*" *came from the man down on her floor.*

"You couldn't do it then and you won't do it now," Jake said. "I love you."

You are one hundred and ten percent crazy.

She leaned her weight on both ends of the knife and kept pushing until the blade reached the carpet on the other side of his neck. She pushed his head a foot away. She wasn't sure, but she thought if she left the head in contact with his body, his Ageless healing ability would reattach it.

Maliha changed her position so she was no longer straddling Jake's torso and slumped to the floor.

"Hound," she whispered. "Hound." Louder.

There was a knock at the door.

"Come in," she said.

As the door opened, Hound said, "Just being polite, in case you and Mr. Hunk were, uh, going at . . ."

She looked up at him, still holding the knife.

"Oh. I see." He knelt down next to her and wrapped his arms around her. "It'll be all right. We'll take it from here."

He turned his head toward the door. "Mickey! Get your ass in here!

"Are you wounded?" he asked Maliha.

"No, just the injuries I already had."

Mickey came running through the door, slamming it back so hard that it crashed into the wall. "What the fuck?" He stood frozen as he took in the scene. "Did you have to . . . ?"

"Yes, she did," Hound said. "I'll explain later. Lock the door before we get a lot of company."

Hound spread out a clean blanket on the couch in Maliha's room, and Mickey carried her over to it. Just then her reward for killing Jake was measured on her scale, and it was a great one. She twisted in pain, pulling apart her pajama top as the scale glowed and moved on her skin. Mickey was frightened and baffled until Hound explained what was happening. Finally she was pulled through time, fading in and out of view, emerging with a few more silver hairs visible within the black braid that hung down her back.

"This woman is extraordinary," Mickey said.

"Took you long enough to realize it," Hound said. "You want to protect her, but it's like trying to protect the sun from being too hot. Hopeless."

I heard that.

"You get some rest," Hound said to Maliha. "You're safe with us."

Although Maliha knew there were threats that only she could deal with, right then Hound's words were a balm to her ragged soul.

Chapter Forty-Two

Three weeks later

Maliha was back in Chicago. She was the only one in her condo and for now, relished the quiet and long hours to think. Amaro was visiting his sister Rosie, Yanmeng and Eliu were still in Switzerland at the clinic, Hound was working on a case, and Mickey had gone back to Phoenix with a fattened bank account and a promise to return soon. Before they'd split up, the team had welcomed Mickey as a new member.

The police found Arnie Henshaw's body after Hound phoned in an anonymous tip. Arnie wasn't just dead, he was Elizabeth-style dead, upping Maliha's pain at the thought of what he went through.

She felt that she'd paid in blood for recent events, and if she dwelled on the past, she could drown in a sea of remorse. It was time to look to the future, to rededicate herself to both her personal quest to redeem her soul from the clutches of Rabishu and to assemble the crystal lens needed to read the Tablet of the Overlord. Her feeling was stronger than ever that she was the only one living who could accomplish that and rid Earth of the seven Sumerian demons. What lay beyond that for humankind, she didn't know, but she wanted to see how it all turned out.

Something that needed her team's attention was that Vice President Cameron had told her there were others like him in politics, sons and daughters of the New Founders. He'd claimed that none was in a position to influence the course of events in the country, as he had been—but what reason would he have had to tell the truth? Lying about the projects of the New Founders would have been second nature to him. He'd told her there were twelve Founders, but what if there were thirty? Or a hundred or more? Rooting out information on the secretive group would be a challenge to her team.

Lucius, her soul mate, her Ageless lover who'd given himself over to a torturous existence to save her, no longer needed to be hidden away in a secret compartment of her heart. Now he lived in her entire heart, and she hoped someday to find the way to bring him back from his demon's hell. She'd never give up trying.

The answer might lie in the Tablet of the Overlord. I have to find the rest of the shards.

There was that mysterious statement Master Liu made to her that kept popping up in her mind, that their lives are linked.

How? Why? I can see how he's important to me, but how could I make a difference to him? He's already so powerful. Is there something on that tablet he wants too?

Maliha raised the shades on the windows of her condo, something she rarely did for security reasons. She stood in front of the expanse of curved windows, looking out at Lake Michigan. Sun glinted off the ice of the lake, searing away thoughts that had saddened and depressed her, searing the hurt from her heart.

It hurt to lose Jake because I still don't understand how I could have been so wrong about him. Now I have to focus on Lucius and how to bring us back together.

A doubt tried to wiggle into her mind. *Could he be hiding something, like Jake? Am I doomed to repeat this kind of failed cycle of love? No, I don't believe Anu would punish me like that.*

December had slipped by while she was in the clinic, and a new year spread out before her. A year of purpose and accomplishment.

Master Liu mentioned that one of his disciples named Daniel Harper has a shard. If I can get Daniel's away from

*him, I'll have four of them. More than half. Master Liu said
to approach Daniel as a woman. I think I can manage that.*

She went into the storage room where the boxes from
Abiyram's apartment were stacked. It was time to tackle
them. She finally knew the story of his death and in her
own way had avenged it. Until now, she'd had neither the
time nor the inclination to handle the items she'd inherited
from him.

Box after box yielded dusty but fascinating artifacts.
She was going to need a special display area in her haven
for them. She would consider donating the better pieces
to museums, but it was impractical. She couldn't produce
authentic provenance, the complete history of the artifact,
because Abiyram had been less than scrupulous in his collecting techniques. She'd have to forge documents, and for
now it was too big a project to undertake.

Maybe later.

A battered leather document tube carried a note in
Abiyram's scrawl: *We'll find this one together.*

Inside was an ancient map. As Maliha held the map that
threatened to crumble in her hands, an image rose from it
into the air and enlarged in front of her. Full of wonder, she
stared at the hovering map that would lead her to the next
shard.

*It looks like I'm going to have to learn a lot about vol-
canoes.*

ACKNOWLEDGMENTS

I'd like to thank the readers of the first two books in the Mortal Path series, *Dark Time* and *Sacrifice*, who responded to Maliha's unique and compelling story, allowing me to bring this next book to you. I love this story and these characters and it's satisfying to be able watch Maliha walk the mortal path.

My agent, Adrienne Rosado of Nancy Yost Literary Agency, has provided valuable support. Thank you, Adrienne! I couldn't make my dreams come true without you.

Emily Krump, my editor at Harper Voyager, helped transform this book from a collection of words into the version you hold in your hands, the one that best represents my vision of the story, for which I am grateful. A special thank you to Emily for her compassion and patience in working with me during a difficult period of my life, the decline in health and passing away of my sister Maxine. A class act, Emily, and one that I'll never forget.

Copyeditor Ellen Leach deserves great credit for smoothing the rough edges of my manuscript. Thanks, Ellen, for a difficult task well done.

My husband, Dennis, makes a rotten critique partner but redeems himself with excellent brainstorming. I get Maliha into trouble, he helps me get her out. On top of that, he makes a terrific egg sandwich with hot pepper cheese. What's not to love?

A special mention belongs to reader Jill Bakkum, who won a contest to name a character in this book after herself. I enjoyed having Dr. Jill in this story.

RETURN TO THE HOLLOWS WITH
NEW YORK TIMES BESTSELLING AUTHOR

KIM HARRISON

WHITE WITCH, BLACK CURSE
978-0-06-113802-7

Kick-ass bounty hunter and witch Rachel Morgan has crossed
forbidden lines, taken demonic hits, and still stands. But a new
predator is moving to the apex of the *Inderlander* food chain—
and now Rachel's past is coming back to haunt her . . . literally.

BLACK MAGIC SANCTION
978-0-06-113804-1

Denounced and shunned by her own kind for dealing with
demons and black magic, Rachel Morgan's best hope is life
imprisonment—her worst, a forced lobotomy and genetic
slavery. And only her enemies are strong enough to help her
win her freedom.

PALE DEMON
978-0-06-113807-2

After centuries of torment, a fearsome creature walks free,
craving innocent blood and souls—especially Rachel Morgan's,
who'll need to embrace her demonic nature to survive.

THE NIGHT HUNTRESS NOVELS FROM

JEANIENE FROST

✦ HALFWAY TO THE GRAVE ✦

978-0-06-124508-4

Kick-ass demon hunter and half-vampire Cat Crawfield and her sexy mentor, Bones, are being pursued by a group of killers. Now Cat will have to choose a side…and Bones is turning out to be as tempting as any man with a heartbeat.

✦ ONE FOOT IN THE GRAVE ✦

978-0-06-124509-1

Cat Crawfield works to rid the world of the rogue undead. But when she's targeted for assassination she turns to her ex, the sexy and dangerous vampire Bones, to help her.

✦ AT GRAVE'S END ✦

978-0-06-158307-0

Caught in the crosshairs of a vengeful vamp, Cat's about to learn the true meaning of bad blood—just as she and Bones need to stop a lethal magic from being unleashed.

✦ DESTINED FOR AN EARLY GRAVE ✦

978-0-06-158321-6

Cat is having terrifying visions in her dreams of a vampire named Gregor who's more powerful than Bones.

✦ THIS SIDE OF THE GRAVE ✦

978-0-06-178318-0

Cat and her vampire husband Bones have fought for their lives, as well as their relationship. But Cat's new and unexpected abilities threaten the both of them.

JOCELYNN DRAKE'S

NEW YORK TIMES BESTSELLING
DARK DAYS NOVELS

NIGHTWALKER
978-0-06-154277-0
For centuries Mira has been a nightwalker—an unstoppable enforcer for a mysterious organization that manipulates earth-shaking events from the darkest shadows. But the foe she now faces is human: the vampire hunter called Danaus, who has already destroyed so many undead.

DAYHUNTER
978-0-06-154283-1
Mira and her unlikely ally Danaus have come to Venice, home of the nightwalker rulers. But there is no safety in the ancient city and Danaus, the only creature she dares trust, is something more than the man he claims to be…

DAWNBREAKER
978-0-06-154288-6
Destiny draws Mira and Danaus toward an apocalyptic confrontation with the *naturi* at Machu Picchu. Once the *naturi* are unchained, blood, chaos, and horror will reign supreme on Earth. But all is not lost as a rogue enemy princess can change the balance of power and turn the dread tide.

And don't miss

PRAY FOR DAWN
978-0-06-185180-3

WAIT FOR DUSK
978-0-06-185181-0

BURN THE NIGHT
978-0-06-185182-7

JD 0411

HARPER VOYAGER
TRADE PAPERBACKS

HARPER Voyager

An Imprint of HarperCollins*Publishers*

www.harpervoyagerbooks.com

SWORDS & DARK MAGIC
Edited by Jonathan Strahan and Lou Anders
978-0-06-172381-0

THE CHILD THIEF
by Brom
978-0-06-167134-0

Z IS FOR ZOMBIE
An Illustrated Guide to the End of the World
by Adam-Troy Castro and Johnny Atomic
978-0-06-199185-1

THE INHERITANCE
and Other Stories
by Robin Hobb
978-0-06-156164-1

THE WATERS RISING
by Sheri S. Tepper
978-0-06-195885-4

GHOSTS BY GASLIGHT
Stories of Steampunk and Supernatural Suspense
Edited by Jack Dann and Nick Gevers
978-0-06-199971-0